RS

The Second Assassination

Other books by Richard Scott

The Reluctant Assassin
A Tony Dantry spy thriller

The Eager Assassin
The Second Tony Dantry Thriller

The Assassin Chip
Another Tony Dantry thriller

Murder on Third Avenue
A novel about murder in corporate America

Salem, the novel
An historical novel about Salem, Massachusetts and the birth of America

Mission in Time
Time travel meets American history

All books are in paper and ebook formats

The Second Assassination

By Richard Scott

Revised November 2014

Published by Winter Island Press
Cover design by Richard Scott

For Jeanne

PART 1

Prologue — I

Washington, DC July 2, 1881
The President's carriage pulled to a stop in front of the Sixth Street entrance to the Baltimore and Potomac railway depot. It was barely 9:30 in the morning, and already Secretary of State James G. Blaine felt uncomfortably sticky from the humidity.

Word had gotten out that the president was expected, and people standing on the sidewalk now began to cluster around the carriage as it neared the curb. Several police officers immediately interceded, urging the pedestrians to keep their distance from the presidential entourage.

"Away from the carriage, folks. Now!" Barked a lieutenant who apparently was in charge." C'mon, move back. Move back. You there, Get back."

The presidential carriage was driven by the same Negro coachman who'd driven it for Presidents Grant and Hayes.
Only a few minutes before, secretaries Lincoln, Windom, and Hunt, and Postmaster-General James, all accompanied by their wives, had preceded the President to the depot. They'd already taken seats in the special railroad car that was to take the Presidential party to New

When the carriage came to a stop, a police sergeant by the name of Kearney stepped forward to open the door. The President said, "How much time have we, officer?"

"About ten minutes, sir."

The President lingered in the carriage, deep in conversation with Secretary Blaine. The few lacy clouds still dotting the morning sky would be gone in an hour or two. By noon it would be hot in the streets of the nation's capital. By mid-afternoon it would be oppressive. You had to expect that in Washington at this time of year, thought Blaine, though he never quite got used to it. One part of him felt fortunate to be accompanying the President up to New York and on to Western Massachusetts. At least in New England the weather was likely to be cooler.

President James A. Garfield was scheduled to deliver a commencement address in Williamstown, Massachusetts, at his beloved alma mater, Williams College. This would be the second time he'd been invited to deliver a commencement address at Williams. The first time had been ten years earlier. It seemed the people at Williams liked him as much as he did them. This time, though, President Garfield was acting the proud father as much as he was President of the United States. He was looking forward to introducing James and Harry, his two college-age sons who were accompanying him on the trip, to Williams with hopes that at least one of them might want to go there.

Secretary of State Blaine viewed the trip differently, though. While he felt fortunate to be looking forward to the fresher air of the northern Berkshires, the cooler weather was the only thing that appealed to him about this trip. He was definitely not eager to spend the next few days in the President's shadow. Blaine was a proud man. His thoughts went back four years to when Rutherford B. Hayes announced he was running for the Presidency. At the time, Hayes had promised that he would serve only one term. Hayes surprised people—though not the ones who knew him well—by keeping his promise. As his four years drew to a close, the Republicans had to scramble to put forth a credible candidate for the next election—the election of 1880.

Blaine himself had been a contender for the Republican nomination in the fall of '80, just a half year ago. It seemed so much longer. He'd challenged Grant, who'd surprised a lot of the Washington politicos by deciding after four years of Rutherford B. Hayes, to try a comeback for a third term. No President had ever held the office for three terms. The Republican Convention had been evenly divided between Blaine and Grant. Vote after vote ended in a standoff.

Then Ohio's favorite son James Abram Garfield began to make his presence known. It was Garfield's adroit maneuvering and spellbinding speeches to the delegates at the convention last fall that had hopelessly deadlocked the convention after a total of 35 votes. On the 36th vote, the delegates had gone for Garfield. Garfield went on to defeat the popular Winfield Hancock in the November election. General Hancock was a West Point graduate who'd served with distinction in the Mexican War and years later commanded a major part of the Union forces at the Battle of Gettysburg.

In a show of party harmony, Garfield had asked Blaine to serve as his Secretary of State. Blaine accepted, but his ego was huge. This was the second time he'd run for the highest office in the land, and the second time he'd failed to achieve it. Playing the role of the loyal party soldier was not easy for him.

Finished with his conversation with Blaine, the President emerged from the carriage. He had to duck in order to make it through the door as he stepped down to the cobbled street. He was followed by Blaine.

Garfield, a hearty, vigorous man of six feet and just under 200 pounds, was clearly in good spirits this morning. Blaine glanced at him. He wanted to resent this charming man who now occupied the office he'd fought so hard for, but he found it extremely difficult to do so. He shook his head slightly as he realized that, in all honesty, he couldn't help but like the President. He found himself making small talk.

"Looks like a fine day to travel, Mr. President."

"Indeed it does, James. Be nice to leave this heat behind us." Then he added wryly, "And Conkling and his gang of Stalwart bloodsuckers." Garfield was referring to Roscoe Conkling, the flamboyant former New York congressman he'd been battling since he'd taken office. Until last month, Conkling and his political "Stalwarts" had run New York's patronage machine virtually without opposition. Then the new president had changed all that, and Conkling had resigned his seat in Congress. But victory for Garfield had not come easily.

"I know it's been draining," said Blaine, "but you can take satisfaction in knowing you've won."

Garfield allowed a trace of a smile, but said nothing as he proceeded toward the ladies entrance to the depot, followed by Secretary Blaine. His staff had chosen the ladies entrance because it was less crowded than the main entrance. The two leaders passed leisurely through the ladies waiting room, Blaine on the

President's right. Their conversation was spirited and cheerful.

The President's sons, James and Harry, followed just a few paces behind the two statesmen. They were close to their father. It had not been easy, of course, as they didn't see him as much as they wanted to, but they admired him and respected him. He was amazingly easy to talk with when he managed to find the time to be at home. It was he who'd suggested they come along for this trip—both for the companionship and for the chance to see Williams College.

Without turning to look at Blaine, the President wiped his brow with his handkerchief and said, "My God, James. Only the beginning of July and already I've had too much of the Washington summer." He exchanged a knowing look with Blaine and added. "I remember twenty years ago, when I was in Congress here how much I looked forward to the summer break to get away from this blasted heat." He wiped his brow. "It never changes here."

Blaine, who was from Maine, said, "Yes, Mr. President. A few days of New England weather will do us all a world of good." Then he added impishly, "Maybe you should move the White House to New England."

Garfield came to a stop and looked at Blaine. There was a twinkle in the President's eye. "You'd like that wouldn't you James?"

"Better than Ohio, Mr. President."

Garfield feigned a frown of disapproval. As they resumed walking, The president threw his arm over the shoulder of his Secretary of State and smiled. It was good to be alive. After his speech in Williamstown and the fresh air of the Berkshires, he'd be ready to tackle the agenda he had for the country.

Blaine interrupted his thoughts.

"I hope Mrs. Garfield is doing well in New Jersey."

"Thanks for your concern, James. I heard from her yesterday. She seems to be recovering quite well. At least that's what she's telling me." Back in May, Lucretia "Crete" Garfield had contracted malaria from the mosquitoes that infested the swamps behind the White House. At the urging of the White House physician, she'd retired from the activity and pressures of Washington to Long Branch on the New Jersey shore in order to convalesce in a healthier atmosphere. She'd taken the couple's three younger children with her.

The President and his entourage had gone only a few more yards when a loud report echoed throughout the large room.

"What the devil?" exclaimed Blaine. He turned and saw a look of surprise on the President's face. It passed quickly though, as everything seemed all right. Seeing that Garfield had given the loud noise only fleeting attention, Blaine caught up with him, as the president had already resumed his brisk pace. Garfield and his Secretary of State were used to noisy demonstrations. It went with the political territory. Neither man noticed a small man with a gun, who, unnoticed by them, was standing just a few feet away.

The man with the gun fired again—this time into the back of the President. Garfield sank to the floor and began bleeding profusely from his wounds. Blaine immediately knelt down and lifted the President's head. James and Harry stood in shocked silence as they looked down at their stricken father.

A nearby janitor heard the shots and rushed toward the scene. On seeing what had happened, he immediately ran off calling for the police. The man holding the gun remained standing in the position from which he'd shot the President. Blaine glanced up for a moment and, for the first time, saw the man who'd done the shooting. He appeared to be below average in height and slender in build. Then James and Harry knelt down, their eyes pleading, looking for direction, looking for someone to make it all right. Blaine told them to keep back and then turned his attention back to Garfield.

"Can you speak, sir?"

Garfield looked white as a ghost, but his eyes were open. "Yes, James. Did you see who did this?"

"Yes, Mr. President. He's standing right over there. The police are on the way. We'll get you a doctor as quickly as we can. Don't move." Blaine felt his heart pounding as he looked again at the man with the gun. He was a pathetic excuse for an assassin. The little man's sunken cheeks were partially hidden by an unkempt mustache and light chin whiskers. His eyes seemed abnormally far apart from each other, giving him a sullen, distant appearance. Blaine was about to return his attention to the president when the man with the gun turned away and began to walk slowly and deliberately out of the room. Before he'd gone five paces, he was apprehended by the same Officer Kearney, who, only minutes earlier, had spoken with the President.

The pistol was still in the assassin's hand when Kearney arrested him. The officer recognized it as being a bulldog, 44 caliber, five-shooter, with three loads remaining. Kearney quickly learned from the shooter that his name was Charles J. Guiteau. Guiteau was hauled off to jail and was behind bars within an hour of the shooting.

Within minutes, the President was taken to a second-floor room above the depot. Soon several physicians arrived to attend to him. The doctors concluded that, because of the President's "nervous prostration," which followed the shock resulting from the shooting, it would not be advisable to probe for the ball. After an hour or so, the doctors talked to Blaine, and told him they'd decided that the President should be moved to the safety and comfort of the White House.

"Have you told the president?"

One of the doctors, the one who appeared to be in charge, said, "Yes, he's in shock, but he's awake and he understands."

When Garfield reached the White House, he was carried to a sleeping chamber in the southeast corner of the building. He was now under the care of the most prominent physicians in Washington. The august assemblage of medical men soon observed that the President had already resumed his normal composed manner, greeting friends, cabinet members, and others who called to wish him well. He was even able to muster a few cheerful words and a warm pressure of the hand to some of these well-wishers. The president seemed to be more concerned with the effect his condition would have on Crete—who herself was convalescing up on the New Jersey shore—than with his own health.

When Lucretia Garfield first heard that her husband had been shot, she was distraught. She was deeply in love with her husband. The Garfield marriage had been a good one, the single exception being a brief affair he'd had back in '62 in New York City with a woman named Calhoun. When Lucretia had learned of it and confronted him, he'd been contrite. She'd forgiven him, and that had been the end of it. Since then, they'd been close, closer, she was convinced, than many couples they knew. For one thing, she could talk to James. They both were intellectually curious. They both were voracious readers.

She smiled as she recalled how her husband had gradually replaced his youthful pugnacity with a mature confidence that most people perceived as charm and wit. She knew he thought of himself as a self-made man, and in many ways he was. He'd come from dire poverty, and he'd gone on to become President of the United States. He'd done this without a father to turn to in his youth, for his father had died when James was not yet two years of age. She took satisfaction in seeing what had become of her man. She'd worked hard to mold him, to smooth away the overt aggressiveness, and to help him convert that aggressiveness to a modest self-confidence. James had said on more than one occasion that he didn't like to blow his own horn. Sometimes, he admitted, this attitude kept him from getting the credit he rightly deserved. Now this man she loved so intensely was close to death. Here she was a hundred miles to the north on the coast of New Jersey. She'd never felt more helpless in her life.

When former President Grant heard about the shooting he telegraphed the following message to Secretary of War
Lincoln:

"Please dispatch to me the condition of the President. News received conflicting. I hope the most favorable may be confirmed. Express to the President my deep sympathy and hope that he may speedily recover."

U.S. Grant

Grant received the following response:

"The President's condition is very serious and excites gravest apprehensions. There is internal hemorrhage. The surgeons are evidently very anxious and guarded in their expressions. He is perfectly clear in mind, and desires me to thank you for your telegram, which I gave to him in substance."

Robert Lincoln
Secretary of War

Secretary of War, Robert Todd Lincoln, remained in constant attendance at the White House. Lincoln seemed to feel the blow more deeply than anyone in official Washington, with the possible exception of Blaine. Lincoln's memories of that terrible night 16 years earlier, when his father was assassinated, were resurrected and magnified by the attack on President Garfield. Lincoln referred to his sad, personal memories several times during the first night's vigil.

"My God," he exclaimed once, "how many hours of sorrow I have passed in this town?"

Postmaster-General James reacted to Lincoln's statement with compassion. "Do you remember how often General Garfield has referred to your father during the past few days?"

On Sunday, the day after the shooting, *The New York Times* said,

"President Garfield's life had been of such a character that it seemed almost impossible for him to have made any personal enemies, and the notion that he had been murdered as a political measure could not be entertained for a moment."

From the first, the President had demanded the truth. At first, Surgeon-General Bliss, thought the President's case hopeless. He told Garfield just that: "Mr. President, your condition is extremely critical. I do not think you can live many hours."

"God's will be done, doctor. I'm ready to go if my time has come," said Garfield firmly.

Later in the day, Dr. Bliss changed his opinion, no doubt because Garfield seemed in fairly good spirits for someone who'd just been shot twice. During the afternoon, though the president was clearly suffering intensely from his wounds, he, on several occasions, gave evidence of his good nature and genial disposition. One of his sons, 16-year-old James, was sobbing at his bedside, and Garfield said, "Don't be alarmed, Jimmy, the upper story is all right, it is only the hull that is a little aged."

At police headquarters, a letter was removed from the would-be assassin's pocket:

JULY 2, 1881

To the White House:
The President's tragic death was a sad necessity, but it will unite the Republican Party and save the Republic. Life is a flimsy dream and it matters little when one goes. A human life is of small value. During the war, thousands of brave boys went down without a tear. I presume the President was a Christian and that he will be happier in Paradise than here. It will be no worse for Mrs. Garfield, dear soul, to part with her husband this way than by natural death. He is liable to go at any time anyway. I had no ill will toward the President. His death was a political necessity. I am a lawyer, a theologian, and a politician. I am a Stalwart

of the Stalwarts. I was with General Grant and the rest of our men in New-York during the canvass. I have some papers for the press, which I shall leave with Byron Andrews and his co-journalists at No. 1,420 New-York-avenue, where the reporters can see them. I am going to the jail.

Charles Guiteau

Investigation by the police revealed Guiteau to be a disgraced lawyer and a disappointed applicant for a government job. He'd been hanging around the White House since March 4th, the day of the President's inauguration. According to White House staff members and military guards stationed in front of the building, some days Guiteau would make political speeches to clusters of people in the area. Other times he'd enter the mansion itself and walk off with stationery, which he later used for petitions and requests of various types—all with political overtones.

* * *

One long July day dragged on into the next as the nation followed the reports of the President's condition in the press. Almost every day the reports from the doctors were optimistic. It seemed only a matter of time before Garfield would be on the mend and able to get back to his routine. On Monday, August 8th, the surgeons performed an operation on Garfield. The objective was to find the ball that was still somewhere inside the ailing President, and failing that, to at least remove some of the diseased tissue to enable the wound to heal more readily. The physicians proclaimed the operation a success. *The New York Times* said, "All the surgeons agree that the operation performed on the President yesterday has been attended with the desired effect and that the wound is now in better condition for steady and unobstructed healing than before the operation was performed."

Unfortunately, the operation and the combined efforts of the surgeons and other doctors before and after the operation were not sufficient to save the President. After 80 days of suffering, James Abram Garfield succumbed on September 19th at the age of 49. He never lost consciousness throughout the entire ordeal, yet he'd only been strong enough during the long summer to carry out one official act, the signing of an extradition paper.

The shooting of Garfield created a near paralysis of government in Washington, as it meant that the nation was essentially without a functioning president during the 80 days that Garfield was bedridden. Most authorities agreed that Vice President Arthur was empowered by the Constitution to assume the powers and duties of the President under such circumstances, but it was unclear whether he should serve as acting President until Garfield recovered or assume the office itself and replace Garfield. The Constitution was ambiguous on the subject, and Congress was not in session, so the issue could not be taken up.

The matter finally came before a cabinet meeting on September 2nd, where it was agreed that no action would be taken without first consulting Garfield. The President's physicians said this would not be possible, so the matter was dropped.

Seventeen days later the President's condition took an unexpected turn for the worse. A few minutes after 10:00 p.m. he complained of a severe pain in his chest. He died at 10:35p.m.

Prologue — II

Salem, Massachusetts   March 1884
Martin Van Zandt, the host, stood at the head of the long, gleaming teakwood table. It was a table he'd imported from Shanghai ten years ago at considerable expense. He remembered vividly the day he first laid eyes on the magnificent piece of furniture when it was being unloaded off the ship down at Crowninshield Wharf. Van Zandt studied each of his five nervous guests who stood awkwardly near the table, waiting for a sign from him. Their discomfort was palpable as his eyes met theirs. Van Zandt was an impressive man, and though barely above average in height, his presence dominated the room.

"Sit, please," he said with a disarming smile. As he took his seat at the head of the table, each of the others followed his cue.

Van Zandt, had been brutally candid about his reason for inviting them to dinner in Salem. His invitation had begun benignly enough by saying he'd be honored to have the pleasure of their company at a little dinner he'd planned at his house on Chestnut Street. Then, almost as an afterthought, the invitation had added that, while they were there, it would give them one last opportunity to air the reasons any of them might have for wanting to sell the magazine. What Van Zandt really meant—and all of them knew it—was that he wanted to see them squirm uncomfortably as they tried vainly to convince him he should vote in favor of selling *Knickerbocker* magazine. Nobody really believed Van Zandt could be persuaded to sell. Nevertheless, no one dared not be there. Just in case.

Van Zandt had founded *Knickerbocker* in 1864 —while the war was still going on. He'd been 48 at the time—too old to serve in the Union Army. He'd tried to apply for a commission as an officer, but Washington had decided that, as a journalist, his skills could be put to better use at home, where he could tell the story of the war—presumably from the Union perspective.

No one in his right mind was starting a business in the middle of the war, but that hadn't deterred Van Zandt in the least. What he'd done was revive a defunct magazine that had been published continuously in New York City from 1833 to 1861. He'd moved the editorial offices to Boston.

Other than the name, everything about Van Zandt's *Knickerbocker* was new and different—thanks to his creative energies. During its first year the new *Knickerbocker* attracted a lot of attention with its photographic profiles of Union soldiers suffering front-line privations and enduring the hell of battle. Van Zandt had scored a coup when he persuaded Matthew Brady to sell him photographs for three different editions. That, plus his aggressive new approach to journalism infused new life into the magazine.

The magazine rapidly rose to prominence. Van Zandt was particularly good at sensing what the literate public wanted. Established publications such as, *Century Magazine*, *Atlantic Monthly*, *Leslie's Weekly*, and *North American Review* had to sit up and take notice. Their editorial content was bland by comparison. *Harper's* was the only serious competition for Van Zandt's *Knickerbocker.*

As brilliant and inspiring a man as Van Zandt was, he also possessed a contrariness of spirit that at times made him impossible. Tonight's dinner was a perfect example. He'd made it clear that he did not want to sell the magazine.

So why was he going through the motions tonight? In part, it was out of necessity. He needed a majority of votes of the stockholders to retain the business. Van Zandt himself owned 39 percent. A plurality, but not a majority. Van Zandt could have held a meeting in the boardroom in Boston to settle this issue, but he had no intention of inconveniencing himself for most of the people in the room. After all, three of them had made known their opposition to him by proclaiming their interest in selling the magazine—his magazine. Why, then, should he make it easy for them? Let them come to him—even if it meant their taking seven or eight hours out of a Thursday evening. He'd added to their inconvenience, of course, by choosing a weekday instead of a Friday or Saturday. He had other plans for his weekend. He was sorry for the inconvenience his two supporters on the board would endure, but better their inconvenience than his.

It annoyed him that he didn't have 51 percent of the stock. Forced him to deal with the other stockholders, when, by rights, he should have had a free hand with the business, a business he'd built by force of his own intellect. Up till now, his five guests—the other stockholders—had constituted what amounted to a rubber stamp board despite the occasional negative votes by two or three members. The sale of the magazine would be closer, but still in his favor. He smiled inwardly, fully confident of his majority, narrow though it might be.

As he stared down the length of the table, his eyes made contact with those of Hugh Trampler, physically the most imposing member of the board. Trampler's steel gray eyes did not look away. As the stockholder with the second-largest number of shares, Trampler was his major opponent on the issue of selling the magazine. Wouldn't it be sweet, thought Van Zandt, if he could turn Trampler around and end up with more votes than he'd started with at the beginning of the evening. He maintained eye contact with Trampler another moment before finally raising his wineglass and smiling.

He was smiling because he knew that, even without Trampler, there were two board members he could definitely count on.

One was Arthur Billingsley, outspoken in his preference for retention of ownership, who held 14 percent of the stock. Billingsley's shares raised the votes Van Zandt could count on to 53 percent.

Billingsley had been with him from the start. He'd believed in the idea of resurrecting *Knickerbocker* back when most people had considered it a hare-brained scheme. Billingsley had been the first outside investor in Van Zandt's magazine, and Van Zandt hadn't forgotten that vote of confidence. Billingsley had always been his own man, though, and while he, Van Zandt, had been building *Knickerbocker* into a formidable publication, his first and oldest investor had been building the import-export business he'd started back in the fifties. Van Zandt not only respected Billingsley, he grudgingly admitted to himself that he'd grown fond of him over the years.
And, of course, there was Margarita Scharf Calore, with her nine percent, who also wanted things to stay just as they were. Recently widowed, she'd inherited her husband's interest in *Knickerbocker* magazine. Van Zandt was just as sure of her votes, but for an entirely different reason.

Hence his arrogance in setting up this dinner of inconvenience. He knew he could count on the votes of Billingsley and Calore. He could therefore embarrass his opposition with impunity. This he would enjoy doing.

"I welcome you all to my home," he said pleasantly. "I hope your trip here wasn't too onerous. Now let's enjoy our meal. Then we can get down to business."

No one at the table, with the exception of the host himself, believed for one second that they would be able to enjoy their meal—knowing, as they did, the business that lay before them, and knowing, as they did, the man they had to deal with. Nevertheless, the meal progressed in a generally relaxed fashion, at least on the surface. The guests nervously pretended they hadn't a care in the world as they forced themselves to enjoy the excellent meal served by Everett Flick, the caretaker-acting-as-waiter, and prepared by his wife Miriam.

All five of his guests were present against their

will this evening; yet none of them would have dared stay home. Van Zandt was aware of their ambivalence, and a hint of scorn formed on his aristocratic countenance as he enjoyed their discomfort.

The guests had more than one reason for wishing they were elsewhere. For one thing, it was not easy to for some of them to get to this part of Greater Boston. Three of the guests lived in Boston—16 miles to the south. They had had to make their way to the Eastern Railway Station in East Boston, either on foot, by hansom cab, or by horsecar plus ferry in order to endure the smoke and ashes of the train that would take them up to Salem.

A fourth guest lived in Braintree, south of Boston, where he had to take a train into South Boston; then take a horsecar or hansom cab to the station in East Boston. Then he had to take another train north to Salem.

The fifth guest lived in Brookline and would need to take a horsecar in to the station in East Boston. All of this was just so they could have dinner before reversing the entire process on their way home the same night. For all five, a meeting in the Boston offices of *Knickerbocker* would have been far more convenient and far less time consuming.

All five of the passengers getting off the train had taken hansoms from the Salem Depot to Van Zandt's house on Chestnut Street.

While getting to Van Zandt's country house was time-consuming, the reason for going there weighed far more heavily on the minds of the five guests than did the travel inconvenience.

Toward the end of the meal, as homemade vanilla ice cream was being served to them, the guests became fidgety. It was already dark out. Here they were on the North Shore, and they hadn't even gotten into the matter they'd come to discuss.

Everett Flick was now removing the last of the dessert dishes, as the men began lighting up expensive cigars. Trampler grudgingly reflected on how decent the meal had been. While he didn't say so to the others at the table, he hadn't expected much culinary proficiency from a servant woman this far outside of Boston. Van Zandt must have read his mind, for he said,

"I notice with interest that each of you did enjoy your meal. Miriam is a rare find—especially up here on the North Shore. Now how about a glass of port. I warn you, you won't be satisfied with just one glass. I was fortunate a few months ago to secure a case of a superb 1870 Ware's Special."

Hugh Trampler exhaled a cloud of blue smoke and cleared his throat nervously. "That would be fine, Martin, but as the hour is getting late for those of us who have to travel tonight, I wonder if we couldn't turn to our business."

"Yes, of course, Hugh. First tell me what you think of that port."

Trampler frowned, and was about to say something he'd probably regret, but he thought better of it. He took an obligatory sip of the proffered port. It was an act of supreme self-control, for his host's deliberate dallying was preventing him from getting to his real interest at this moment. The sale of the magazine had been his only serious interest in recent weeks—every waking moment. For him, the sale was not some philosophical issue, but rather a highly visceral one. He needed money—and fast. He took another sip and said, "Quite good, Martin. Excellent in fact. But you didn't bring us up to Salem just to taste your port."

"Indeed I didn't," smiled Van Zandt mischievously. "I invited you up here for two reasons actually. First, I wanted to give you a final chance to change my mind on the matter of selling *Knickerbocker*. Now what I find interesting is that you actually came. I wasn't sure all of you would. I'd have thought that some of you would have had more sense. My God, you all know I'm not likely to change my mind on this subject."

“This is just some kind of cynical game with you, isn’t it Martin?” It was Margarita Scharf Calore, easily the youngest member of the board. She’d inherited her directorship from her husband a few years earlier after he’d succumbed to tuberculosis.

“I don’t know if it’s cynical or not, my dear. I do admit to being fascinated by the behavior of humans who smell the scent of money.”

“Damn it, Martin, that’s vile and unfair,” roared Trampler. “We have every right to be concerned about our financial interests without being labeled mercenary by you. *Knickerbocker* is a business, not a charity. We’re all in this to make money. Nothing wrong with that. Certainly the magazine has been good to you.” Trampler took a deep breath before plunging ahead. “I might add that I don’t see you giving away any of your money.”

Van Zandt remained expressionless a few seconds. Then he slowly folded his hands in his lap, jutting his jaw forward a half inch. He returned Trampler’s look with a chilling stare.

“What I do with my money is my business,” he said coldly. “Furthermore, what I do with my business is also my business.”

A portly, heavily jowled man leaned forward in his seat. It was Sebastian LaRue, a successful attorney in the Boston business community. His fleshy cheeks were ruddy and covered with scaly reddish blotches. His face was not reddened by working out of doors, though, for he was known for his avoidance of anything to do with the outdoors. LaRue began slowly and deliberately, “Martin, with all due respect for your having made this business what it is today, it is not your business. It belongs to all of us in this room. Perhaps, that is the heart of the problem. You view this business more paternalistically than do the rest of us.”

“I started *Knickerbocker*, and I built it into what it is today,” exploded Van Zandt. “Without me, it wouldn’t even exist.”

"True, Martin," said Trampler from the other side of the table, "and you own 39 percent of the stock. That's a lot, but it's not enough to make *Knickerbocker* yours. As Sebastian says, it's our magazine, and some of us think it's time to sell."

Van Zandt smiled mirthlessly, "I suppose you still feel that way, too, Winnifred?" He was addressing Winnifred Neustadt, the other widow on the board, and, when he was honest with himself, the only director he respected besides Arthur Billingsley.

"Indeed I do. It's time to sell. I wish you would reconsider your position, Martin. After all, with the biggest block of stock, you'd have the most to gain."

Van Zandt turned away from his perceived enemies. His gaze now fastened on the two allies he felt he could count on. He looked first at Arthur Billingsley, a genteel man in his late fifties, and then at Margarita Calore, a seductively attractive woman in her late thirties—the two board members he considered, for lack of a better term, his allies. Calore may not have been an ally out of choice, but that was beside the point. The muscles in his face relaxed. "I assume you two are still with me on this?" It was more of an assumption than a question.

Billingsley nodded resignedly, hating to side with Van Zandt on anything.

Calore said, "Yes, of course, Martin, though I must say sometimes I'm tempted."

"Don't give in to it," said Van Zandt, adding mysteriously, "else I, too, might be tempted." He shot Calore a meaningful look.

Calore returned his look, unable or unwilling to hide the hatred she felt for the man. But her defiance evaporated quickly, and she dropped her head submissively, drawing in a deep breath before saying, "I'm with you, Martin. I'm with you."

"Good, I knew I could count on you," said Van Zandt contemptuously. Then, raising his voice, he continued, "Well now, it appears as if nothing's changed. Three of you want to sell, and three of us don't. Ha! Just as I thought. You're all quite predictable. Still, I'd hoped at least one of you would have surprised me with an original thought."

"Damn it, Martin," said Billingsley, "I know you're our host, but that's insulting. If I were you, I wouldn't take the votes of Mrs. Calore and me for granted." Billingsley was trying to avoid self-emasculation in front of his colleagues, while at the same time maintaining a modicum of self-control.

Van Zandt studied him for a moment before responding. His hooded eyes were almost slits. Billingsley had been against selling the magazine from the very first time it was mentioned. As a successful businessman, he didn't need the money that would immediately accrue to the stockholders if the sale went through. Still, Van Zandt reasoned, if pressed too far, Billingsley might abandon his position in favor of the status quo on principle alone. He was that kind of person. Best not to push him too much. Van Zandt was confident that he could manipulate greed, self-interest, and the other baser human instincts, but he was unsure of how to deal with people who were motivated by principle. He smiled at Billingsley as he spoke.

"I would certainly never take your vote for granted, Arthur."

Then, turning to Margarita Scharf Calore, he leaned back in his chair self-importantly, a trace of disdain on his patrician features. He interlaced his fingers under his chin and stared ominously into the eyes of a face that had bewitched many a man before him. Van Zandt, however, was not about to be bewitched. A wry grin formed on his formidable countenance.

"As for you, my dear—" His words were meant to suggest levity to the others, but it was clear to Calore, that there was deadly serious meaning behind what he'd deliberately left unsaid. The others just shook their heads. Humor for Van Zandt was always at the expense of others.

"You mentioned two reasons for having us up here, Martin." It was LaRue speaking, rubbing tired eyes. "We know what the first reason is. What was the second one?"

"I was about to get to that," said Van Zandt soberly. "What I'm about to say will come as a shock to all but one of you. Believe me, what I'm going to say, I don't say lightly, for I know how serious my accusation is." He paused to take a deep breath before continuing, "It has come to my attention—don't ask me how—that one of you collaborated with Guiteau." There was a collective gasp from the group around the table. The room fell silent, and the quickened breathing of the guests was palpable.

Van Zandt scanned their faces—starting on his left and ending on his right. Was that a look of panic in the eyes of one of his guests? "I know who you are," continued Van Zandt ominously. "Here is what I propose to do."

* * *

There wasn't much blood at the scene. What there was had formed a dark amorphous stain beneath the head of the deceased—less than a foot long and no more than six inches wide. When fresh, nine or ten hours earlier, it had been a viscous deep crimson flow, slowly spreading outward beneath the white-haired head of the pale victim. In the ensuing hours, much of the vital fluid had been absorbed by the expensive oriental carpet. The blood was a much deeper red now—deeper even than the darkest maroon filigrees of the rich carpet on which the dead man lay—more like a rich claret seen through the imperfect glass of its bottle in a dimly lit room. The stain appeared to be completely dry now.

Chief Chester Gormley of the Salem Police Department bent down in order to get a better look at where the dead man had been hit. The tangled mass of white hair of the victim was matted with dried blood. It looked sticky. Gormley frowned. It looked as if there'd been several blows. "Crushed his skull," he said, shaking his head. He placed one hand on his knee and slowly got up. "Where's his wife?"

"He's a widower," said Sergeant Kevin O'Leary. "Mrs. Van Zandt died a couple of years ago, according to Mrs. Flick, the housekeeper. The Flick woman and her husband live here in a small apartment on the third floor at the other end of the house." O'Leary's eyes widened in awe. "Some house. Must be twenty rooms. Always wondered what it was like in here. Anyway, Mr. Flick's the caretaker, gardener, what have you. Also drives the buggy for Mr. Van Zandt when he needs to go somewhere."

"Who discovered the body?"

O'Leary jerked a thumb toward the couple across the room. "Mrs. Flick. She also does the cooking. When he didn't show up for breakfast, she got worried and went up to his bedroom to see if he was okay. Door was open. Bed hadn't been disturbed, she said. Didn't know what to make of it. She knew Mr. Van Zandt had been home last night. She'd cooked a big dinner for him and a bunch of fancy guests. Her husband helped her serve them."

"You have a list of the guests?'

"Yep. She gave me their names. I don't have all of their addresses, though."

"Have any?"

"Just one. A Mr. Billingsley. Lives in Boston. Back Bay." He raised his eyebrows and passed a piece of paper to Gormley. "Here."

"Good. What time did the guests leave?"

"About eight-thirty, according to the Flicks."

"A little early for a fancy dinner party to be breakin' up, wouldn't you say, Kevin?"

"I s'pose," said O'Leary. "But don't forget, they all had to go back to the Boston—or even further for a couple of 'em."

"How'd they get to the Salem Depot?"

"Flick took 'em in the family carriage." O'Leary rolled his eyes. "You should see this carriage. Must've cost a fortune. Took all five of 'em in one trip." When he got back to the house—it was around ten 'cause he waited at the depot with the five of 'em till the train came in—he and the missus went up to their rooms in the other end of the house.

"Then this morning, when she discovered that he hadn't slept in his bed, she got worried. Looked everywhere. Thought maybe he'd fallen or had a problem with his heart. Finally, after searching most of the house, she stumbled onto him here in the sitting room."

"That's them, you say?" Gormley nodded in the direction of the tired-looking middle-aged couple standing silently at the other end of the sitting room.

"Yep. Told 'em to stick around."

"Ask 'em to come on over."

Everett Flick was a short, stocky man with a full mustache that covered much of his thin-lipped mouth. His graying hair showed traces of its original light brown color, though it was nearly white at the temples, and receding in the front. His round face had the creased, weather-beaten look of a man who worked out of doors a lot. He was wearing faded blue overalls that looked to be at least a size too big for him.

Miriam Flick was plain looking and pasty faced, and an inch taller than her husband. She wore a clean blue and white-checked housedress—also faded. Her waist was equal in size to her hips and her ample bosom. Despite her dowdy appearance, though, it soon became clear that she did most of the thinking for the couple. Chief Gormley nodded to the couple as they came over. It was obvious that Mrs. Flick had been crying.

Gormley dwarfed the apprehensive Flick couple. Standing a head taller than either of them, and wearing a rumpled, but clean uniform, he seemed aware that this was no ordinary investigation. Crime in Salem tended to be limited to occasional burglaries, rowdyism in waterfront bars, domestic abuse and youthful vandalism. In his 26 years on the force, he'd only handled a few suspicious deaths and even fewer murders. He'd never had a deceased as prominent as Mr. Van Zandt.

Gormley addressed the cowering couple: "I know you've already talked with Sergeant O'Leary and Patrolman Kilmartin, but I'd like for you to tell me what you told them, if you don't mind."

"That's just it, don't you see," said Mrs. Flick, wiping a tear away from under her right eye. "We don't know very much at all. I know Mr. Van Zandt was still downstairs after his guests left. Saw him myself sittin' there in the parlor with a glass of whiskey or sherry or something. I poked my head in one last time to tell him I was going up to bed. Asked him if there was anything else. No, he said. He'd see us in the morning at breakfast."

"Do you know why he stayed downstairs by himself?" asked Gormley.

She got a far-off look in her eyes before she continued, "Mr. Van Zandt was good to Everett and me, but he had some strange ways."

"Like what, ma'am?"

She turned her head away modestly. "I'd best not say."

"At a time like this, ma'am, you'd best tell us everything you can."

She nodded her understanding. "Well, like I said, he had some strange ways."

Gormley nodded encouragingly. "Such as?" He tried to keep from sounding threatening.

"Like when he had company for dinner or a party, he had this strange habit. Instead of going up to bed after they left, he'd stay in the parlor by himself, sometimes for hours at a time. He did that last night. Done that for years. Leastways, ever since Mrs. Van

Zandt passed away."

"What'd he do there by himself?"

"Just think about her, I spose. If it was me, I'd go up to my room soon's they left." As she said this, her eyes grew misty. "Maybe he'd be alive today."

Gormley turned to Everett Flick. "Where were you while Mr. Van Zandt sat in the parlor last night?"

"I was takin' those people back to the depot so's they could catch the train to Boston."

"He was gone for over an hour," interjected Miriam. "Weren't you, Everett?"

"Yes, I was. Waited till the train come. They asked me to. Said they didn't want to be stuck there in case it didn't come. When I got back, the house was dark—'cept for a light in the parlor and one in our apartment at the other end of the house. Can't wait till this rainy spell lets up so's the streets dry up. You know how messy they get in the rain. Damn, I'm rambling. Anyway, when I came back to the house I peeked into the parlor and said good night to Mr. Van Zandt."

"What time was that?"

"Must have been a little after ten."

"Did he say anything to you, Mr. Flick?" asked Gormley.

"Yes sir, he did. Said, good night, Everett. Then he thanked me for taking those folks back to the depot."

"How many?"

"Why, all of 'em."

Gormley shook his head impatiently. "How many was that?"

"Five. Three men and two women."

"Then what'd you do?"

"I checked in the kitchen to see if Miriam was still there. Didn't think she would be. Didn't see no light in there. She wasn't there, of course. I could still smell the kerosene, so I knew she hadn't been gone long. Then I went up to the apartment. Miriam was already in bed. As I said, the house was dark when I got back here. 'Cept for the parlor."

"Then what happened?"

"Why I went to bed."

"Go on, continue with what you did till Mrs. Flick discovered that Mr. Van Zandt was dead."

"This morning," said Flick in his monotone, "when Mr. Van Zandt didn't come down for his breakfast like he always does, Miriam went up to knock on his door. He didn't answer so she opened the door and found that he hadn't slept in his bed. She didn't know what to make of it. Looked in every room on the second floor. Finally came downstairs, and when she came into the parlor, there he was, just lying there." He put his arm around his grief-stricken wife's shoulders. Gormley noticed that she seemed truly comforted by this.

Gormley continued with his questions.

"What time is that? When he normally comes down?"

"Eight o'clock. Mr. Van Zandt always comes down for his breakfast at eight o'clock. On the weekends when he's here, that is."

Then, as if to clarify the obvious, Miriam added, "He's not here every weekend, and he hardly ever comes during the week. This week was unusual. He came up from Boston on Wednesday. Said he was taking a few days off."

"Oh," said Gormley, his curiosity aroused. "He doesn't. . . or didn't live here all the time? Where did he live during the week?"

"Boston. That's where he lives. Mr. Van Zandt has...oh my goodness." She put her hand to her mouth as she realized that she'd been talking in the present tense. "Mr. Van Zandt *had* a townhouse on Beacon Hill, I believe. His business was there, you know. Boston, I mean."

"And what was his business?"

"*Knickerbocker* magazine. He was the publisher."

Gormley raised an eyebrow at hearing the name of the well-known periodical.

"He didn't own all of it," interrupted her husband, proud to have something to contribute. "Had partners. They were the folks that came to dinner last night, I believe."

"Well, yes, Everett, that's right. But he was the main owner, You know that," Miriam Flick added authoritatively.

Gormley then asked, "How'd the evening go?"
Miriam Flick furrowed her brow. "I'm afraid we can't say, Mr. Gormley. He didn't talk to us about his business."

Gormley pursed his lips and tried not to appear impatient. "Surely you can give me some idea what it was like last night. Was the mood at the table pleasant? Was there any squabbling or arguing? Did anyone lose his temper?"

"I was in the dining room more than Miriam," offered Everett, a bit tentatively, not sure he wanted to be the one to explain.

"And?"

"It started out pleasant enough, but..."

"But what?" prompted Gormley impatiently.
"Wasn't long before they started bickering among themselves. No, that's not quite right. It seemed to be them against Mr. Van Zandt."

"Who do you mean by *them*?"

"Seemed like all of them. Most of 'em, anyway."

"Could you tell what it was about?"

"It wasn't my business, you understand. I try not to eavesdrop..."

"Yes, of course. Still, you must have heard something, Mr. Flick."

"There was talk about selling *Knickerbocker.* Some of the others wanted to sell, and Mr. Van Zandt didn't. He felt very strongly about it. You could tell from his voice that he was angry. Very angry."
"How about the others—the ones who did want to sell? Were they mad, too?"

"Yessir, they most certainly were."

"Do you remember which of the guests were for selling?"

"Wouldn't swear to it, but it seemed like that big gentleman Mr. Trampler, I think—and one of the women were for it. As I said, I tried not to stare."

Miriam Flick said, "I was in the kitchen most of the time, so I'm afraid I can't help you, Mr. Gormley."

She then sat down on a satin-upholstered straight chair that was placed with its upright back against the wall. She wiped her forehead with her apron. "I can't imagine anyone doing such a thing, can you, Mr. Gormley?"

The chief smiled patiently, "No ma'am, I can't. Tell me, is there any evidence of someone breaking in—through a door or a window, I mean?"

"No sir, said Everett Flick. I've looked. Wouldn't have needed to break in, anyway."

"Why do you say that?"

"Doors weren't locked."

PART 2

Chapter 1

Boston — December 1884 Thursday the 4th

I'd been back in Boston for barely a week when my long-lost cousin Samantha dropped in on me out of the blue. What she had to say was pretty shocking. Seeing her for the first time after all those years was itself a shock, but nothing compared with what she had to tell me. But I'm getting ahead of myself.
It was early December, and I was just getting used to my new digs. Samantha didn't write or send a telegram in advance. She simply materialized at my front door that cold, gray afternoon in early December.

Oh, she brought one additional surprise with her—Edward.

My Uncle Martin, the eccentric, difficult man who left me this house, had liked chimes. Exquisite chimes. No doubt he'd acquired this taste for door chimes in his lifetime of travel to every corner of the globe. I'm sure that during his frequent trips abroad he'd heard the ringing of more church chimes and village chimes and cathedral chimes and basilica chimes than a Vatican bishop.

Uncle Martin's chimes play a short passage from Tchaikovsky's *Waltz from Swan Lake*. The passage plays whenever someone presses the oval mother-of-pearl button next to the rather large and extremely heavy solid oak front door. They're actually quite nice. The chimes, I mean. I have no idea how they work, but I do know that only someone like my uncle could have afforded them. (I suppose, now that

I've become the beneficiary of nearly half his estate, I would have to include myself.) When he had the chimes installed four years ago, there was nothing like them in Boston. He knew what he wanted and had them designed to his own specifications by someone referred to him by one of his many contacts here in the city. No one ever accused Uncle Martin of not being well connected.

The chimes interrupted my concentration. I was trying to complete the third in a series of articles I was writing about Mr. Cleveland for the *Salem Gazette*. Upon leaving the paper, I'd worked out an arrangement with the editor that provided for my writing an occasional article for them on a freelance basis.

The series of three pieces had to do with our new President, Grover Cleveland. He'd be taking office in March, and people wanted to know about him. Most people I knew had high hopes for the man, especially after the so-so performance of Chester Arthur. Arthur had been Garfield's vice president and became president after the assassination. Not being elected in the first place, Mr. Arthur had faced an uphill fight just to gain the country's acceptance. Let's face it, some considered him unfit to be vice president, so how could you expect him to handle the rigors of the presidency. Still, I didn't judge him quite so harshly. Mark Twain was positively effusive recently when he said,

> *I am but one in 55,000,000; still, in the opinion of this one-fifty-five millionth of the country's population, it would be hard to better President Arthur's administration. But don't decide till you hear from the rest.*

President Arthur surprised both his enemies and his friends. He wasn't so awful, really. He put an end to the spoils system—at least he made a valiant effort. But in the end, he was never fully accepted. He lost out to Blaine on the second ballot at the convention, and Blaine went on to lose to Cleveland in the election last month, which brings us to where we are now.

As I said, the chimes startled me. I wasn't expecting visitors. I was curious, too, since not many people knew that I lived in this house, which I'd so recently inherited from my Uncle.

I hauled myself out of my chair and made my way out of the library and down the wide hallway towards the front door. The door, which must weigh a couple of hundred pounds, swung open surprisingly easily. My uncle wouldn't have accepted anything less. I found myself facing a young couple—if you accept my age as young. They were smartly outfitted in the latest fashions of the day. The young lady was dressed in a stylishly bustled royal blue dress with a cheviot mantle of a slightly darker hue placed lightly upon her shoulders. A pale blue parasol was poised gracefully over her left shoulder.

The gentleman's flawlessly tailored dark suit complemented his trim physique as he stood nattily by the lady's side. He was clearly *à la mode* as he rakishly held the brim of one of the new top hats that had taken the country by storm in recent years.

They were not at all what I would have expected to find gracing my doorstep that afternoon. Certainly she was not what I would have expected. I don't know what I would have expected, but she was not it. Not that I was disappointed, mind you. To say that she was pleasing to the eye would be an understatement. As I said, she appeared to be about my age—maybe a little younger—and possessed that combination of nubile feminism and latent energy that, for me, at least, was really quite exciting. She offered me what appeared to be her icebreaker smile.

"Hello, are you James Christopher?" Her voice was perky and confident. Not at all the self-effacing mode of today's young women.

"Guilty." I tried to match her smile without letting her know that, at that moment, she could have gotten anything from me. As it turned out, her first words weren't all that demanding—and weren't a request.

"I'm Samantha Van Zandt. Your long-lost cousin. Remember?"

She couldn't have surprised me more if she'd claimed she was Queen Victoria. There'd be no mistaking the two of them, though, for my purported cousin was clearly much prettier than the dear old monarch.

Samantha Van Zandt was indeed my cousin, though I hadn't seen her in at least ten years. She'd been nineteen, maybe twenty at the time. A year or two later she'd broken her parents hearts by eloping with some young man she'd met at school. I looked at the smartly dressed man standing beside her and wondered if this were he. Before I sought clarification (God knows how I would have managed that), she came to my rescue.

"Oh, darn, forgive me, James. I'm being bad mannered. This is Edward Ridley, my husband."

"A pleasure," I said, extending my hand.

"I've heard a good deal about you...all of it good," said Ridley urbanely.

"Yes, James, Edward is the same fellow I ran away with ten years ago. As you can imagine, we've both changed a great deal. Edward and I were both too young. And both rebellious." Edward shot her a look, as if to say he wasn't sure he agreed on both counts. What she'd done with herself in the intervening ten years must be quite a story, I thought.

Samantha's elopement had been the scandal of the family. Good girls simply didn't elope, especially girls from privileged families, which hers certainly was. The disgrace nearly killed my Aunt Grace and my Uncle Martin. After she ran off, they hardly acknowledged that they had a daughter. Apparently Edward had taken her out West to Illinois. He'd had this lust for frontier adventure. I have no idea what he did out there. To look at him, he didn't seem the outdoor type to me. I do know that Samantha ended up teaching in a one-room school somewhere on the plains near the Mississippi. She wrote home, occasionally, but didn't come home. Travel was too difficult, and they had no money.

About six or seven years into Samantha's estrangement from the family, Aunt Grace actually did die—from tuberculosis, I think. She was always volunteering to help the needy. I suppose she caught it from being so close to the unfortunates on the street. Her do-gooding ways used to drive Uncle Martin crazy, but he was so much in love with her, he never made much of a fuss over it. I suppose he was secretly proud of her. After her death he was never quite the same person.

But back to Samantha. Believe me when I tell you that she'd changed in ten years. No longer the gangly tomboy I remembered, or the simple frontier schoolmarm I'd imagined her to be out there in the wilds of Illinois. Now, as I stood staring at her, she looked very much the eastern sophisticate. She was properly dressed and had the bearing and poise of a thoroughly modern woman. It didn't appear to be an affectation, either. I must have stared at her a full twenty seconds before I finally managed to speak.

"Samantha. My God, how long has it been?"

"Ten years, James. Are you going to invite us in?"

"Why...yes, of course," I said awkwardly. "Come in. My God, you've changed. I mean really changed."

"For the better, I hope."

"Definitely for the better."

"Was I that bad before?"

I felt my cheeks flush. "I didn't mean it that...what I meant was..."

"I know, James. I know. I was rough around the edges. My hair was wild. Never cut it. Wore ugly old clothes—though I didn't have to. Daddy never denied me anything. But by that time I was rejecting everything and anything if it came from him *or* from

Mother. Weird, huh."

"Guess you were going through a stage," I offered weakly, not knowing exactly what to say.

She grimaced, shaking her head wistfully, "That stage lasted three or four years. Thank goodness Edward rescued me from my wicked ways." She glanced up at her husband, who seemed uncomfortable with the conversation. Edward finally managed a polite, but reserved smile. Samantha did a slow pirouette, inspecting her surroundings as we stood talking in the foyer. "Place looks pretty much the way I remembered it."

"Just moved in a week ago," I said. "Can I get you something to drink?"

"Oh, no, James. Nothing."

"Surely you'll have some tea?"

She looked at her husband. "Tea sounds good, doesn't it Edward?" He smiled a reluctant assent.

"Tea it is, then" I said. "Be right back."

A few minutes later the three of us were sitting somewhat awkwardly in my front parlor. We really didn't know much about each other. I know Samantha and I were cousins, but most people grow apart when they don't see each other for ten years—especially if they're relatives. And I knew exactly nothing about Edward, a deficit that was destined to be corrected in the very near future, though I didn't realize it at the time. As she completed a cursory examination of the exquisitely furnished room, she turned to me.

"Same furniture. What is it, Chippendale? I never bothered to ask when I lived here."

"Queen Anne I think. Though I'm not sure." I was beginning to tire of the awkwardness, so I decided to move things along. "Bring me up to date. It's been a long time, Sam."

"Would you believe, I'm now a lady of leisure. Edward is a banker, you know. Boston Bank of Commerce.

"You've come full circle," I said with a grin.

"Yes, I suppose I have. We just built a new house on Commonwealth Avenue out in Newton."

"That's quite a trip for Edward, isn't it?" Turning to him, I said, "I assume your office is in downtown Boston?"

"School Street. Yes, it's a good trip," agreed Edward seriously. "We don't live out there during the week, though. Have a little apartment here in Boston —on Beacon Street. Just a few blocks from here. We go out to Newton on weekends."

I whistled silently. Two houses—within ten miles of each other. Probably not that far apart. I could see that my cousin had recovered more than adequately from the indiscretions of her youth. Before I could give more consideration to this ironic turn of events, Samantha quickly turned her attention to me, and her assessment of my good fortune.

"So you got the house," she said. "Both of them, as a matter of fact." The irony of both of us ending up with two houses didn't escape me. I'm sure it didn't escape her either.

I said, "I never expected it, Samantha. I never expected anything, really."

She shot me a look of disbelief. "Of course you didn't."

"Really, I never expected him to leave me anything. And I didn't expect him to die at 68. He was so alive, so active. I guess I expected him to go on forever."

"Well, he probably would have gone on for 10 or 15 more years if someone hadn't hit him with that jade statue." I think Grandfather was 85 when he died. She studied me carefully before going on. "So Daddy never told you he was going to leave you almost half of his estate—not to mention the houses I grew up in?"

I wasn't sure where she was going with this, but I didn't like the direction she appeared to be heading.

"Believe it or not, it's true. His leaving me the houses and the money was a total surprise. Oh I suppose if you'd asked me before he was killed, did I think he'd bequeath me anything, I would have said he might leave me a few dollars. I knew he liked me. But, did I think he'd leave me close to a million dollars, if you include the stock, the two houses, and the land? No. Absolutely not. He was always unpredictable. A hard man to figure."

She eyed me suspiciously. "Liked you. James, he adored you. Treated you like the son he never had."

"You didn't seem to have any trouble with that when we were young."

"You were a fairly decent chap then," she grinned impishly. Edward looked sour. He didn't seem to appreciate the easy relationship that had developed so quickly between Sam and me. To Edward, the relationship must have appeared to be a revitalization of a long-standing mutual affection.

"But not now?" I said provocatively.

"I didn't say that, James. Don't put words in my mouth."

"Well, what are you saying, Sam? Do you resent the fact that your father left me the two houses and a lot of money?"

She stood up and walked to the big mullioned window that looked out upon Mt. Vernon Street. She stood there for a moment with her hands on her hips. Edward watched her from where he was sitting. He seemed to be trying to read her thoughts. Finally, she turned and faced me. "No, I don't. I really don't. There's really no one else more deserving. Besides," she said with a wide grin, "I've known for over a year now that you were getting the houses. Daddy told me in a moment of weakness—just a few months before he died. Any resentment I might have felt is long gone."

I was flabbergasted. "And neither he nor you ever told me. Why? Why didn't *he* tell me?"

"Why didn't he do a lot of things, James? My father was a contrary unpredictable man. You know that."

I shook my head at the truth of her statement. Martin Van Zandt was indeed a contrary unpredictable man. "What about you? You don't think he should have left it all to you? Including the houses?"

"He left me a great deal, as you well know. Of course I was surprised when he told me that I wasn't getting the houses. At first I was disappointed. But I'd disappointed him, too. I realize now just how much." She turned to me then and said, "I've grown up, James. I really have. You don't know this, but on more than one occasion when I was a girl, I told him I hated these houses. Both of them. I know he loved them, and my rejecting them hurt him more than anyone could have imagined. I suppose I'm lucky he left me the money and the company stock."

"He did leave you a great deal. . ."

She dropped her head and sighed, "Under the circumstances, it was more than generous."

She was right, of course. Martin Van Zandt had left his only daughter 25 percent of his company's stock. The way I figured it, that came to somewhere between six hundred thousand and a million dollars. A fortune when you consider that the average income in Boston was somewhere between two and three hundred dollars a year. She could live like a queen for the rest of her life. Not bad for a daughter, who, ten years earlier, had rejected materialism in general and specifically everything else her parents stood for. I'd always liked Sam, though. She was fun and had a generous spirit. Spunky, too. Clearly, she had a mind of her own.

Now, though, it seemed as if she'd finally gotten her life sorted out. Edward may have been a bit serious, but he appeared to be a man of substance with a good future. I hoped I was right about both of them. Samantha *was* my cousin, after all. I looked her in the eyes and said, "Yes, it is a lot, especially in light of your view of money a few years ago." I smiled, hoping she'd take it the way I meant it. Simply as a little good-natured teasing.

Her face reddened as she grinned back at me sheepishly.

"I told you I'd changed, James. Maybe not as much as Daddy would have wanted, but I've changed."

"So is this visit just an informal house warming, or do you have an agenda?"

"Both. I did want to get a good look at you after all these years. After all, you are living in my house." She quickly held up her hand and added, "Don't get your dander up, James. Just teasing. I really don't have any problem with it. Honest. Though I do hope you'll invite Edward and me to visit here once in awhile. I have some good memories about this place, despite what you may have heard."

I relaxed a bit. "Of course. I'm glad you want to visit. It's a big house for one person. I can use the company once in awhile."

"You'll have plenty of company once people learn you live here. I wouldn't worry about being lonely, James."

Her expression then grew serious. "I do have another reason for seeing you today. It's about my father's death. Everyone believes he was killed by a burglar. They say that Daddy caught him in the act of burglarizing the house." She was talking about the other house I'd inherited the rambling 18-room house up in Salem.

"That's what the Salem police report said."

"Yes, I know, but I don't believe it."

"You think the police lied?"

"No. I don't think they lied. But I do think they made a mistake. They're not that experienced with this sort of crime, James. How many murders do they have? You know what I mean. You used to spend time up there, when you were younger."

"Yes, I spent time up there as a boy visiting Uncle Martin. But I've spent a couple of years up there recently, too, working at the local paper. I'll tell you more about that later. But, yes, I know Salem well. And yes, you're right. They don't have a lot of murders in Salem."

She grew thoughtful, her brow knitted pensively. I found myself looking at her full, sensuous lips. "They could have lied," she said. "You can't rule that out."

She had my attention now. "What motive would they have for lying?"

"To cover their incompetence. What if they simply had not idea what happened. Isn't it possible they might come up with the idea of a burglar rather than admit they were stumped?"

"If it wasn't a burglar, who was it?"

She took a deep breath, "I have no proof, but I think it's one of the board members."

I felt as if I'd been kicked in the stomach. "That's a rather serious accusation, Samantha. I assume you can back it up?"

A sheepish look appeared on her creamy smooth face. "Well, yes and no. That is, I have reasons for saying it, but I don't have any proof."

"Have you gone to the Salem police with your suspicions?"

"No, I wanted to speak to you first. I'm not sure how to proceed, but I thought you'd know what to do."

"You haven't seen me in 10 years, and you're willing to trust my judgment over that of everyone else you know?"

"I'm sort of limited in my options, James. It has to be someone with an interest in the company. And you, as a member of the family and its newest board member, certainly qualify."

"So does everyone else who works for the magazine or owns shares of it," I countered. Then I looked at her husband. "How about you, Edward? What do you suggest?"

He hesitated, clearly reluctant to express his opinion, and then Sam intervened before he could say whatever he was going to say.

"It has to be someone with a great deal at stake, James. Someone like a major stockholder or a board member. You know what's involved, James. If Edward asks questions people will resent it. They'll say it's none of his business."

"As the husband of Martin's most important heir and a new board member? I rather doubt that, Sam. I'm sure people would listen to him."

"Perhaps, but Edward feels somewhat uncomfortable with that role." She looked down at her feet. "Besides, he doesn't entirely agree with me on this, do you Edward?"

Edward shook his head. "Not at all." It was louder and firmer than I would have expected from him. "Frankly, I think it's nonsense. The police did their job. Best to leave it alone."

"So you see, James, it's *my* suspicious nature; not Edward's. I'm really asking you to indulge your cousin for old times sake. Edward thinks I'm crazy and the average employee doesn't know much about this at all, and probably doesn't care, either. They're not affected. At least not as directly as a major shareholder. The problem is, I can't trust most of the shareholders, because I have the feeling that one of them could be the murderer."

"Well, now that I'm a major shareholder and member of the board. What does that make me?" I said smiling.

She started to respond, but I continued talking because I knew what she was going to say. "But I wasn't here when your father was killed," I said. "So that let's me off the hook, right?"

She smiled warmly, "Right."

"Otherwise I'd be a suspect, too."

"Yes, I suppose so."

I feigned a pout.

"C'mon, James, you had a lot to gain from my father's death. Look at the money you ended up with. And the house. Not to mention being appointed to the board directors of one of America's most successful magazines."

In one sense she was right. *Knickerbocker* magazine was enormously profitable. It had made Martin Van Zandt rich and famous. And now I had a good portion of his money and owned a goodly portion of his business. And I was only 36.

Twenty-one years earlier my uncle had founded the now famous periodical. He'd been a regular staff writer for *Harper's*. As a writer, he'd seen much of the world, and he'd done it on a shoestring. Freelance writers don't get paid very much. They do it because they love to write. If they're good, and if they're sought after—as he was—it's one way to get around on someone else's dollar. That is, when they're sent on assignment somewhere to cover an important event or to interview an important person. But they don't travel first class.

Anyway, my uncle finally got fed up with being in debt constantly and decided he could make more money publishing his own magazine than he could writing for other publications. In writing for *Harper's* and certain other magazines and newspapers, he'd covered the banking and financial professions. Unlike many other writers at the time, he'd gone rather easy on the tycoons. Not that he catered to them, but he wasn't out to get them. Tried to present a fair picture, he'd always maintained. I was never quite sure what his motivation was, but suffice it to say, he made a lot of friends in the banking and financial world.

When he decided to start his own magazine he went to some of these moneyed people and they helped him. And the rest, as they say, is history. That is, until nine months ago when Uncle Martin was murdered.

Samantha's assessment still hung in the air like a brash challenge, threatening me to prove it wrong. I understood how she felt, too, but if she'd given the matter any thought, she'd have seen that she was all wrong about me.

"Sam, you're forgetting something very important. I didn't know I would inherit your father's money. I didn't know I was even in his will. God knows, he was unpredictable as hell. And I certainly didn't know that the board was going to ask me to sit with them."

She leaned forward and cradled her face in her hands. When she raised her head, her eyes were red.

"I know. I know. I still speak before I think sometimes. Old habits are hard to break, James, and this is a very emotional subject for me. I know you're being patient with me. My God, you could have reminded me that I, too, have just been made a member of the board."

"The fact hadn't escaped me," I said with a wry grin. "I would have reminded you, if I'd found it necessary." I could see that she didn't quite know how take that. She apparently decided to let it pass.

"I know you would never hurt Daddy," she said, almost on the verge of tears.

"Look, I understand," I said. "Just believe me when I tell you that I did care for Uncle Martin." God, how insincere this must have sounded to her in view of her suspicions. Still, I did mean it. At least I thought I did. "In his own strange way he was good to me, Sam, long before I ever benefited from his will. Oh, I know he could be difficult, and at times harsh, even cruel, but he always seemed to like me. I have no idea why, because I certainly didn't play up to his vanity. As a matter of fact I recall disagreeing with him on more than one occasion."

"I think that's why he left you all this. He respected you for not being like all the sycophants who surrounded him."

"Well, he was a remarkable man, in spite of his temper and even, at times, ruthlessness."

"Then you'll help me?" As she said this, I looked

over at Edward, who seemed disinterested, and remained expressionless.

"If you want someone to test your ideas on, I'll be more than happy to oblige," I told her.

"I was kind of hoping you'd do more than just offer an opinion, James. I need someone to help me look into this."

"Wait a minute. Whoa. I'm your basic writer cum publishing director, cousin; not an investigator."

Edward cleared his throat and harrumphed. Clearly he had serious doubts about the value of any help I could give, but he remained silent.

Samantha shot a quick look at her laconic spouse and capitulated, "All right, all right, James. I'll settle for advice."

She'd given in too quickly, I thought, but I left well enough alone.

Chapter 2 *Thursday the 4th*

I made another pot of strong tea and resigned myself to falling far short of my goal of writing the better part of the first of my three articles for the *Salem Gazette.* I'd been particularly eager to write today, especially since I'd just gotten one of the new writing machines made by Sholes & Glidden, the people who made the sewing machines. I'd been fascinated by these type writers, as Sholes & Glidden called them, since first seeing one last year at the newspaper where I was working up in Salem. The *Gazette* was an old established paper, and it had been a good opportunity for me to take on a job with some responsibility. The publisher had offered me the position of assistant managing editor, and I'd taken to it like a fish to water. Anyway, the managing editor had let me try the type writer machine once, and, to extend my tired old fish metaphor, from that moment on I'd been hooked.

Now that I had my own writing machine—it arrived just yesterday afternoon—I can't tell you how frustrating it was to have to leave it. On the other hand, I liked my cousin, and we hadn't seen each other in ten years, so there was no question that the type writer and my manuscript would have to wait. When I rejoined Sam and Edward in the sitting room, she looked up at me expectantly.

"Tell me what you know," I said.

"For one thing, nothing was stolen from the house the night Daddy was murdered."

"Nothing?"

"Nothing. Now, James, you tell me there's a burglar anywhere in the world who breaks into a house and leaves without taking anything."

"If he's caught in the act and he panics, I could see him leaving empty handed."

"Then why would he kill Daddy? He had nothing to gain. James, burglars don't break into a house when it's occupied. What happened was not a typical burglary. Not even a typical bungled burglary. It wasn't a burglary at all, James. Whoever killed my father came into the house through a door. It had to be someone Daddy knew."

I couldn't argue with her reasoning—assuming her facts were right. And they'd be easy to confirm. Still, assuming she was right about all this, it was a big leap from pseudo burglary to a deliberate murder by one of *Knickerbocker's* board members. I told her that, too.

"I know that, James. But think about it. You believe what you believe because you've been conditioned to believe it. The police said it was a bungled attempt at burglary. The newspapers then spread the word. That's now the accepted explanation. I believed it myself until I started thinking about it."

"All right," I said, "I've conceded that the break-in or so-called break-in is a little hard to accept, especially since there was no evidence of forcible entry. No need for a forcible entry, since the doors were unlocked. But you haven't shown me how you go from that to blaming a board member for the murder?"

"You've worked for newspapers, James. You've written about murders. You tell me. Why does someone kill another person?"

"Is this really necessary?"

"Humor me."

"Money's always a good motive."

"What else?"

"Love. Or more accurately unrequited love, or jealousy, or some kind of triangle, or adultery."

"Go on."

"Blackmail. To put an end to it, that is."

She nodded, encouraging me to continue.

"I suppose, too, that someone would commit murder to prevent another person from doing something, from taking some action."

"Exactly," she beamed.

"So that's where you're headed. Okay, don't keep me in the dark. Who wanted to prevent what?"

A flicker of a smile flashed over her face. Then she shook her head. "I don't know who, but I think I know what. That is, I don't know which person, but I'm almost certain it's a board member."

I tried to appear patient, but she could see I was skeptical.

"You said you'd listen. Look, I can't fill you in in five minutes. It'll take longer than that." Suddenly a flash of realization crossed her face. "Goodness," James, "I'm sorry. We've descended upon you like this, and haven't even asked if you were busy." Edward just rolled his eyes as if to acknowledge the typicality of such behavior on the part of his wife.

She was right. And so were Edward's eyes. But she'd always been like this—impulsive, unthinking about how her actions affected others. Still, there was no point in postponing this.

"You've got my attention," I said. "So let's stay with it." I looked at my watch. It was five thirty. "Why don't we walk over to Union Oyster House and get a table. We can have a bite to eat, enjoy a bottle of claret, and talk about this without feeling pressed."

"I interrupted something, didn't I?"

"Don't worry about it, Sam. I was writing. It'll still be there in the morning. I did leave the lights on in the library, though. Just let me go turn off the gas. Then we can walk over to the restaurant. It's only on Water Street near the wharf. After we order, we can catch up on things. I'll treat you to Boston's best sea food." I grinned at my cousin. "I can afford it now. While we're eating we can drift back to the subject at hand. How does that sound?"

Samantha welcomed the idea, so long as she

and Edward paid. I said I wouldn't hear of it. Edward acquiesced rather quickly, I thought.
I started towards the library, and then turned and faced my two visitors. Before we left, I had to show them my new writing machine.

* * *

It had turned dark in the hour-and-a-half my visitors had been with me in the comfortable old brick townhouse. When we left the building we were greeted by a gray, misty night. A light rain was developing. As we stepped onto Mt. Vernon Street, our ears were assaulted by the familiar metallic sound of iron wheels squealing and squeaking upon steel rails as overcrowded horsecars made their way noisily along Beacon Street two blocks away. The familiar cacophony was punctuated by the sharp staccato of horses' hooves on the cobbled streets—most of which in this part of town were quite narrow. As we left the relative quiet of Beacon Hill, we were accosted more and more by the racket of carriages and carts careening too fast for the traffic on streets that were too tight for the traffic. At times, because of the din, it was hard for us to talk. We turned the corner onto Court Street, trying to avoid dirty puddles and piles of garbage clogging the gutters.

It was difficult to navigate the sidewalks in this part of town, as one had to wend his way past numerous cinder barrels, trash containers, vats of slops, and other vile-smelling wastes. At points, it was necessary to use the street in order to avoid these filthy obstacles, for they often clogged the entire width of the sidewalk.

The street wasn't much better. Aside from the horse droppings, garbage was strewn liberally and without consideration for carriages or pedestrians. Occasionally we had to navigate a cautious path through the middle of the thoroughfare, since every few feet we found ourselves circumnavigating stinking piles of trash or offal in the gutter. I felt for Samantha, as she'd not come prepared for the rain. Her women's shoes were no match for the filthy streets, now made sloppy by the light shower.

A handsome black carriage with polished brass fittings rounded the next corner and headed directly towards us. It was occupied by a well-dressed gentleman and his lady. Court Street was quite narrow, and I could see that we'd most certainly be splashed unless the vehicle slowed down quickly. This it had no intention of doing. Carriages hardly ever slowed down for pedestrians. It was too hard on the horses. They'd have to change pace too often in the city traffic and congestion. As he neared us, the driver of the oncoming carriage laid his whip to the horses, and the coach accelerated. We had no recourse but to turn our backs to the street as the carriage thundered by, splashing us with slops from the street as it clattered past.

"You bastard," cried Edward, shaking his arm angrily. In the short time I'd known him, this was by far the most passionate I'd seen him. I must say, I shared his sentiments.

Alas, our battle with the streets was not yet done. As we approached the corner of Kilby Street we were met by a band of roving pigs coming directly toward us on the run. Unfortunately, pigs are far too common in American cities. They have been for years. Boston must have thousands of them. In some parts of the city, they roam at will.

The three of us ran for the nearest doorway. Edward didn't quite make it and suffered the indignity of being brushed aside rather rudely by an overlarge porker who never looked back as he continued on down the street with his porcine friends.

Five minutes later, our short, but eventful walk behind us, we rounded the corner of Congress and Union and were soon seated comfortably in the 60-year-old restaurant I'd come to appreciate so much from the first time I'd moved to Boston. The place claimed to be the oldest restaurant in America, and from what I understood, no other place had challenged that claim. Herman, our waiter, was a close-cropped, red-faced man of average height and deeply etched features. It was impossible to tell his age, though I'm certain he is older than me. He approached with his usual dour expression, looking tired and curmudgeonly as he stood before us, wiping his hands on his white half-apron. I recognized him just as he saw me.

He broke into a warm smile, "Mr. Christopher. Good to see you." His personable manner belied the morose impression he'd made moments before. I vowed then and there what I'd vowed a dozen times before: that someday, when the conditions were right, I would explain to Herman how off-putting his expression was when he moved from table to table, when not dealing directly with the customers. It was as if it took effort to be friendly, and he only had so much effort in reserve.

But I digress. The truth of the matter was that Herman was a friendly waiter. After I ordered a bottle of my favorite claret, an 1878 Chateau Branne-Mouton, he took our food orders graciously. At my suggestion, Samantha ordered the filet of sole. Herman beamed approvingly. I ordered the baked lobster. Edward ordered the roast beef. I know Herman disapproved, but he scarcely let on.

"The Union Oyster House is the only place in Boston that carries this claret," I said, purposely directing my comment to Edward, who thus far had said next to nothing since I'd met him two hours ago. Nothing, that is, but his apt curse when we'd all been splashed by the passing carriage out in the street.
The corners of Edward's mouth twitched upward for something like a split second. "Quite good," he grunted. It was becoming rather apparent that Edward was not a talker.

"Mmmm," beamed Samantha appreciatively, apparently aware that Edward and I were not communicating and wanting to make up for it with her own enthusiasm. As I studied the striking features of my cousin's face across the table, I felt an unexpected stirring in my loins. I found myself casting a furtive glance in the direction of the laconic Edward. I have no doubt he sensed the feelings that were stirring inside me for my attractive cousin—a woman who happened to be, not inconsequentially, his wife. I was beginning to think the reason for his reserve towards me might be resentment and perhaps with some justification.

"Okay," I said, settling back with a glass of wine in my hand, "convince me the killer is a board member."

She took a sip of from her glass, and swallowed nervously. "Did you know that for almost a year before his death, Father was being pressured to sell the magazine?"

"I had no idea. By whom?"

"Several of the directors. Probably most of them."

"But why? The magazine was doing well, at least from what I've heard."

"It was, and is. And because it *was* doing so well, several of the board members saw a chance to make a quick killing." She caught my eye and added nervously, "no pun intended. A group of former editors and executives from *Harper's* and *The New York Times* wanted to buy *Knickerbocker.* As far as I know, they still do. I remember at the time Daddy saying that they'd offered eight times earnings. Apparently that's considered quite generous in the business world. It would have nearly doubled the value of the stock overnight. A lot of the board members found that very appealing, as you can well imagine."

Harper's, of course, was the behemoth of the publications world. It was first published in 1850 and was the brainchild of the people at Harper & Brothers, the New York book-publishing firm. Oddly enough, the *The New York Times* newspaper was also started in

1850. For many years it was well respected, though that reputation has slipped a bit lately. It's not as well regarded now as *Harper's*, but it does have a loyal following. If these people acquired *Knickerbocker*, they'd have the second most powerful magazine in the country—next to *Harper's*.

"I take it your father was against selling."

"Vehemently. He wouldn't hear of it."

"If most of the board was for it, then they had the votes. Why didn't they just vote to accept the offer from the *Harper's* and *Times* people?"

Samantha's face reddened. She started to lose her composure. "Because my father made sure some of them couldn't." She saw the puzzled look on my face and continued in a more deliberate manner. "James, despite what you know and despite what you may have heard about me, I loved my father." She hesitated before plunging ahead. "I know I disappointed him ten years ago. I was far from the perfect daughter. But Daddy wasn't perfect, either. As you no doubt know, he wasn't always so nice in business. He could be hard when he felt it was necessary. Actually he could be ruthless. I know that."

I nodded. "Sometimes in business you've got to be tough."

She paused for a few seconds, as if considering whether to continue. She seemed to be searching for the right words. "I'm afraid it was more than just tough, more than just hard business tactics. As I said, Father could be ruthless. I've heard that if he had something on you he would threaten to use it in order to get you to do what he wanted."

"Blackmail?"

"I don't like that expression, but I guess you could call it that, James."

"You're saying he got people to vote the way he wanted them to by threatening to expose their secrets."

"Daddy was a very persuasive, very charismatic

man. I'm sure that simply by force of his personality he convinced some board members that they'd be making a big mistake if they voted to sell. But...and I don't know it for sure, but it probably is also true that...*if they had embarrassing secrets*, Daddy would threaten to reveal them. He would use whatever he had at his disposal to get his way. He was that kind of person. I know that. Lord knows, when I was younger, that's what I resented most."

By now we'd made serious inroads into our excellent meals, and were doing a good job on a second bottle of wine. After swallowing the latest of several rather healthy quaffs, I set my glass down on the table and found myself staring into my cousin's eyes. They were the most unusual blend of gray and blue I'd ever seen in a person's eyes. I know that that sounds like the hyperbole of one under the spell of youthful infatuation, but believe me, they really were different. And, of course, I was not exactly youthful. Even as an adolescent, though, I remember being mesmerized by those eyes. Samantha'd changed a great deal in the past decade, but not those eyes.

I'd always found her to be different. There was something about her that set her apart from other girls when she was a child, and whatever it was, it was still there.

You're probably thinking that these are not healthy observations for a cousin to be making. You'd be right, too, if it weren't for the fact that Samantha had been adopted as an infant. She wasn't the natural daughter of Martin and Grace Van Zandt. They'd never been able to have children, and as they found themselves closing in on forty, they'd decided to adopt. I'm glad they did. The road in the Van Zandt household had been rocky, but it looked as if Samantha had finally rounded the bend.

She was staring back at me now. I knew I should avert her gaze, so I forced myself to return to the subject at hand.

"I have to confess, Sam, That I'm pretty much

in the dark about the board. I know their names, and I know a couple of them ever so slightly, but that's about it."

"You're a member of the board now, James. You should know these people."

"I'll get to know them. I'll make it my business to know them. So far, though, the only board meeting I've attended was eight weeks ago, when they asked me to join them as a director. By the way, you weren't at that meeting eight weeks ago. When did they officially ask you to join the board?"

"A month ago. Don't ask me why we weren't asked at the same time."

I shook my head in amazement at the eccentricity of the board. I then reflected on that time eight weeks ago when I'd been asked officially. I'd taken the train down from Salem to meet with the board after receiving a letter from Mr. Friedman, the attorney for the board. He'd been Uncle Martin's personal lawyer, and he represented the magazine in any legal matters routine and otherwise. The meeting with the board had been fairly cordial, or so I'd thought at the time. Basically my qualifications came down to one thing: I owned 14 percent of the magazine. I quickly learned that that percentage put me in third place among all the shareholders. Only Samantha, with 25 percent, and Hugh Trampler, with 16 percent, had more shares.

"Immediately after the meeting I returned to Salem and the *Gazette,"* I explained to Sam, adding, "I spent three of the last eight weeks training my replacement. Obviously, I haven't had any time to get to know any of the directors, except very superficially."

"Didn't you know any of them from before?"

"I'd met Arthur Billingsley once, and Margarita Calore a couple of times, but I can't say I really know them. Frankly, Sam, I never cared for the business part of the business. Until now, the thought of sitting as a director on the board of a commercial business was rather unattractive. Truth be known, I forced myself to learn what I had to about the business world in order to be a decent journalist, but my first love has always been editorial. No, even that's not totally accurate. Editorial is fine, but my first love is writing."

She looked at me quizzically. "So why did you accept the directorship? You certainly knew that by becoming a board member you would have to get involved with the business end of the magazine."

I acknowledged all that with a sigh of resignation. My day definitely wasn't going as planned. I'd gotten up early in the morning with the intention of getting in seven or eight hours of writing. I wanted to get as far into my first article as possible before assuming my new responsibilities as a member of the board. And doing the writing with my new writing machine had made the prospect of an all-day writing session all the more attractive.

Some might think that board activity is limited to once-a-month meetings with the occasional in-between consultation with other directors. Perhaps that's the way it would go, but I wasn't taking any chances. Knowing myself as I did, I could see myself getting involved in the magazine business up to my elbows. I knew that once that happened, my writing time would be limited. That is, unless I wanted to get up before dawn or write into the wee hours at the end of a long day.

And now, a relative, who'd suddenly materialized from the past, was asking questions I'd avoided dealing with for weeks.

"That's a good question," I said. "Clearly the obvious answer is that I accepted in order to protect my interests. But if you want me to dig a little deeper, I suppose that, as much as I love writing, I probably didn't want to pass up the chance to live in more comfort than I've been able to as a journalist. Now that I have what I inherited from your father, I can afford to devote more time to the kind of writing I like."

I couldn't tell from her expression whether she believed me or not, so I gave her more to chew on. "Or, maybe I saw it as a personal growth opportunity. Sort of a challenge, to see if I could survive or even flourish in the world of business and commerce."

"But you'd still rather be writing?"

"Yes." I reflected for a moment before continuing. "And I suppose there's another method to my madness, too. I suppose I accepted the directorship because I felt an obligation to Uncle Martin. He'd been good to me...despite our occasional differences...and now he'd left me this huge inheritance...so I felt obligated to do what I could to help protect what he'd created."

The icy gray-blue eyes melted. "I hope you succeed, James. Don't take this the wrong way, but I'm amazed that they'd ask you to be a director instead of someone from outside of the family—someone they could control. Someone less committed to the Van Zandt interest in retaining the magazine."

"I have the shares. They couldn't very well exclude me. And maybe they think they can control me better if they can see me. Besides, if what you say is true about one of them being a murderer, they probably didn't all agree on asking me to serve. I imagine there's at least one director who didn't want me on the board."

"I would guess you're right," said Samantha. Then, without further comment on the matter, she asked a different question, "When you met with the board two months ago, did you detect any animosity from any of the members?"

I shook my head silently before responding. "Either you're wrong about one of them being a killer," I said, "or the guilty party is one hell of a good actor. I honestly don't remember anyone being unfriendly or even sounding reluctant or hesitant about appointing me. At first, when I got the call from Mr. Friedman, asking me if I'd be interested in coming to Boston to talk about a directorship, I was dumfounded. Why me, I thought. Then he reminded me that my newly inherited shares entitled me to it."

Sam leaned forward in her chair. She seemed fascinated by what I was saying. “So what you’re telling me is that nobody on the board gave any indication of animosity towards you.”

“None that I could sense. But I suppose, if you’re right about your suspicions, a very clever person could hide his feelings. I will, of course, be attending the next board meeting on Monday. Looks like I’ll be attending most of them from this point on. I’ll make it a point to pay a little closer attention to the behavior of each director.” I could see that this pleased her. I was taking her seriously. I still felt that the burden of proof was on her, though.

“Sam, if, as you suspect, one of the board members did your father in to keep him from blocking the sale of the magazine, why hasn’t the board proceeded with the sale? After all, your father is no longer an obstacle.”

“It’s a good question. I think it comes down to timing. Can you imagine the killer, whoever he was—“

“Or she.”

“Yes, or she. Can you imagine the killer having the temerity to suggest selling the magazine in the wake of murdering daddy?”

“I see your point.”

“Whoever did it would most likely lie low and wait, hoping, I would think, that one of the other directors who’d originally been in favor of selling would broach the subject first. But I wouldn’t expect the innocent ones to be too quick to bring up the idea, either out of respect for my father and out of fear that they’d look suspicious. Eventually, though, with the passage of time and with new board members, the risk of proposing the sale would be minimal. Once my father’s will had cleared probate, it was likely that his heir or heirs would become board members. These new members, as it turned out, you and I might not have the same passionate commitment to retaining the magazine.”

What she said made sense. I nodded my

agreement and asked my next question.

"So whom do you suspect. . .and why?" I asked.

"Trampler is a good possibility, though I can't prove it."

Hugh Trampler was in his early sixties—though he looked more like a vigorous fifty. He was principal owner of a construction firm in Charlestown. He seemed a little rough around the edges, but I couldn't believe he was a murderer. In the short time I'd known him, I'd found myself liking him. He was a big burly man—close to six-foot-three. He must have carried well over 230 pounds on that tall frame of his. I suspect that even at his age it was mostly muscle. To me he'd seemed like a big friendly bear. "Samantha, I just can't believe it. Trampler of all people. He just doesn't fit."

"Who does fit, James? This is not a professional assassin from the underworld. Look, I know Trampler seems like a nice man. And I'm not sure he is the killer. All I'm saying is that he has to be considered a possibility. Don't raise your eyebrows at me, James. Just listen for a minute, will you."

"I'm listening."

"Try to keep an open mind."

"My mind is open. Go ahead." As I spoke I could see that Edward was helping himself to more wine. He'd already had several glasses. It was hard to tell if he was following the conversation or not.

"Trampler needs money in the worst way," said Sam. "He's nearly bankrupt."

"I thought he was rich."

"He was quite well off, that is until recently. Not long ago—two or three years I would guess—he and another contractor from Charlestown became partners for the purpose of putting up a large commercial building in Lynn, I think it was. The problem was, after they'd gotten it about half done, the partner backed out. Ran out of money or something. Trampler's only chance of salvaging the venture and the money he'd invested was to buy out his partner's share. But he didn't have enough money, so his company failed. He's ruined. Apparently he's protected some of his personal assets, though not all of them. I understand he had to sell his house in Braintree. He now lives there in a rather modest three-room apartment. His days as a building contractor are over. He's convinced that, if Daddy had been willing to sell *Knickerbocker* when the *Harper's* and *Times* group wanted to buy, his share of the proceeds would have enabled him to weather the storm. Obviously he was one of the directors who wanted to sell. All I'm saying, James, is that he had a good motive."

"I suppose so, but I still don't see him as a murderer."

"We've addressed that, dear cousin. Who does seem like a murderer?"

"Okay," I sighed, "what other candidates do you have?"

"I hope you're not dismissing Trampler."

"I'm not, but you said there were other possibilities. Let's hear about them, too. Then maybe we can sort them out some way." I noticed out of the corner of my eye that Edward had poured himself still another glass of wine. I hadn't been keeping a strict accounting, but I knew he was way ahead of Sam and me.

"I've got one that will knock your socks off, James." she grinned wickedly. "Did you know that Margarita Calore used to be a high-priced prostitute?" I was thunderstruck. "No, I did not know. This board is full of surprises. Does the rest of the board know this?"

"As far as I know, no one knows. My father told me this two or three years ago. One of the few times he and I were on speaking terms."

I hesitated before asking my next question. "How did Martin happen to know this?"

Sam feigned a frown of shocked disapproval. "You are a wicked one, James Christopher. It so happens one of his editors heard it from a journalist at the *Atlantic Monthly*. Don't ask me how the journalist happened to know."

"And you think your father was blackmailing her?"

"I'm fairly certain of it."

"That would certainly be a motive for killing him."

"Right you are. You see, James, I'm not so crazy."

Chapter 3 *Thursday the 4th*

"How does Edward feel about all of this, Sam?" I would have asked the man himself, but he seemed to be off somewhere in his own oenologically induced stupor. We'd only met a few hours earlier, so I was quite surprised that he would let himself become so inebriated. Samantha glanced quickly to her right where he was slouched against the wall. Then she answered, a look of embarrassment on her face.

"He doesn't agree with me, frankly."

"Even after hearing the arguments you've presented to me today?"

She stole another look to her right. It was more a disdainful look than a surreptitious one. "Edward is not one to stir the waters, James."

At this, Edward did in fact stir from his apparent stupor.

"So that's what you think!" he exploded thunderously. Several eyes at neighboring tables turned our way. One rather portly man with fleshy jowls seemed particularly fascinated by what he was seeing.

Unfortunately, Edward was not about to let the matter drop. "Because I disagree with you," he barked viciously, "You think I'm a do-nothing."

Startled that he'd been listening, and suspecting that he'd been feigning his inebriation, Samantha recovered quite well, I thought.

"That is not what I said, Edward, and you know it."

"You've always had a vivid imagination, Samantha, and you've come up with some bizarre notions in the past ten years, but this is by far the craziest one yet. My God, you're the last person to be accusing me of being unwilling to take action. Your problem is that you're just the opposite. You're impulsive and want to take action even when it's completely uncalled for."

Edward was most certainly awake now. I liked him better asleep. Of course, I now realized he'd been pretending to be asleep all along. What kind of a vile person could lie in wait for his wife to say something in order to catch her at it? And then to attack her publicly like this.

"Leave her alone, Edward," I said, trying to control my own rising temper. "Calm down, man. The whole place is staring at you." As I was saying this, Herman materialized at our table. He was clearly uncomfortable as he spoke. "Is there a problem, Mr. Christopher? The other guests..." He motioned helplessly towards the room behind him.

Something had taken hold of Edward's mind. He was more than merely agitated. He spoke before I could answer, "Mind your own business, man. Leave us alone." Then he turned his suddenly feral eyes in my direction—ignoring Herman. He'd clearly gone off the deep end emotionally. "Don't take her side. Can't you see how she distorts things?"

"I'm afraid I don't see any such thing. What I do see is that you're making an ass of yourself in front of your wife, me, and everyone in this place—a place I might add, that I happen to frequent. I don't know what your problem is, but I think you'd better get control of yourself."

I waited to see if he'd digested any of what I'd said before adding in a more conciliatory tone, "Look, you've had a great deal to drink. I'm sure in the morning you'll regret having said all this. Why don't we have some coffee and put this behind us."

Edward nodded sheepishly. As quickly as the madness had come over him, it had left. His demeanor became docile, and he attempted a half-hearted smile.

As the cessation of hostilities slowly matured into a state of precarious rapprochement, I noticed that the heavyset gentleman I'd seen peering at us earlier was making his way over to our table. It wasn't easy for him, as his bulk made negotiating the narrow spaces between tables somewhat of an exercise in physical dexterity—an exercise he clearly was not good at. Samantha noticed him for the first time as he neared the table. She recognized him, too, and spoke first.

"Mr. LaRue. What a surprise." Sam acted as if everything were perfectly normal, ignoring the fracas at our table that moments ago had occupied all eyes in the restaurant. LaRue was not quite so tactful, though.

"So this is how our two newest directors behave in public. Dear God, I fear the rest of us made a grave mistake in inviting the two of you to join the board. I told the others you were too young. And far too radical as far as I'm concerned." Samantha was speechless. All she could do was stare at the ill-mannered LaRue. Edward tried to hide a smirk. It was left to me respond to the adipose intruder, whom I'd recognized as one of the board members I'd met eight weeks earlier.

"Mr. LaRue," I said firmly, "I won't pretend to defend our loud performance of a few moments ago, but I'm afraid your bad manners do yourself no great service either." I waited for the explosion that was sure to follow. The stout man stared at me in disbelief, his shiny pate reflecting light from the gas lamp on the wall near our table. I couldn't help noticing, too, that he had a terrible skin condition. Slowly his heavy face was transformed into a broad smile.

"Hah!" he bellowed. It was a laugh that seemed to originate from deep inside his massive body. "You're absolutely right Mr. Christopher. I was out of line. You have every right to berate me." Then he broke into an orotund laugh that seemed to ripple all the way up from his toes, shaking every roll of fat on his not inconsequential body. "Good God, you thought I was serious, didn't you?"

"I must admit, sir, I did." I studied him carefully. The man was truly an enigma.

"Hell, I saw you young people over here all in a lather, and thought I'd have a little fun. Must say, you reacted about the way I expected. People generally do," he observed sagely, but with a twinkle. "By the way, what's your position on selling the magazine?"

"I'm against it," said Sam without hesitation.

LaRue frowned and quickly turned his attention to me. "And you, sir?" His gaze bored into me.

"I haven't decided, yet," I said. "I need to give it more thought,"

LaRue's expression hardened. "You do that, Mr. Christopher. And, you, Mrs. Ridley, maybe you could give it more thought, too." His eyes assumed their twinkle again, and he motioned with his hand to Herman, who was standing with a somewhat relieved expression two tables away a tray suspended from his left hand. "Bring these nice folks another round of whatever they're having, Herman. See that you put it on my bill." Turning back to the table he beamed at the three of us, savoring the minor triumph of having taken full control of the situation.

"You folks enjoy yourselves now. I'd better get back to my group." With that he dipped his chin a half inch, first toward Sam, then toward me completely ignoring Edward. Then he turned, and began his return trip through the obstacle course of tables.

I stared at Samantha with a quizzical look. "Isn't that the damnedest. What do you make of it?"

"That, dear cousin, is Sebastian LaRue. Now you've met a board member away from the boardroom. He's a hard one to figure out. But don't underestimate him."

"Do you trust him?"

"I don't know."

"Do you think he was serious—at first, I mean?"

"As I said, it's hard to figure him out. I don't

really know him. Somehow, though, I got the feeling he was dead serious. But how do I know, really. The male members of the board are not going to tell a woman much—especially a young woman. Monday will be my first full meeting, too. You and I, James, should be quite the curiosities on Monday."

"Yes, I expect so," I said with a chuckle."

"I'm glad you were home today, James." She glanced nervously at Edward. "I'm going to be in Springfield this weekend, but I expect to be back in time for the meeting."

I raised my eyebrows. "You're a busy woman, Sam."

Edward frowned. "Isn't she. She should stay home, if you ask me."

"I'm attending a conference there. Mrs. Stanton is speaking." She could tell from the puzzled look on my face that I had no idea what she was talking about. "Elizabeth Cady Stanton, the woman who speaks out for the rights of women. You've heard of her."

Then it dawned on me. *The* Mrs. Stanton. She'd been a prime mover in the women's rights movement for years—a movement that I had thus far only read about. "Yes, of course I have. You're involved in such things?" I suppose the surprise in my voice was palpable.

"Edward thinks I am. And he doesn't approve. Do you, Edward?"

"Radical nonsense," he harrumphed.

"How about you, James. Do you approve?"

"It's not for me to approve or disapprove," I said evasively. "You're not my wife." I saw Edward nodding vigorously at this.

"Yes, of course, but on general principle do you approve or disapprove of women being granted more rights?"

I'd never really had it put to me before. "I suppose it's a good thing. How active are you anyway?"

She smiled teasingly. “That’s a whole other subject, James. I don’t think we’ve time for it tonight. Perhaps another time—if you’re really interested.” Edward frowned throughout this entire exchange.

In a way I was interested. As a journalist and as citizen I was always interested in what motivated people. And when I took the trouble to think about it, women really had very little power in American society. “Yes, I’ll look forward to that. Well, before we call it a night, let me ask you another question about our friend LaRue. Is he one of the directors who wanted to sell?”

“I think so, but I’m not certain.”
“Sounds as if he is. If so, though, why would he risk alienating the two newest directors? For all he knew, we might have been in favor of selling.”

“I don’t know, James. Maybe he, too, had too much to drink. More likely, though, he’s so arrogant that he thinks he’s assuaged us by pretending it was all a big joke. He’s very bright, and I think he sometimes underestimates others. Especially young people.”

“Interesting man,” I said matter-of-factly. “Very interesting. Tell me about the others now.”
“Well, we’ve talked about Trampler and Margarita Scharf Calore. And you’ve now met LaRue. We still haven’t talked about Arthur Billingsley and Winnifred Neustadt.”

“Before we get to the those two, tell me anything else you can think of about LaRue?”

“Actually, Edward knows him better than I do, don’t you Edward?”

“Yes, I suppose I do,” said Edward soberly—more soberly than I would have expected twenty minutes earlier.

“What’s he do?” I asked.

“He’s an attorney. Has a practice here on Tremont Street,” said Edward.

“How is it that he doesn’t represent the board

on legal matters—instead of Myron Friedman?"
Edward frowned, "My father-in-law preferred Friedman as the corporate attorney."
It occurred to me that Uncle Martin's decision might have been influenced by LaRue's abrasive manner. What I said, however, was, "I imagine this didn't sit too well with LaRue."

Edward smiled sardonically. "You imagine right. Sebastian was quite put out at first."

"At first?"

"Yes, eventually, he came to accept it. Considered it a blessing in some ways."

"How so?"

"As attorney for the magazine his actions would be judged more harshly by his fellow board members. His every move would be scrutinized closely, don't you see?"

I wasn't sure I did see. "I'm not certain that would be the case, Edward. Sounds as if Mr. LaRue might be a little unsure of himself."
"I don't know what was in his head. All I know is that he seemed to be relieved after his initial pique. Still—"

"Yes?"

"I suppose he could have been hiding his true feelings."

"Would you suppose he was angry enough with Martin to have killed him?" I asked.

"Good Lord, man. What a thing to say."

"I'll take that as a no."

"I didn't say that exactly. It's just that I can't imagine him—or anyone on the board for that matter —killing anyone."

"Of course," I allowed, more tactfully, than he deserved. "By the way, how is it that you know him?"

"He's done some work for us at the bank. I met him at a closing, I believe. We've run into each other on more than one occasion. We're not close. Just business acquaintances."

"Isn't he known for having a temper, Edward?" said Sam, who'd been following closely.

He looked unhappy. This interruption from his wife seemed to annoy Edward. He apparently wasn't in the habit of discussing business with his wife. "I suppose so," he said, trying to remain calm. "Why do you ask?"

"Just that people sometimes act irrationally when angry. They might even be capable of murder."

I could see Edward's temper rising. "That's rubbish. How many times must I tell you that this suspicious mind of yours is going to get you into all kinds of trouble. You haven't the slightest evidence that Sebastian LaRue was even near your father's house the night he died."

"That's not true. He was there for dinner—with the rest of the board. You know that, Edward."

I could see that, if I didn't move this along, we were on the verge of another contretemps. "Look," I said to both of them, "it's getting rather late, and since Edward has to be at work in the morning, and I want to visit the offices of *Knickerbocker* tomorrow, (Edward's eyebrows rose up at this) could either of you tell me what you know of Winnifred Neustadt?"

A smug look appeared on Edward's nearly perfect countenance. "I'll defer to Samantha on this one," he said with satisfaction.

"Edward is enjoying this, James." She took a deep breath before proceeding. You'll understand why in a minute. "Winnifred Neustadt was widowed a few years ago. Her husband was in manufacturing—coal stoves I believe—and he left her quite comfortable. She still owns a large block of shares in the company, I'm told. They've now begun making those new kerosene stoves that are becoming so popular. My guess is that the value of her stove company stocks will grow." She paused to take a breath. She pursed her lips before plunging ahead, "What Edward is so smug about is her affair with Daddy."

"That's not fair, Samantha," said Edward. Then,

turning to me he said, “She thinks I delight in her father being put in a bad light. That really isn’t true.”
“Oh come on, Edward,” said Sam. “You know it is. You and father never got along. Admit it.”
“Well, we did have our differences, but I certainly don’t take much pleasure from having his sordid affair discussed.”

“Dear God, Edward. You do have a way with words. Let’s just drop it.” She shook her head in exasperation, before turning back to me.

“It went on for some months,” she said, “Then one day she appeared at a board meeting in a vile mood. The explanation for this wasn’t hard to understand. It soon came out how, I don’t know that the affair was over. Word quickly spread that my father had lost interest in her. She was embarrassed by this, as you might imagine, and was not very good at hiding her anger.”

“Classic case of the rejected lover,” I said.

“Exactly.”

“Did she hate your father enough to kill him?”

“I wish I knew, James.”

“So do I,” I said. “What about Billingsley?”

“Arthur Billingsley is in the import/export business. It so happens that he exports those coal and kerosene stoves that Winnifred Neustadt’s husband used to manufacture. As I told you, the company still makes them and does very well. So does Billingsley.”

“Board’s rather inbred, wouldn’t you say?”

This brought a smile to Edward’s lips. “Indeed.”

Chapter 4 *Monday, December 8th*

The meeting had been set for two p.m. Monday. We were to meet in the second-floor boardroom at the magazine's offices on the corner of Milk and Broad Streets.

Rather than use the stairs, I opted for the elevator recently installed by the Otis Company. While passenger elevators were not common, (I believe there were fewer than a hundred of them installed in all of Boston) these new contraptions were no longer the novelty they'd been 25 years earlier when they began appearing in office buildings.

As I exited on the second floor from the wrought iron cage, I heard voices from the boardroom just across the corridor. I soon realized that the other board members were already there. I pulled my watch from my vest pocket. One fifty-five. I was glad not to be late for my first meeting as a board member.

All eyes were upon me as I entered the room.

"Welcome, Mr. Christopher." It was the booming voice of Arthur Billingsley, the chairman. He'd been elected after Uncle Martin was killed. "Please take a seat. We're about to begin." He motioned to one of only three remaining stuffed leather chairs at the long mahogany table. I took one near the middle. As I sat, I made a quick inventory of those present and noted that Samantha was not there. Then I noted—why I should have noted this is beyond me—that I was the only man present who didn't sport a full set of whiskers. I suddenly felt very young. The hirsute look had been the fashion for several decades now. Men considered a beard, or at least a mustache with full side-whiskers, a sign of masculinity. My mustache sans beard or full side-whiskers made me a bit of a curiosity in most circles. Odd, really, because the Founding Fathers clearly didn't lack virility or strength of character, but I can't think of one who wore a beard. Simply wasn't the fashion a hundred years ago. "Do you know if Mrs. Ridley will be joining us, Mr. Christopher?" It was Sebastian LaRue.

"I know she intends to be here. Something must have delayed her. Perhaps the traffic. It was unusually heavy on my way over here."

"The meeting has been scheduled for a month. Traffic is no excuse for being late," admonished LaRue acidly. "One should allow for traffic. Perhaps she over-indulged last night."

Any doubt as to this man's true nature was now laid to rest. I'd had about enough of this boorish man. "That, sir, is uncalled for," I said angrily, realizing as I said it that it was not a good way to begin my tenure on the board of directors of *Knickerbocker* magazine. I looked around the room and sensed that the other board members were withholding judgment for the moment. They must have known LaRue for what he was, but they also must have formed some opinion of Samantha. Now they would be forming one of me.

Chairman Billingsley leaned forward in his chair, trying to bring some order to the assemblage. "I don't think it was uncalled for," continued LaRue audaciously. "I saw with my own eyes the way she and that loutish husband of hers carried on last night at the Oyster House. Disgraceful."

Finally, Billingsley stood up and took charge. "Gentlemen, gentlemen. Please let's not lose our tempers. I'm sure Mrs. Ridley will join us shortly. In the meantime I think we should begin. You know how I like to follow Mr. Roberts. That includes beginning our meetings on time."

The Mr. Roberts he was referring to was *Pocket Manual of Rules of Order for Deliberative Assemblies*, a new book of rules of parliamentary procedure the board had adopted last year. The rules of order had been written in 1876 by an enterprising army engineer named Henry Robert. What he'd done was adapt the rules of debate used in the U.S. House of Representatives. His idea was that he'd produce a set of rules that could be used in any type of public debate so that new rules wouldn't have to be created for each organization. His book had been catching on lately. Even businesses had begun to adopt it in order to bring about a degree of order to their deliberations. Billingsley gaveled the meeting to order at five minutes past two. I got the distinct impression that he was more concerned about not starting late than he was about any dissension on the board. He then addressed me directly, with only the trace of a smile on his craggy, avuncular face.

"Mr. Christopher, on behalf of the board of directors I'd like to welcome you to membership in our group. We had hoped to welcome Mrs. Ridley at this time, but I see she still has not arrived. So be it," he concluded magisterially. With that, he turned and faced the table. "Will the secretary please read the minutes."

This was done quickly and efficiently by the secretary of the board, Winnifred Neustadt. A surprisingly diplomatic Sebastian LaRue then gave the treasurer's report. Old business was promptly disposed of, and then Billingsley called for new business.

Hugh Trampler cleared his throat, shifted his bulk in his seat, and began somewhat cautiously. "Now that we have our two new members in place despite the fact that one is unfortunately not present this afternoon I'd like to propose we reconsider an issue that was discussed well over a year ago, and then dropped. I think you all know what I'm talking about. Yes, I mean the sale of *Knickerbocker* to the group of publishers. I suppose you could call it old business in a sense. But since it has not been on our agenda for over a year, I think it does qualify as new business."

"How do we know these *Harper's* and *New York Times* people are still interested?" It was the rather sultry voice of Margarita Scharf Calore. She spoke with a hint of a Mediterranean accent. Someone, I can't remember who, had told me that her mother was from Spain. Others had told me Southern Italy. No one seemed to know for sure. Calore was a small woman, and quite attractive—in a Mediterranean sort of way. She was probably close to forty, but could easily have passed for someone in her early thirties. I could see how men would have been willing to pay for her sexual favors.

"I know because I've spoken with Gerald Robinson as recently as last Friday," said Trampler confidently. Robinson was a former editor at *Harper's* and one of the group that had made the original offer over a year ago.

Trampler continued, "They've about given up hope, but he said that if our board, with its new make-up, were to reconsider the matter, the offer would still stand."

From my perspective it seemed as if Trampler's little speech was no surprise to the others.

"I agree with Hugh," said LaRue. "I think we should reconsider selling. Can we poll the membership—unofficially that is?"

Billingsley frowned. Apparently he'd feared something like this. "I suppose an informal poll is in order. Those of us in favor of selling please......"

"Excuse me," I said, "Being new to the board, I'm unfamiliar with the details of the offer. It would help if I could be provided with more information before I make a decision. Then I'd feel more comfortable telling the board which way I'd be inclined to vote. I'm sorry to delay the process, but—"

"That may not be necessary," interrupted LaRue. "Let's proceed with the informal vote. If we have enough votes, we won't need to wait for Mr. Christopher to educate himself." Was I imagining a slight sneer directed at me?

Billingsley made a quick visual survey of the room. Seeing no apparent objection, he said, "All right. Let's proceed. Those in favor of selling please raise your hand." LaRue's hand was up before the chairman finished speaking. Trampler's hand was next, followed by that of Margarita Calore.

"According to my math," said Billingsley, "that falls short of the fifty-one percent needed to pass the resolution by—let's see now—I believe that would be fourteen percent." He paused to let it sink in; then continued with a wink, "Looks like you'll get your chance to educate yourself on this matter, Mr. Christopher."

LaRue was clearly unhappy. He turned to Billingsley.

"Arthur, I thought you were with us?"

"I don't know where you got that idea, Sebastian."

"Well, I just thought—"

"I'm afraid you thought wrong."

Hugh Trampler leaned over the table in the direction of Winnifred Neustadt. "Winnifred, I thought you wanted to sell?"

"I did at first—last year. Now though, with Mr. Christopher and Mrs. Ridley on the board and with Arthur as chairman, I think I'd like to wait and see how things develop."

"That's ridiculous," barked LaRue. "Isn't it just like a woman to change her mind."

"My decisions are my own business, Sebastian," snapped Neustadt. "And they aren't gender related. I'll thank you to mind your own business. You know nothing of my affairs, and I'll thank you to stay out of them."

"Of course, Winnifred, of course. You're absolutely right," said Trampler unctuously. "But the offer hasn't changed. You were in favor the first time we received it. I don't see why you should be against it now."

"I told you," she replied impatiently, "I want to see how things progress with the new board members and with Arthur as chairman."

"My God, woman," broke in LaRue, "Arthur has been chairman for almost a year. You can see what kind of a leader he is. As for our two new members, they're green and inexperienced. I doubt the magazine will fare as well under this board as it did under the Van Zandt board. Can't you see that we'll all be better off if we sell while the magazine is still in demand?"

I could not believe my ears. Could this man have been any ruder? How could he have become the successful attorney everyone said he was? And if he was looking for votes from Samantha and me, this was a strange way to get them.

"You're entitled to your own opinion, Sebastian," Neustadt said crisply. "I, for one, am willing to wait and see."

At that point, Chairman Billingsley addressed me directly.

"Mr. Christopher, it appears that the decision to sell may well hinge on either your vote or that of Mrs. Ridley. Essentially, the situation is this: A small group of former editors and executives from *Harper's* and *The Times* are interested in buying *Knickerbocker.* They've offered $5,000,000. When they first made the offer—that would be over a year ago—it amounted to eight times earnings, which happens to be a very favorable offer indeed. If we'd accepted then, the value of our shares would have doubled overnight. Or nearly so. Today, company earnings are a bit higher, so the ratio is not as favorable, but still quite good. If we were to accept the offer today, each share would be worth nearly one-hundred-fifty percent of its present value."

I nodded to convey my understanding. It was more or less what I had been led to believe prior to hearing his explanation. Naturally it raised other questions in my mind.

"Mr. Trampler, in light of our increased earnings, are the buyers willing to offer more than

$5,000,000?" I could see by the expressions on the faces of Trampler and LaRue that they were surprised and heartened by my question.

"That wasn't discussed on Friday," said Trampler. "I'm not sure they'd offer more, but I suppose we could ask."

"Not yet, if you don't mind," I said. "I have another question, though?"

"Yes," said Billingsley, with growing respect.

"What are the arguments for not selling?" I noticed that LaRue dropped his head and shook it disconsolately. One moment he'd found encouragement from my words; the next moment his optimism was dashed. Trampler, too, looked crestfallen.

Billingsley was more than happy to explain. "One argument against selling is tradition. *Knickerbocker* has been in existence nearly as long as *Harper's*, and for that matter, *The Times*. Some board members feel it should continue as it has and carry on the traditions that have made it so distinctive."

"Ridiculous. Sentimental nonsense," blurted LaRue. "This is a business, and we're in it for profit. Selling the magazine is good business. For all of us. You'll make yourself a lot of money overnight, Mr. Christopher. What's wrong with that?"

"I'm aware of the arguments for the sale," I said. "If you don't mind, Mr. LaRue, I'd like to hear the other arguments *against* selling."

Billingsley cleared his throat. "Of course, Mr. Christopher. Happy to oblige. Another argument against is the fact that the magazine is doing better every month. Some of us think that, if the present trend continues, we'll eventually do so well that our stock will be valued higher than it would be worth if were to accept the offer from the group."

"That's just your opinion, Arthur," interjected Trampler. "In my opinion, it's far too optimistic."

Billingsley smiled confidently and turned to me, "As Mr. Trampler so eloquently puts it, it is a matter of opinion. You'll want to examine the language of the offer, the company financials, and perhaps even talk with some of the staff before you make your decision. In the meantime, I'll see that Mrs. Ridley has access to all of that information, too. We can vote on the offer at the next board meeting in January."

"That's ridiculous," blurted LaRue. We've waited far too long already for this vote. I move that we set a special meeting for next week?"

Billingsley replied firmly, "The matter has been tabled for over a year. We now have two new members on our board. They're so new they haven't had a chance yet to become fully conversant with the issues that concern us. There's no reason we can't wait one more month before we vote. It's only fair to Mrs. Ridley and Mr. Christopher."

"That's just the point," said Trampler. We've put this off for over a year. To some of us, it's a matter of urgency. And has been for some time. Out of fairness to the majority of the board, I say we vote next week." Billingsley frowned and pursed his lips as he looked around the big table. "Let's compromise. We'll meet two weeks from today." Getting no objection other than a glare from Trampler, he continued, "Is there any other new business?" As he asked the question, he was distracted by a knocking on the boardroom door.

"What is it?" Asked Billingsley, sounding annoyed. A young woman was standing in the doorway trying to catch his eye. "Come in my dear, come in," said the chairman. "What is so important that you have to interrupt our meeting?"

The young lady approached deferentially, and Billingsley motioned impatiently for her to lean closer to his ear. She seemed agitated as she whispered what she had to say. I could see that Billingsley was shaken by what she told him. He interrupted her once to say, "Who told you this?" Then he thanked her and turned his attention back to us at the table.

"I'm afraid I have some bad news. Mrs. Ridley

has been attacked by someone in the street. She's now under doctor's care at her home." I heard a gasp from Winnifred Neustadt.

"How is she? Is she all right?" I asked, feeling my heart beat faster.

"Apparently she's not critical, though Mary didn't have any details. It happened this morning, about four hours ago, up on Boylston Street, near Berkeley. The police believe it was some young street hoodlum trying to rob her. She was struck several times."

Margarita Scharf Calore gasped.

"Good Lord," cried Hugh Trampler.

"The police took her home. Her husband wasn't there. They sent for a doctor and then tried to reach Ridley at the bank, but he wasn't there. Apparently visiting a client or something. Mrs. Ridley had her maid make a telephone call to us. They have a telephone, you know. Ridley told me about it the last time I spoke with him. God knows what they do with it. I dare say there can't be more than a dozen homes in all of Boston that have one. Who could you talk to? Still, good thing they have it, as the maid was finally able to get through to us here at *Knickerbocker.*"

Billingsley quickly adjourned the meeting. I flagged down a hansom cab and told the cabbie to take me to Mt. Vernon Street as quickly as possible. Fortunately traffic was light, or I would have gotten out and run the dozen or so blocks to my cousin's house.

Chapter 5 *Monday the 8th*

I had expected worse, so I was somewhat relieved to find Samantha sitting up when I got there. There was a bandage over her right eye and one on her right cheek. She said there were two more on her shoulder, but these, of course, I couldn't see. Sam told me the doctor had just left. She was alone except for Elizabeth, her Irish maid, a pleasant-looking middle-aged woman from County Clare. Her black hair was streaked with gray and there was a hint of a dimple on each cheek. She'd opened the door for me and held out a modest silver salver, expecting me to place my visiting card on it. It was one of the more pretentious customs of the day in polite society, but it was rather silly here, since I could see my cousin across the room. Elizabeth and I exchanged introductions, and I quickly discovered that Samantha's ordeal weighed more heavily on her than it did on Sam.

"Oh Mr. Christopher, I'm so glad you're here. What a sight she was when they brought her here."

"Elizabeth, don't carry on so." It was Sam, sounding better than she looked. "You've been a dear, but stop fussing. You can see now that I'm all right. These bruises will heal in a few days. I'll be fine."

"Shall I leave you then, Mrs. Ridley, so you can visit with Mr. Christopher?"

"Yes, of course, Elizabeth. I'll call you if I need anything. And thank you."

I tossed my hat on a chair and sat down opposite her.

"My God, Sam, you had a nasty experience.

What in blazes happened?"

Her face began to redden. A tear formed and began making its way down her bandaged cheek. She wiped it away with the back of her hand. "Oh, James. It was terrible. I didn't want Elizabeth to see me this way...I, I... Oh dear God. He, he came at me out of nowhere." She sniffed and buried her face in her hands. I got up and went over and sat beside her. I put my arm over her shoulder and tried to calm her.

"Take your time. Take your time. Are you up to telling me what happened? Or would you prefer that we do this another time?"

"No. I'll be all right." She wiped her eyes with her handkerchief.

"By the way, where's Edward?" I asked.

"I don't know. They tried to reach him at the bank, but he wasn't there. Must have been visiting a client or some such. I'm sure he'll come home when they tell him, though I don't expect much comfort from that quarter."

This comment came as a bit of a shock. Not that I was totally surprised at the sentiment, for I'd come to view Edward as a rather disagreeable fellow. But I wasn't aware that Sam shared my view. I looked at her expectantly, waiting for what she'd say next.

"Oh, don't be so surprised. You've seen him." She closed her eyes and lowered her head. Then she looked up, dabbing at her eyes as she did so. She met my gaze without flinching. "You haven't seen the half of him, either."

"Has he always been like this?"

"Not the first two or three years. Oh, he showed signs of it. He was always the jealous type, I suppose. But he treated me well. He was a sweetheart really. Looking back, now, I realize it was because he needed me. He had no career. Edward always wanted to be an outdoorsman, a man's man. He thought he could find what he was looking for out West, but he was out of his element on the frontier. He tried his hand rounding up cattle in southern Indiana, but it wasn't his thing. Then he worked in a saloon in Ohio, but that wasn't for him either. Then he worked at a logging camp in Southern Illinois. He was always a fish out of water. He liked his creature comforts too much. Finally, it dawned on him, and he decided to return East. And that's when it all began."

"You mean he changed?"

"Yes. When we came to Boston, he got a job as a teller in a bank. I could see from the very beginning that he was good at it. He received one promotion after another. With each promotion he became more arrogant, and more impatient with anything I said or did. The more successful he became at work, the more he looked down upon me.

"Now he has nothing but contempt for me. Any opinion I voice is ridiculous. Any thought I have he considers to be stupid. I'm his possession, and he expects me to shut up and look like a lady. My thoughts are not valued. Better yet, I shouldn't have any thoughts, unless it's what Elizabeth will prepare for dinner.

"He does like to take me to functions. Benefits, dances, that sort of thing. I think he approves of the way I look. But if I even speak to another man at a social function, he quickly drags me away. If I protest, or, God forbid, the gentleman should, Edward becomes moody and belligerent—verging on the violent—saying horrible things to the other man. Dammit, James, I get so embarrassed, I dread going to these affairs."

"Christ, Sam, how do you stand it?"

"What choice do I have?"

"You could leave the man? You have ample means, now that you've come into your inheritance. You don't need his support."

"You're not being realistic. I'd be a divorced woman, and divorced women are scorned. You know that. People would call me all sorts of names behind my back and even to my face."

"Now that you've come into all this, does he treat you any differently? I would think that he'd show a little more respect, if only out of selfishness."

"You would think so, but he doesn't seem to care. Oh he cares about the money all right. But he's confident I would never divorce him."

"Has he ever struck you?"

"Only once. He was terribly drunk. He didn't know what he was doing, James."

"Good God, Sam."

"Forget Edward, James. I can handle him." She tried to smile, but I could see that it was painful because of her bruises. "I haven't told you how good it's been seeing you again after all these years."

"You're a remarkable woman. You know that, don't you? You can think of me when you've been through such a terrible ordeal."

"Forget about that. I'll heal. It was frightening, but such things do happen on the streets of Boston. They happen all the time. I'm lucky a policeman came along to stop him."

I shook my head at her resilient spirit. "Tell me what happened?"

"I was out shopping for bread and a few other things."

"Elizabeth doesn't shop for you?"

"She does most of it, of course, but I enjoy visiting the shops myself once in awhile. I like to talk with the shopkeepers. You can't imagine what it's like being cooped up in this house all day."

I wasn't surprised. Sam was never one to let others do for her when she was perfectly capable of doing for herself. "So tell me what happened."

"Well, I was on Boylston Street, and as I was coming out of Huber's Bakery carrying bread and some sweet rolls, someone came out of the alleyway—it's right next to the bake shop—and came at me with a club or something. Fortunately, I caught sight of him in the corner of my eye just as he was about to hit me. I turned away, but it was too late to avoid the first blow altogether. Here's where he hit me." She pointed to the bandage over her right eye. "I think it glanced off my forehead and got me here, too." She pointed to the bandage on her cheek.

"The bastard."

"Before I could recover he hit me again, and I honestly think he would have killed me if a policeman hadn't come along just then."

"What happened to the man?"

"He ran off down the alley. The policeman tried to follow him, but he was too fast."

"Did he take anything?"

"No."

"He didn't try to take your bag or anything?"

"No. Nothing. That's the strange thing, James. He didn't try to take anything. He just seemed to want to hurt me. I honestly think he wanted to kill me." She swallowed before continuing. I could tell she was reliving in vivid fashion the horrible experience she'd gone through a few hours ago. Finally she was able to continue. "Thank God for the policeman. I know they have a bad reputation, but I can't say enough for this one."

"Did this man who attacked you say anything? Anything at all."

"Nothing. I do remember that he was breathing heavily, but he didn't say anything."

"Did you get a good look at him?"

"Not a good one. He was tall—I could see that. And, oh, I stepped on his shoe. I know I stepped on his shoe. Funny that that should stay with me."

"This whole thing is strange, Sam."

"What do you mean, strange?"

"Why would a perfect stranger attack you if he had no intention of robbing you?"

"It does make you wonder, doesn't it? I've been thinking about it a great deal since I got home. Sort of like with Daddy. Both of us attacked and nothing taken in either incident. One can't help wondering..."

"Now hold on, cousin. You're not saying the two attacks are connected?"

"I'm saying they could be."

"What's the motive for the attack on you, Sam?"

"Precisely my question. It wasn't robbery, so what was it?"

"The man might have been crazy. Who knows what a mad man will do? There's a lot of street people these days who aren't quite right in the head."

"Even a mad man has to be provoked, James. This man attacked me without provocation of any kind. No, I have this feeling he was after me. Not just the first person who passed by, but me."

"So what *was* his motive?" I asked, already thinking that I knew what she would say, for I was beginning to think the same way myself.

"If I'm right, it was the same motive my father's attacker had to prevent me from voting against the sale of *Knickerbocker.*" She put her fist to her lips, looking at the floor thoughtfully. Finally she continued. "And if I am right, you, too, could be in danger, James."

"I don't think so. I haven't yet made my intentions clear. Besides, you have more votes than I do. But that's assuming you're right. I hope you're not making too big a leap here."

"You think I'm wrong about this?"

"I didn't say that. But we don't know for sure, do we?"

"No, we don't. But hadn't we better err on the side of caution."

"Of course. You'd best not go out alone until we've had a chance to look into this."

"You will look into it then, James?"

"I'll do what I can, Sam. I can't promise too much, though. I'm not an investigator."

"No, you're a journalist. That's better."

"Thank you for the vote of confidence. But

before I do anything, I think I'll talk to a friend of mine at the Boston Police department. In the meantime, Sam, I hope that husband of yours will take measures to see that you're safe."

"I wouldn't count on that, James."

Chapter 6 *Monday the 8th*

John Holland was a detective inspector for the Boston Police Department. I'd met him last year in the course of doing a series of stories for the *Salem Gazette.* It was a series about corruption in the Boston Police Department, so, at the time, when a friend had put me onto Holland, I admit that I had some doubts. I had to be cautious. I trusted my friend, but I didn't know this cop. He could very well have been as crooked as any of the others I'd be writing about.

My friend had told me Holland was a good cop —one of the honest ones. On that basis, I plunged ahead—cautiously. My gamble paid off. Holland turned out to be a good source. He'd been willing to talk to me, provided we met somewhere away from the main station house at Pemberton Square, where he worked. He couldn't afford to be seen talking to the press, and he certainly couldn't afford to be quoted in a newspaper—especially the *Salem Gazette.*

The first time we met was at the South End Grounds at Columbus and Walpole. My friend had suggested that the three of us go see a professional baseball game. The Boston Braves sometimes known as the Red Caps or the Beaneaters, were playing the Philadelphia Quakers. Holland and I had gotten along well that day. I found that I really liked the fellow. He was hard not to like.

It wasn't easy for an honest cop to survive in Boston, let alone be promoted in a force that had a high percentage of crooked cops. Somehow he did survive, though. He'd done better than that—he'd made it up through the ranks to detective inspector. And he was only my age or a year older, which was young for a detective inspector.

I suppose it was his political instincts that kept him going. He went about his job in such a way that most of his colleagues—honest and crooked alike—couldn't help but admire him. And, as I said, he happened to be a damn likeable chap.

Holland had admitted to me that the hardest thing he did on the job was to look the other way. Like when he saw cops demanding handouts and protection money from innocent shopkeepers. He never took anything himself, but he didn't snitch, either.

He did draw the line at physical abuse. When other cops beat up vagrants and other street people, he'd step in and stop it. Somehow, through it all, he'd managed to build himself a career, and retain some self-respect.

I met him at a busy porterhouse on Winter Street. We didn't have time for one of the steaks for which these alehouses were famous. We had to settle for a couple of pints. Holland told me that it was unlikely any of his fellow officers would frequent this particular place. They had their customary haunts, and this wasn't one of them. Neither of us thought that anyone from the department knew that Holland had given me information and ideas last year when I was doing my story, but you never knew. Someone could have seen us together. I didn't want to get John in trouble. It was hard enough for him in the department without that.

"James, m'boy, good to see you. Jesus, that was some exercise you put me through last year. Never squirmed so much in my life. Deal with the scum of the earth ten times a day, but them I can handle. You, however, forced me to examine what I was doing. Wasn't easy, believe me. Thanks for sending me a copy of your story. Damn good, too. Shook a few people up around here, believe me."

"Seen any changes?"

"Don't get carried away, Jimmy. You made 'em sweat a bit, but it'll take more than a story in the paper to change the system." Then, with a wry grin, he added, "Of course, if it'd been in the *Evening Transcript*, or the *Globe*, or even the *Post*, they might've felt the heat a bit more."

"I know," I said, "The *Salem Gazette's* readership is a lot smaller than the readership of the Boston papers."

"Exactly. And it's 16 miles to the north. Might's well be the moon."

"It is an influential town, though, Jimmy. Lot of powerful people live there. You'd think the legislators would feel pressured to take action when they read something in the papers that reveals a situation as scandalous as what's going on in the Boston Police Department. Even if they read it in a Salem paper."

"Not as much as you might think, James. Hell, you've covered the statehouse. Everybody wants a favor and everybody has friends. Better to have friends in the police department than enemies. So how do you like living up in Salem?"

"It's nice, but I don't live there anymore. Just moved back to Boston."

"Well I'll be damned. That is a surprise. What brought you back?"

"It's part of why I wanted to talk to you. Finish what you were saying, John, and I'll bring you up-to-date." I could tell by the expression on his face that he was pleased that he'd have a chance to finish what he'd started. He forced an embarrassed grin and continued.

"Almost through, James. You lived in Salem, so you know that the legislators from the farming areas and small towns and cities outside of Boston control the legislature. Most of 'em hate the city.

"And you can't expect much from Governor Butler. They say he's going to run for president on the

Greenback ticket. With his reputation I wouldn't expect it to very far, though." Holland paused, and a smile formed on his rugged features. "I'll never forget what Lincoln said about him when he was an officer in the Union army. Said he considered Butler "as full of poison gas as a dead dog."

I hadn't heard that one, and couldn't help chuckling. Then I said hopefully, but I suppose rather naively, "But surely some legislators must care."

"Remember, Jimmy, this state and this whole fuckin' country are run by agriculture. Folks out in the Berkshires don't care if the cop on the beat charges protection money from some whorehouse in Boston." Holland was getting wound up now. Patches of red were forming on his neck under each ear. His eyes had widened and were glistening like live coals. He wasn't finished, either.

"City governments aren't much better, either. They're run by the bankers and the big businessmen. The mayor can't get the people a five-cent fare on the horsecars, can he?"

"No, he can't, John. But he did at least try."

"Lot of good it did."

I held up a hand and smiled, "I need a favor, John."

"Sorry, get me on this subject, and I get carried away," he said sheepishly.

One of the things I liked most about John Holland was that he cared. Sometimes he cared too much for his own good, but he cared. He cared about issues, and he cared about people. And in truth, he did have a point about how politics in Massachusetts came down to rural districts versus the city of Boston. When I finally spoke, Holland was listening attentively.

"John, I need your help. It's about a murder."

"A murder?"

"Happened last March."

He frowned, "Where?"

"Up in Salem. Victim was my uncle. His name

was Martin Van Zandt. Killed in his own home."

"He have money?"

"Yes, plenty. The house in Salem has eighteen rooms."

I told my story in as much detail as I could, right down to how I'd inherited a large part of my uncle's estate. Holland tried not to interrupt too much. When I was finished, he leaned back in his seat and studied me. I could see that he was wrestling with what I'd told him. Especially the part about the murderer being one of the dinner guests.

"So what do you want me to do, James?"

"Do you think I'm out of my mind?"

"Could be," he grinned. "No, seriously, I think you might be right. I don't believe in that kind of coincidence. Things don't happen like that, a burglar just happening to come by after a dinner party, especially a dinner party where most of the guests hated the host's guts."

"So you agree that it could be one of the board members?"

"Could be. Could be. Like I said, I don't believe in that kind of coincidences. Still," he dragged the word out slowly, bringing his steepled hands pensively to his chin as he seemed to be considering the possibilities. "It is possible. Unlikely, but possible." He scratched his black, walrus-like mustache contemplatively. "You see, my friend, I don't know the police up there. If I did, I'd feel more comfortable evaluating their conclusions."

"What would you do if you were me?"

"Maybe nothing." I started to protest, and he held his hand up. "Wait, let me finish, James. First of all, what're you looking for? If you pursue this, you could be letting' yourself in for a hell of a lot of trouble. Especially if you're wrong. Which *is* a possibility, whether you like it or not."

"I know," I said, "but if I'm right, I'll get the bastard who killed my uncle."

"Hell, you wanna be crass about it, the killer did you a favor. Sounds like you're a rich man now, thanks to him." Holland broke into a wide grin. "You sure you didn't do the old man in, yourself?"

I didn't see the humor in it. Not that Uncle Martin was so lovable God knows, it was despicable the way he treated some people. But he'd always been good to me, even when we disagreed. With many people, he was intolerant to the extreme; yet I always sensed that he respected me.

He was extremely bright, and knew it. He had a tendency to measure others by his own intellect. Often they came up wanting. Add to that the fact that tact and empathy were not among his strengths, and you had a man who simply had no patience with weakness or slow-wittedness. I guess he didn't place me in either of those categories.

So, while I didn't feel the loss the way I had for my own father—God rest his soul—I did feel a strong loyalty to my irascible, but brilliant uncle. Hence my annoyance at what I felt was Holland's intemperate attempt at humor.

It suddenly occurred to me that John might actually think I *had* done my uncle in. From his perspective I certainly had a motive. I had to set him straight immediately.

"Christ, John. Why would I be here if I'd done him in?"

"Don't get your nose out of joint, Jimmy. Just a little joke. From the looks of your face I can see it wasn't such a good one, either. Look, all I'm saying is, if you start looking into this, you may wish you hadn't. Hell, if you're right, the killer might go after you."

"So you won't help me then?"

"Jesus, there you go again. Jumpin' to conclusions. If you're going to investigate your uncle's death, you'd better be a little less emotional and a little more objective about it. As for me helping you, I don't know what I can do from here. The crime was committed in Essex County. I can't go snoopin' around up there. Not my province. And I'll tell you, James, those coppers up there in Salem are not gonna take kindly to you if you go sniffing around in their backyard. I'd tread lightly, if I were you. If you must question them, show a little respect, even if it hurts."

I nodded, though somewhat impatiently, "Can you get me any background information on some of these board members? Before I talk to them, I'd like to know as much as I can about them."

"Give me their names. I'll see what I can do. But if they've never been arrested, we may not have anything on 'em." He grinned mischievously, "We don't make it a habit of keeping files on law-abiding citizens, Jimmy."

I gave him a list of the board members and their addresses.

Holland folded the list and put it in his coat pocket. "Do what I can, James." He then added, "If I were you, I'd check newspaper files. You must know someone at one of the city papers. Most of your board members must have been in the papers at one time or another."

I told him I planned to do just that, but I'd still appreciate his checking the police files.

Chapter 7 *Monday The 8th*

I doubt if there was anyone in all of Boston whose life had changed more dramatically in the past two months than mine had. It all started when Uncle Martin's attorney notified me that I was to get a sizable part of the Van Zandt estate. Within weeks of learning this, I'd gone from barely getting by each week on my journalist's salary to honest-to-goodness wealth. It was all too new to me to fully come to grips with. I still found myself counting my pennies and hesitating before making the smallest purchase. Force of habit, I suppose.

But my changed economic status was only a part of the transformation that had come over me. I'd also become a director on the board of one of America's most prestigious magazines, resigned from my job as assistant managing editor of the *Salem Gazette*, and moved from North Shore back to Boston. And if that weren't enough, I'd taken on even more by accepting my cousin's challenge to find my uncle's killer.

When I got back to the townhouse on Beacon Street, it suddenly hit me. My life was unrecognizable. Did I know one person who could cope with that much change? And living alone only made it that much worse. I had no mate to discuss these matters with, nor to share the stress with. It occurred to me that I might have bitten off more than I could chew. But my confidence quickly overcame my doubts. As I look back now, I realize that I was seduced by the excitement of it all.

It's the kind of situation that I would have discussed with my father or mother, had they still been alive. How I missed them both. Father had been the first journalist in our family. He'd been one of the best in Boston, maybe in the entire 38 states. He'd been my inspiration from as far back as I could remember. His name was James, too. I'm a junior. He'd been with the *Boston Globe* most of his journalistic life, a vocation that came abruptly to an end four years ago when he was covering the second biggest story of his celebrated career, the defeat of the great Sioux chief, Sitting Bull, out in the northern plains.

Five years earlier Sitting Bull had helped defeat General Custer at the Battle of the Little Bighorn. From the perspective of the white man, Sitting Bull was a problem. White settlers from the East, eager to take advantage of the Homestead Act and actually have a piece of land they could call their own, were constantly being harassed and attacked by Sitting Bull's braves. He had to be stopped. My father understood this.

But my father understood a lot more than that. He was one of the few people I knew who ever considered the Indian's point of view. That kind of objectivity was what made him such a good journalist. My father's biggest story, of course, had been his coverage of the Civil War. For three years he'd actually been at the front lines surviving with hardly a scratch. Then, four years ago, he'd persuaded his editor at the *Globe* to let him accompany that ill-fated Army contingent sent to defeat Sitting Bull once and for all.

It's a little unclear how it happened, but two months after my father left home, the Army notified my mother that he'd been killed by an encounter with the Indians. Hit in the chest by an arrow launched by one of the chief's warriors. He'd bled to death within an hour. That much we did learn. Ironically, his death and his coverage of the encounter became almost as big a story here in the East as the defeat of Sitting Bull. That's how famous my father was.

It was natural, then, that I would experience pangs of conscience about resigning my post at the

Gazette. Was it a rejection of my journalistic heritage? Was it a rejection of my father? Ridiculous, I told myself. I worshipped my father. Besides, I wasn't abandoning journalism. I was just participating in a different way. And, of course, I was still writing when I found the time, that is.

I'd been home less than an hour when my ruminations were interrupted by the rousing strains of Waltz from Swan Lake. The last time I'd heard the chimes, I'd found myself squarely in the middle of a murder investigation. What surprise could I expect to find on the other side of the heavy oak door this time? I didn't have to speculate long. When I opened the door, I found myself staring into the smiling visage of Hugh Trampler.

I was surprised, but not as surprised as I would have been a few days ago. I'd begun to realize that my fellow board members were full of surprises. I could tell from the look on his face that he, too, was rather surprised—surprised, that is, to see me answering my own door. As a man of some means, I'd be expected to have a man or a woman on staff assigned to the task. I would have to take someone on fairly soon.

The standard ritual was for the visitor to present his visiting card, and for a servant (How I hated that word. I preferred domestic.) to take it to the master or mistress of the house.

In Boston, no gentleman or lady who could afford it went without at least one domestic. I could easily afford it now. Actually, I could afford several people, but that wouldn't be me. When I was a boy living up on Marlborough Street, my parents had employed two full-time servants. After finishing up at Tufts, though, I'd been on my own and hadn't had a place big enough to warrant a staff. One or two rooms hardly require servants. Besides, I couldn't have afforded it. Despite father's fame as a journalist, he hadn't died a rich man. What he left, he left to my mother. It wasn't much.

But things had changed dramatically. I did

need someone now. I couldn't run two big houses by myself. Trampler's presence reminded me that I now had obligations I'd never dreamed of just a few weeks ago.

"Mr. Trampler, what a pleasure," I gushed, more than a little hypocritically. "Please come in."

"Sorry to drop in on you without notice, Christopher, but I must see you. Do you have a few minutes you can spare?"

"Yes, of course." I led him into the front parlor and directed him to the same spot I'd guided Samantha to so recently. He settled himself into his seat like a much younger man. For someone who must have been in his early sixties, he seemed unusually fit. He declined tea or coffee, which was a good thing because I had none ready.

"What can I do for you?" I asked, easing myself into my favorite stuffed chair directly opposite my large, powerfully built guest. He seemed more than a little uncomfortable.

"Now I hope you don't take this the wrong way, Christopher. Don't want you to think I'm pressuring you. It's just that I know there isn't much time before the next board meeting, and, since this vote is so damned important to all of us, I thought maybe I could help you decide. Maybe answer a few questions." He leaned back and nervously inhaled a great quantity of air.

"That's very considerate of you," I said warily. "Very considerate. I do understand that this vote is very important to you and the others. It's important to me, too." I was inclined to come out and tell him that I'd about decided to vote for keeping the magazine, but I decided to take another course. Might as well begin my investigations immediately. I forced a wry grin. "I have the feeling that if I were to let it be known before the vote that I was in favor of keeping the magazine, I might be putting myself at risk."

Trampler looked confused. I couldn't tell if he was acting or not. "I don't understand," he said.

"Well, some people believe that Martin Van Zandt was killed to keep him from voting for retaining *Knickerbocker.* If they're right, I could be at risk for the same reason. And so could Mrs. Ridley. As you know, she's already been attacked. Perhaps that's because she's already let her intentions be known."

"You don't think the attack on Mrs. Ridley had anything to do with *Knickerbocker*, do you? My God, that was just a madman on the streets."

"That's what people are assuming. We don't really know, do we?" I stared hard into his dark, deeply inset eyes, looking for something, anything.

"No, I suppose we don't. Not for certain, anyway. But we'd be jumping to conclusions if we assumed someone attacked Mrs. Ridley with the purpose of keeping her from voting against the sale of *Knickerbocker.* My God, who would do such a thing?"

"That's what I intend to find out," I said grimly.

"If it wasn't a madman on the street, who was it?"

"That's just the point. It couldn't be anyone else. The only people who'd benefit from selling the magazine are the board members."

"Exactly."

His eyes bulged as my comment registered. "You don't mean to sit there and tell me you think one of us could have killed your uncle?"

"That's not what I'm saying. What I'm saying is, if it wasn't a street vagrant, then by process of elimination it would have to be someone else. It was you, not I, who pointed out that the only people to benefit from my uncle's death would be board members. I certainly hope that's not the case, but the possibility can't be overlooked. Tell me, since you were at my uncle's house the night he died, I assume you traveled back to the Salem train depot with the other guests?"

"Yes, we all left the house together. Martin's houseman took us over to the depot in the buggy. Why do you ask?"

"It's just that, if someone left by himself, he could have gone back later and killed my uncle. Or he could have waited nearby until the rest of the guests had gone."

"Good grief. Do you know what you're saying?"

"Yes, I think I do."

Trampler ran his hand through his hair, unaware of the unruly wisps he was leaving. He looked positively distraught. "Look, it's no secret that I want to sell *Knickerbocker*. But as much as I want it to happen, I don't want it *that* much." He leaned closer and went on.

"I can't say that Martin and I were close. That would be a lie. But I did respect the man and his abilities. Besides, I could never kill anyone intentionally." He drew in another deep breath, before continuing. "To be honest, my desire to sell the magazine is completely selfish. You've probably already heard that my business has come upon hard times. I've lost a good deal of what I once had, and stand to lose the rest if the magazine isn't sold soon. I know it's selfish. I'm not even sure it's the best thing for the magazine and the staff, but it would save me. Not very pretty, is it?"

I looked down at my feet, but said nothing.

Trampler had become fidgety in his chair. If he was the killer, he was uneasy in the role. He sat back and appeared even more uncomfortable. Then he moved forward in the chair, fixing me with an intense look, appealing to my practicality. "Set my gain aside for a moment. Don't you see, everyone else on the board would gain, too, so what's the harm if I gain? Why should anyone be against nearly doubling the value of their shares?"

"For one thing, some of us don't really need the money. I know that's not what you want to hear, and if I were in your shoes, I wouldn't want to hear it either. Aside from that, though, I think there are better reasons for not selling."

"I know, I know. Tradition and all that. All very

nice, but that doesn't put food on your table."

"As I said, that's not at issue for some of us. But it's not just tradition I have in mind. It's good journalism. Peter Zumbach (I was referring, of course, to our editor-in-chief) and his editors have created about as close to a perfect editorial formula for a magazine as I could envision. I'd hate to put that at risk." I could tell by the look in Trampler's eyes that a fine editorial formula was the least of his concerns.

"Another reason for not selling, in my opinion, is that the stock may well be worth more in the future than it is now. If that's true, why cast that aside for the promise of a short-term gain?"

"That's all speculation, Christopher. You think it'll happen, but you don't know that. What you do know is that the stock would immediately jump in value if we accept the group's offer."

"It may be speculation, but it's not some wild guess. I've seen the books. Circulation is growing steadily. Income is on the rise, and profits are getting better every year. The value of the shares is already up from a year ago. There's every reason to believe the magazine will prosper."

"Sounds like you've made up your mind," said Trampler bitterly.

"I think maybe I have."

"Aren't you afraid it'll be the death of you?"

Chapter 8 *Tuesday the 9th*

The next morning I awoke to a steady rain. It wasn't cold for December, but the rain looked like the sort that would last all day. I prepared a simple breakfast of oatmeal and toast and was about to sit down with the morning paper when a smartly uniformed young messenger came to my door with an envelope addressed to me. I recognized the familiar scrawl on the outside as that of John Holland and asked the messenger to wait while I scanned whatever was inside in order to determine whether I needed to reply. I quickly tore open the envelope and gave the four pages inside a quick read. Holland's hand was not easy to decipher, but I could see that he'd uncovered some information about two of my fellow board members. He certainly hadn't wasted any time. I thanked the messenger for waiting, and said there'd be no response. He smiled when he saw that I'd given him twenty cents, far more than I should have, but I was feeling rather flush lately.

I retired into the kitchen, threw some coal on the dying embers in the big cast iron stove, and made myself some tea to go with my now cold oatmeal and toast. Sitting near a window that looked out upon a microscopic garden and then beyond to the rear of a building facing out on Branch Street, the gray morning light made it easier for me to read. I proceeded to study what Holland had sent me. He prefaced his notes by saying that he'd been able to find something on only two of the board members.

The first surprise had to do with my recent visitor, Hugh Trampler, who, according to the police files, had been involved in an accidental death incident in 1870. According to the police report, Trampler and one of his construction workers had been arguing while standing on the third floor of a building that was under construction. It was only a skeleton or framework when the incident occurred. Apparently the two men had been standing on a girder when the worker fell to his death. His family accused Trampler of deliberately pushing him. Some of the other workers later testified that Trampler and the worker had fought on several previous occasions. It wasn't clear whether these fights were physical or merely arguments. It never went to trial because the prosecutor didn't feel he had enough evidence to make a case. The case was closed quietly, and according to Holland, there were no other incidents reported to the police involving Trampler.

The second and bigger surprise concerned Samantha, or more accurately her husband, Edward. I say Samantha because she's the board member. Edward, it seemed, had more dimension than I'd given him credit for. It wasn't a very attractive dimension, either. If the police reports could be believed, it appeared than our Mr. Ridley was a bit of a knave. The first thing Holland's report mentioned was something that allegedly happened a year ago during the mayoral election campaign. According to Holland, Edward's bank, the Boston Bank of Commerce, was backing Martin for Mayor. No surprise there. So was every other bank in the city. As I read on, though, it got more interesting. Apparently the bank had put pressure on its big borrowers to contribute to the Martin campaign fund. Either contribute or you won't get your loan. According to the police report, Edward Ridley was one of the bank officers who'd helped formulate and implement the bank's policy. Apparently one company filed a complaint with the police, and an investigation was started. The bank quickly reversed its policy, and the company withdrew its complaint.

As if that weren't interesting enough, another police report told of a mysterious visit by the police to the home of one Edward Ridley. It turned out to be

Sam's Edward Ridley. Seems that Sam had filed a complaint. What it was about was unclear, as she dropped the charges after the police came. This, I found to be even more interesting than his extortion scheme at the bank.

Chapter 9 *Tuesday the 9th*

I was now eager to dig deeper into the mysterious death of my uncle. At last I had some hard facts to consider. It was too early to tell whether these facts would have any bearing on my uncle's death, but I could already see from what John Holland had sent me that facts were a much better starting point than mere supposition or suspicion. I'd been asking around for just a few days, and I'd already come up with some very interesting information. I was convinced there was a great deal more to be learned, and with more inquiry and just a little bit of luck, I would find myself closer to the answer I was seeking.

I decided to devote a couple of hours to studying the corporate financial papers I'd been given by Arthur Billingsley prior to yesterday's board meeting. I felt the need to become more conversant with the income and expense part of the business than I already was—though I must confess that I'd already become fairly familiar with the magazine's finances. I took the thick sheaf of *Knickerbocker* papers and made myself a cheese sandwich and another cup of tea and spent the better part of two hours learning a great deal.

By then, I was ready to get out of the house and continue my inquiries. I looked out the front window and was delighted to see that the day had improved considerably. A day that had started out rainy and dark had now turned sunny, brisk, and invigorating.

I would have to travel uptown to pursue my investigations. At a time like this, I suppose I envied the Ridleys their telephone. They were the only family I knew that had one. I knew that families that could afford it were beginning to get them. Not many, but more than the dozen or so Arthur Billingsley had estimated. Probably a few hundred at least. The telephone had become the new symbol of status. I sensed that it would be many, many years, though, before very many homes had one of the devices. Businesses and doctors with large practices were about the only ones that could afford telephones for the foreseeable future. And, of course, people with considerable means. The Ridleys had theirs, and I could have one, too, I realized. I'd been living the Spartan life so long that thinking like a rich person didn't come naturally. I could afford a telephone now. Another thing I would have to attend to when I had the time.

I walked briskly out to the street and waited for the next horsecar. As one slowed for traffic at the intersection, I hopped aboard and took it all the way to my destination on State Street. Traffic seemed unusually heavy for early afternoon, and the trip took nearly a half hour. It was about 2:30 when I entered the Globe offices and asked for Justin Case. Justin was an editor at *The Globe* and a friend of mine. We'd been classmates at Tufts, and, because of our mutual profession, kept in touch. We'd actually covered a number of the same stories in recent years. Occasionally outside of Boston, but usually when my paper in Salem had seen fit to foot the expense to send me to Boston for an important news event.

The directory in the lobby said that Case was on the third floor. I could see that the single elevator car was on the fourth floor and not moving, so I took the stairs, two steps at a time, and found myself at the top of the landing, surrounded by doors with opaque glass panels. I went for the one with the words City Room painted in on its frosted glass rectangle.

When I opened the door I was greeted by the familiar cacophony of newsroom sounds—a semi-chaotic farrago of men yelling and type writers clacking. I could see immediately that *The Globe* had many more of the new writing machines than we'd had up in Salem. I went up to the first person I came to, a stocky, balding man with handlebar mustache, florid complexion, and red suspenders. The man, who clearly was in a position of some authority, was standing in one of the narrow aisles formed by what seemed to be an endless number of desks. He was engaged in heated conversation with a younger man, waving two or three pages of typed copy with each point he made. Finally, he noticed that I was standing there and turned to me with an annoyed look on his face.

"Yes?"

"I'm looking for Justin Case. I'm a friend of his."

"Back there." He turned to his left and pointed with his thumb to a slightly larger desk at the back of the large room. The man behind the desk was indeed Justin. He was hunched over his type writer, hammering away at the keys in a way only he could do.

"Thanks," I said as the man turned his back. I began threading my way to the back of the room through the tightly spaced desks.

Even when I was virtually upon him, he continued writing. This was the Justin I'd come to know. Intense, competitive, and fiercely industrious. After standing before him for a full half minute, I finally reached my hand out and placed it over the keys. Needless to say, he looked up.

"James. What the hell are you doing here?"

"That's a fine greeting for an old friend."

He grinned, "I thought you were up in Salem. What brings you to the big city?"

"I've moved down here. Quit my job up there."

"Aha! You've landed yourself a big job here with the *Transcript* or the *Post*. I can feel the competition already."

I smiled, then became serious. "Justin, is there someplace we can go to talk? I'll bring you up to date on everything."

He looked at the half-finished copy in his type writer. I know how he must have felt. He had too much to write and not enough time to do it. I could feel his mind deciding—the same feeling I'd had when Samantha had interrupted my writing last Thursday. "God, I'm sorry, James. I'm on deadline, but I can take a few minutes. When I get past this, we can relax, maybe go out on the town. Right now, though, I sense that you have more to talk about than just old times." I nodded, and he pointed to a closed door at the far side of the city room. I followed him through it into a smaller room where newspaper people were relaxing with cigarettes and pipes, or simply drinking coffee. The room was thick with blue smoke. Most of the people were standing, but there was a motley assortment of beaten-up wooden chairs scattered around the periphery of the stark room, so we found a relatively remote corner and sat down.

Justin began filling his pipe. He leaned forward in his chair and waited expectantly for what I had to say.

"Look," I said. "I know what it's like to be on deadline. My timing is bad, I realize that. I won't take much of your time now. And I will take you up on your offer to go out on the town one of these nights. Right now, I need your help."

"Name it, James."

I told him briefly about Uncle Martin's death and how he'd left me the two houses and a great deal of stock in the company. He seemed truly pleased at my good fortune. I told him about Sam's suspicions, and how I'd come to share those suspicions. Finally, I asked him if he'd mind checking the newspaper morgue for the names of the board members. I then pulled out a type-written list of the names.

He gave me a wry grin. "You were pretty sure of yourself weren't you old boy?"

"I was pretty sure of you."

He shook his head. There was a trace of a smile on his face. "When do you need this?"

"By Friday, if possible."

"I'll see what I can do, James. I do have a few other things to do around here."

Chapter 10 *Wednesday the 10TH*

A plan was beginning to unfold in my head. It felt good to have taken some action, first by asking John Holland to check on the names I'd given him, and then knowing that Justin was going to search the morgue at *The Globe*. It wasn't much, but I felt it was a good beginning. Clearly I had a long way to go before I knew who killed Uncle Martin. But at least I'd set some things in motion. This morning, I hoped to accomplish a number of things I'd been meaning to do, among them household things and checking on Samantha.

Later, in the afternoon, I would get back to my plan.The first item on my agenda for the day was to visit a domestics agency. I'd decided that I needed someone to keep my Beacon Street house in order. It wasn't that I considered myself above such work. After all, I'd attended to my own household chores most of my adult life. An aspiring journalist has little choice. Recently, though, my circumstances had changed dramatically. With my newly acquired wealth came obligations—business and social—that simply didn't allow time for doing routine household tasks. I had enough money to pay a servant without even feeling it. I'd already notified the Flicks up in Salem that I wanted them to stay on. They'd been loyal, and frankly, had no place else to go. There wasn't much for them to do right now, but I needed time to decide what I was going to do with the house. They'd been living there for nine months with the approval of Mr. Friedman, Uncle Martin's executor. The will had stated that they could stay on until the will had gone through probate and the heir (myself) made a decision on their fate. In the meantime, they were being paid out of the proceeds of the will.

At times, selling the estate had seemed the wisest course. Then, something would happen to persuade me that I should keep the place, even if I only used it a few times a year. In any event, until I decided, I planned to keep the Flicks on salary. It was a good thing, too, because they were essential to my immediate plans.

I had good luck at the first agency I called on. It was on Tremont Street, only a fifteen-minute walk from my house. The tinkle of a bell announced my arrival as I entered the dimly lit office. Two male job applicants and a number of women of all ages and description were sitting in battered wooden chairs placed against opposite walls of the crowded room. All eyes stared at me expectantly before I'd even closed the door. They seemed to know that I was a potential employer, and not another applicant.

I'd decided before I left the house that I'd hire a manservant rather than a female. When the matronly woman who appeared to be in charge of the agency told me that both men waiting were unemployed manservants with excellent credentials, I was delighted.

I wanted someone who would live in—someone who would reside in the servant's quarters on the fourth floor. I needed a versatile person who could serve as butler, prepare and serve three meals a day when necessary, and do a number of other household chores as well. It would obviously have been inappropriate for a woman to live in, and I didn't think the place was quite big enough for a husband-and-wife couple. The agency lady told me she hadn't yet interviewed either of the men, but that I could meet with them separately in the back room, if I liked. If I found either of them suitable, she could assure me that they both came highly recommended by previous employers and that I would probably be pleased.

I'm not one for long deliberations and exhaustive inquiries—with the possible exception of my investigations into my uncle's death—so, after a brief session with each of the two candidates, I chose the first of the two. He said he'd be able to report to work first thing the next morning. I was somewhat taken back by his immediate decision, since he hadn't even seen where he'd be living, but it seemed more his risk than mine. Besides, I'd offered him a dollar a week more than the going rate. I suppose six dollars a week looks quite good when you don't have rent to consider. His name was Charles Trimble, and he was fifty-five years of age.

Having taken care of household business, I was free to go to Mt. Vernon Street and see how my cousin was faring in the wake of her narrow escape on Boylston Street two days ago. It was a bright, crisp December day, with no threat of foul weather, so I decided to walk the twenty-or-so blocks rather than fight the crowds on the horsecars.

Elizabeth greeted me with a hearty welcome as she reached for my coat and hat. "I'll tell the missus you're here, sir," she said with a smile and a Gaelic lilt to her voice. "Back in a moment. She'll be delighted you're here."

I stood in the foyer while she went to tell Sam that I was there. I couldn't help noticing while I waited that the house seemed cold. Not for lack of a stove, mind you, but for lack of the little things one usually finds in a house that's lived in. There were no pictures on the walls or on the tables. None of those personal things you expect in a home. I knew Sam was the type of person who'd make a house warm. The Samantha I remembered was a spontaneous, passionate person. What I'd seen of her the other day only reinforced that impression. So why did I get the feeling that the house was unlived-in? It was neat as a pin, but that in itself proved nothing.

Before I could reflect further on what I'd sensed, Samantha entered the room. Not surprisingly, she looked much better than she had on Monday. The bandages that had covered large areas of her face and arms were gone—except for one small dressing on her forehead. She broke into a broad smile when she saw me.

"You are a sight for sore eyes, James. What brings you here?"

"I had to see how you were doing. You were quite a sight Monday, you know."

"Yes, I imagine I was. As you can see, I'm much better now."

I stood there looking at her, experiencing stirrings I hadn't expected to feel, and feeling a bit awkward because of them. No doubt sensing my hesitation, she came to me and planted a warm kiss on my cheek. It was somewhere between a cousin kiss and that of a lover.

"You look like a new woman. I hope you feel as good as you look."

"You journalists do have a way with words." She motioned to a chair, "Here, sit down and be comfortable."

"So, I imagine Edward was upset when he found out what happened to you." From what I'd seen and heard of Edward, I wasn't at all sure this was true, but I wanted to find out what his reaction had been.

"Yes, but not so much because I was injured, but because I'd acted foolishly, as he put it, by going out into the streets by myself. Said I should have known better. Believe me, James, Edward is not your typical husband. At least I hope not for the sake of America's women." She looked away, as if she were thinking about something. Finally she said, "I never should have gotten married."

"Divorce him, Sam."

"It would only be worse. I told you before, divorced women are pariahs. I'd be shunned and scorned by everyone. At least this way most of the people I know treat me decently."

"But not your husband." Then, on a hunch I asked, "Does he mistreat you physically, Sam? Does he hit you?"

She brought her hands to her face and looked down. For a moment she said nothing. Then she dropped her hands and looked up at me. Her eyes were red. She nodded.

"Did you tell the police?"

"Not the first time. I threatened to. But the next time, yes. They spoke with him, but they did nothing. They didn't actually side with him, but they certainly didn't seem that upset. Now, of course, he holds it against me that I called them in. Men are supposed to rule their households, after all. I could sense that in the way the policeman reacted. The attitude in modern America is that sometimes a woman needs to be taught a lesson. God knows what lesson I needed, but that's the way men think."

"No, Sam, that's not the way all men think."

"Too many do. You know it, James."

I shrugged. "I suppose, but not everyone. You must leave this man, Sam. You can afford to now. Find yourself a decent place and get out."

"I told you, it's not that easy for a woman. Besides, he hasn't struck me recently. As a matter of fact, we hardly talk now. We just share the same house."

"I'm going to have a talk with Edward. He'll answer to me if he ever lays a hand on you again."

"No, James! Please, I appreciate what you're trying to do, but it would only be worse. I can handle it. Please." She brushed a wisp of hair away from her face and tried to look calm.

"I can't stand this, Sam. This is not a life for you." I was surprised at my emotions. I hadn't seen Samantha in years. I'd gotten by fairly well without her, too. But now, her welfare seemed the most important thing in my life. "Think about leaving him, Sam. Just think about it."

She nodded mechanically. "I'll think about it, James, but sometimes we must learn to accept our fate."

"I can't believe it's you saying this."

"James, you remember me as a young girl. When I was young, I was a free spirit, but this is 1884. When girls grow up, it's important that they understand their place in the family. In order to maintain their mental health, most women learn to grow inward. They learn to make a life for themselves that does not conflict with the men in their lives, for if it should conflict, they would come out the loser." She sighed resignedly. "Maybe someday, things will be different, James, but I don't expect that to happen in our lifetime." I could tell that she'd come to terms with this, and that, I think, was what disturbed me the most. She could see that I was troubled, and she made a willful effort to brighten up and change the subject. "We received your invitation, James. Surprisingly, Edward wants to attend."

She was referring to the invitation I'd sent to the board members and their spouses, inviting them to my Salem house for a holiday dinner next Sunday—just four days before Christmas. I must admit that it wasn't solely the holiday spirit that motivated me to invite these people to Salem for wassail and dinner. I had a method to my madness, though I hoped the occasion would at least be pleasantly festive. Getting to know the board members and their spouses a little better probably wasn't such a bad idea, though becoming close friends with some of them was not high on my list of priorities—Samantha excepted, of course. I decided, at least for the moment, not to pursue the issue of her virtual servitude to her scoundrel of a husband. I forced a smile.

"Wonderful, I'm delighted you'll be coming. I hope we'll have a chance to catch up on old times. It'll also get you out of this house and among other people for awhile."

"Yes, you're right, though one never knows how Edward will take it."

"Take it?"

"Well, he doesn't like it when I socialize with

others—especially other men."

"I was about to make a pointed comment, when the front doorbell interrupted jarringly. It wasn't a pleasant chime like the one I'd inherited from Uncle Martin, or even the cheerful tinkle of those bells you so often find attached to the top of shop doors. Rather, it was one of those awful squawking things that tortured the ears each time a caller twisted a knob on the front of the door. Elizabeth materialized from somewhere in the house and opened the door. A young tousle-haired Western-Union messenger with cap in hand handed her an envelope and announced in a voice louder than necessary, "Telegram for Mrs. Edward Ridley."

A moment later, Samantha was opening the envelope Elizabeth had given her.

"Excuse me a minute, will you? I wasn't expecting anything. I'm curious." She deftly slit open the envelope and withdrew a single folded sheet of paper. As soon as she unfolded it, her brows narrowed and her expression turned pale.

"What is it?" I asked. Whatever it was, it was not good.

She held the message so that I could see it. It was brief and to the point:

NEXT TIME YOU WON'T BE SO LUCKY STOP IF YOU KNOW WHAT'S GOOD FOR YOU, VOTE TO SELL STOP

I reached for her wrist and spoke quickly. "I'm going after that boy. We have to know who sent this. Keep the doors locked until I come back."

"No, James, you'll never find him. And if you do, he may attack you."

"I have to try." As I was going out the door, I added, "Remember, don't open the door for anyone."

There was no one on the street save two urchins playing some sort of game with a ball. "Hey," I yelled to the nearest, whose tattered gray cap kept sliding back on his head. He stopped and studied me. As he stood there, he removed the dirty cap, pushed a great pile of blond hair back on his head, and replaced the hat in a futile effort to control the unkempt mane. Seeing that I had his attention, I yelled out, "Did you see the messenger who just left this house?"

The young fellow must have sensed the urgency in my voice, because he was clearly startled. When it registered on him what I'd said, he pointed in the direction of Charles Street. I started running in that direction.

"Ain't no point in trying to find him," he shouted after me. I stopped and turned to face him.
"Why do you say that?"

"He was ridin' a bicycle. You'd never catch him, I reckon."

I shook my head. He was right, of course. There was nothing to do but return to the house. A few more questions proved only that the two boys had not paid much attention to the messenger. They were unable to provide much by way of description.

Inside again, I could see that Sam was beginning to feel the full impact of the menacing message she'd just received. She was visibly shaken.

I was livid. "The bastard! If there was ever any doubt, now we know there's a killer on the board."
She didn't respond for almost a minute. When she did speak, what she said came as a shock. "No we don't, James."

I looked at her with astonishment. Had I heard right? Only moments ago she'd been in a terrible state. But now, apparently through an enormous effort of will, she appeared calm—far more composed than one would expect a person to be after having received such a missive.

"How can you say that, Sam?"

"You may be right," she said. "It's just that we don't really know what's behind this, do we?"

"You'd better explain. I think we do know."

"Think about it. There was never any doubt in my mind that the murderer was on the board. That's not what I'm questioning. What I'm saying is that whoever sent this note might not be the murderer. It might be the person who attacked me on the street, but he might not be the murderer. Am I making any sense, James?"

"I think I see where you're headed. The killer could be an entirely different person..."

"Or my attacker could be someone hired by the killer. Or—"

"Or," I interrupted, "the letter writer could be someone who heard that you'd been attacked and decided to take advantage of the situation. If it were a perfect stranger who attacked you, that person would never know about the vote. But a board member could exploit your misfortune without risking exposure. And he wouldn't have to resort to violence. When the tramp on the street attacked you, he may have inadvertently set the stage for one of the board members to further intimidate you."

"Yes! That's possible." Then she looked away. "You realize, don't you, that there could be two board members to concern ourselves with. One could be father's killer; the other could be the letter writer."

I convinced Sam that the telegram should be reported to the police. I told her we should see John Holland, and right away. She really didn't think the police would do much about it, but when I pressed and told her I'd accompany her, she finally agreed. Before we left the house, she went and talked with Elizabeth to let her know she was going out.

"Did you tell her about the message?"

"No, just that I was going out to visit a few shops."

"Shouldn't you tell her what happened so she can inform Edward when he comes home?" I asked. "Won't he be concerned?" By now I should have known the answer.

"No, he'll be more upset to find that I've gone off with another man. Besides, I'll be back before he gets home. He never comes home before seven or eight.

Sometimes much later."

"He works that late every day?"

She sniffed contemptuously. "I wish that were the case."

I was almost afraid to ask the next question. "Then what does he do that keeps him out so late?"

"He used to claim that he was working, but I smelled alcohol on his breath so many times that he finally admitted that he has drinks with clients or colleagues. Says it's part of the business." She shook her head sadly. "You may as well know. I'm pretty sure that it's more than just drinking with his gentlemen friends."

"A woman?"

She nodded.

"How can you be sure? Maybe it is only drinking with clients."

"No, James. It's not my imagination. I can smell the scent of her on him."

"Have you confronted him about it?"

"Of course. He denies it or merely laughs it off. I don't really think he cares anyway. What could I do about it?"

"I told you before. You could divorce him. My God, the man really is a scoundrel."

"And I told you that women never do well in a divorce. The judge always rules for the man. The woman is considered unappreciative of how well the man has provided for her. Even if he's beaten her, she must have deserved it."

"Sam, what do you care now? You have money. You can create a life for yourself."

"And live as an outcast."

I reached for her and held her close to me. It happened naturally enough. She was so close that I could feel her chest heave as she tried to stifle sniffles of anguish.

I knew there was a great deal of truth to what she'd been saying. I felt frustrated, and I must confess, probably more concern than I would have, had I been hearing about the plight of some woman I didn't know.

But Sam I did know. Sam, I cared about. I was beginning to realize just how much I did care. I put my hand under her chin, and gently pulled her head up. She looked at me, and I could see tears beginning to form under reddened eyes. Before I had time to think about the propriety of what was happening, our lips met—tentatively at first; then with a passion I hadn't expected.

I'd kissed more women in my thirty-four years than I could put a number to—usually after carefully wooing and pursuing them. This was different, though. It was completely unplanned, and, therefore, all the more evocative.

"I'm sorry," I said. "I don't know what came over me."

She wiped a tear away. "I do."

I grinned sheepishly, "I suppose I do, too. Come on, we'd better get ourselves over to the station house so we can meet with John Holland."

"And forget this ever happened?"

"If Edward were a decent chap, I'd say yes."

"If Edward were a decent chap, this never would have happened."

We agreed that we needed to revisit the matter, but later, for meeting with Holland was, at least for the present, the highest priority.

When we arrived at the police station he was just leaving the building, which, as it turned out, was fortuitous. I caught his eye as he was about to set off on foot down Tremont Street towards Court Street.

I hailed him with a yell, "John, have you got a minute?"

"James. How the devil are you? And who's your beautiful lady friend?"

I introduced Samantha as my cousin. He looked at me with a curious expression, as if he wasn't sure he believed me. Under other circumstances, I would have enjoyed the situation. Instead, I plunged ahead and told him we had a police matter to report to him. He nodded and said in a relieved tone of voice that he was glad that we'd met each other outside the station house. I understood what he meant. As the journalist who'd written the scathing series on police corruption, I was still persona non grata to a lot of his colleagues. It was best for his sake that we not be seen together. We agreed to stroll down Tremont Street and then onto Court. Since it was cool, but not particularly cold for December, that's what we did.

We showed him the note and explained about my chasing after the messenger.

"So you never did catch up to him?"

"No, by the time I got out into the street he was gone."

"And the two boys in the street couldn't describe him for you?"

"Just that he was young, probably fifteen or sixteen and was wearing a Western Union uniform. No details beyond that. Basically what Samantha and I remembered seeing. That might be enough if one of your detectives visits the Western Union office. They should know which of their boys delivered to the Ridley house, wouldn't you think?"

"I suppose we could also ask the members of your board of directors a few questions. Not sure we'd get much, though." He scratched the side of his head thoughtfully. "Got to think about that one. I'll definitely send someone out to check with the Western-Union office. See if they can tell us who sent the telegram."

"Yes, that could give us the name of the sender."

"Don't get your hopes up. If our boy is smart, he may have sent someone else to order the telegram. Or he may have used a disguise."

I nodded my understanding. "Still, it's worth a try isn't it?"

"Sure, it's worth a try, James. Let you know

what we turn up. If we get something, then we can take it from there."

"At least now, I hope you believe that our suspicions may have some merit?"

"I believed you the first time, my friend. And I agree that this might be serious.

Chapter 11 *Wednesday the 10th*

My article on Grover Cleveland for the *Salem Gazette* was not progressing well. As a matter of fact, it was not progressing at all. I hadn't written a word since that fateful day last week when Samantha had so unexpectedly made her reappearance after all those years. It now looked as if it would be, at the very least, a few more days before I could get back to my type writer.

How quickly my priorities had shifted. What mattered now was that I find who'd killed Uncle Martin and that I protect Samantha from further harm. The latter was beginning to take precedence over the former. What had seemed so important less than a week ago, now seemed insignificant by comparison to the commitments I'd made in the last few days.

My hopes rested on a couple of things: I was hoping that Justin at *The Globe* would come through with some useful information from the paper's morgue before my holiday dinner party on the 21st. I wanted to be as prepared as possible for that important get together.

My other hope lay with John Holland's efforts. If he could find out who sent the telegram, we'd be a lot closer to clearing up a lot of things.

I knew that, in the meantime, I should be working away on the *Gazette* piece, but I just couldn't concentrate on it now. My mind was on other things.

It was ironic that so much of my life seemed to revolve around newspapers and magazines. Not so long ago I was contributing on a regular basis to the *Salem Gazette*. All of a sudden, though, instead of being the one who did the contributing, it was I who needed something from a publication—actually from two publications. The first was *The Globe*. But the obvious had taken a little longer to dawn on me. That dawning, of course, was that *Knickerbocker* magazine was, for me, a far more accessible publication than *The Globe*. A visit to *Knickerbocker's* offices seemed in order. There was still time this afternoon.

I decided to start with Peter Zumbach, *Knickerbocker's* editor-in-chief. There was no point in going home for a quick midday meal, as I had nothing in the pantry. Not that I was much of a cook anyway. Hopefully, this sorry situation would be remedied tomorrow, when Charles Trimble would take up his duties. In the meantime, I got by by stopping at a grocer's for a roll and a piece of New York cheddar, which I proceeded to eat on the way.

By the time I'd reached the magazine offices at Milk and Broad, the edge was off my appetite, and I was ready to meet with Zumbach. Only now did it occur to me that he might not be ready to meet with me. I should have sent a note with a messenger to alert him that I was planning to call on him.

I'm usually not so capricious, but in my zeal to get to the bottom of my uncle's murder and do it before something happened to Samantha, I'd been operating mostly on impulse. Still, since I'd neglected to send a messenger, or a telegram, my only other option would have been to place a telephone call. That, of course, was ridiculous. I didn't have a telephone. I'd just have to hope Zumbach would be there and that he'd take the time to see me. I knew that the magazine had at least one phone (yes, the other day I'd heard someone use this shortened form of the word). That's how Elizabeth had contacted us to tell us about the attack on Samantha.

A young man sitting at a desk in the lobby went back into the editorial department to fetch Zumbach. Two minutes later he'd returned with the editor-in-chief. It was obvious that Zumbach was a working editor; not one of those gentlemen-executive types who sat back and read the reports of others who actually did all the work. He cut a rather dashing figure with his shirtsleeves rolled up, standing there waiting to see what I wanted from him. He would know that I was a board member, so he would, no doubt, be guarded until he found out why I was there. He was an impressive man, probably an inch taller than me, but appearing much taller, no doubt because of his relaxed manner and gangly carriage. He didn't appear to be much older than me. There was something about him that I found hard to define. It had a lot to do with self-confidence. He seemed sure of himself without the slightest hint of arrogance. His sharply delineated rather longish face was topped with a thick mop of hair, so blond that it was nearly white. Before he spoke a word, I had the feeling I would like him.

"Ah, so you're James Christopher," he smiled broadly. "I've been looking forward to meeting you."

"And I you," I said, relieved to find that my initial reading of him seemed to have been vindicated. "Do you have a few minutes now, or would another time be better?"

"Now's as good a time as any, as long as you don't mind if we get interrupted from time to time. Let's go into my office.

His office was nothing special, but far nicer than what you'd find in most newspapers. Magazine people apparently cared more for esthetics than newspaper people, for Zumbach actually had a couple of framed pictures on his walls. One appeared to be a prize-winning *Knickerbocker* cover with Lincoln's face on it. I got up in order to note the date of the issue. It so happened that it was the issue for the week just prior to the assassination.

I told Zumbach that I had two reasons for calling on him. The first was that I thought it only appropriate that I get a closer look at the business I now owned stock in. I was hoping that I might even meet a few of the staff members, if that didn't interfere with things too much.

Zumbach smiled. He said that he was delighted to know that I cared about the magazine and that he'd be pleased to show me around and introduce me to the staff. He said most of the other board members seemed to care only about profitability—not that he didn't understand their concern, mind you.

My other reason, I explained to him—and with some trepidation—was that I had a few questions to ask concerning what he knew about my Uncle Martin and his relations with the board of directors. My trepidation stemmed from my not knowing Zumbach or what his relations were with Martin Van Zandt or the board. For all I knew he would resent my inquiries or, worse yet, give me misleading information. Or he might consider me a meddler who should stick to his board affairs and leave the magazine to him.

Zumbach frowned as I explained this second reason. He hesitated for just a few seconds before responding. "I know you're a journalist, Mr. Christopher."

"Call me James, please."

"As a journalist you're used to seeing things objectively—more so than the average person. But as Martin Van Zandt's nephew—apparently a favored nephew, in light of his leaving you a big portion of his estate—you may not like what I have to say. Are you sure you want to hear it?"

"I know my uncle had his faults. I'd still like to know what you can tell me about what he was like when he dealt with people here at the magazine—regardless of how it makes him look."

I could see that he was wrestling with himself. I was, after all, an unfamiliar commodity. After weighing his options, he came right out with it.

"He was a bastard. Treated people miserably. He actually treated me better than most, for some unknown reason."

"I suspect I know why."

"I'd love to hear it."

"He respected you. He had no patience with people he didn't."

"Perhaps you're right. Whatever his reasons, the man was insufferable. To my mind, he had only one redeeming virtue."

"And that was?"

"He loved *Knickerbocker* magazine. He was a serious journalist as much as he was a businessman. Despite his unpleasant personality, I can't deny that the magazine always came first with him, which was what kept me here. It certainly wasn't the pleasure of working with him. I stayed in spite of his abrasiveness because he allowed me to do serious journalism. That's not always easy to find. If I wanted to do something bold or different, he'd usually support it. He had a nose for what was big news and for what would sell. I can't deny him that. So if you could put aside your sensitivities, this was a good place to work. We did a lot of good stuff here in the past few years, in large part because Martin Van Zandt was willing to go out on a limb and try new things."

"How did he relate to the board members?"

"The way you'd expect. He was always fighting one or two of them over some issue. Or maybe they were fighting him. To be honest, I wasn't always sure which. I have to admit that most of the board members seemed more interested in earnings than in editorial content." He paused for a moment as he considered me. "I don't know where your sentiments lie yet. I'd like to think, though, that with your background, you might care as much about *how* we earn our dollars as you do about how many we earn."

I smiled. "Did he get along with any of them?"

"I suppose he got along with Arthur Billingsley. Billingsley, you know, was one of Mr. Van Zandt's first investors, back in the early days when he needed support. He was about ten years younger than Mr. Van Zandt, but they became fairly close, nevertheless. Billingsley never wanted to sell *Knickerbocker* the way some of the others did. I think your uncle appreciated that loyalty."

"So they got along well?"

"I didn't say that. Mr. Billingsley often disagreed with your uncle over certain matters. Mr. Billingsley is a strong-willed person—and successful in his own right. He owns that import/export business, you know. Between his financial independence and the fact that he'd known Mr. Van Zandt so long, he simply wasn't intimidated the way most of the other board members were. And, don't forget, he was the third largest stockholder. All I'm saying is that your uncle got along with him better than most. I think he respected him, to use your word." He pulled out his pocket watch and stole a peek at the time.

"I realize you have deadlines," I said understandingly. "I won't take much more of your time. Which board member did my uncle have the most disagreement with?"

"I suppose Mr. Trampler. He was the most vocal advocate for selling the magazine. His business was—is—in trouble. He needed, and still needs money. Who doesn't? Anyway, everyone knew he needed money. Your uncle, of course, wouldn't hear of selling. Thank God for that, too. But your uncle showed no sympathy for Mr. Trampler's problem. None whatsoever. Apparently his attitude was that Trampler should have known better than to take on a partner he couldn't trust."

"Did you hear him say that?"

"No, but that's the word that leaked out around here. It's hard to keep a secret, you know. Especially about bad news. It certainly wouldn't have been out of character for your uncle to say it."

"Can you think of another board member he fought with?"

A smirk formed on Zumbach's face. He raised his head an inch or so, stared at me through narrowed eyelids, and nodded knowingly. "What are you *really* after, Mr. Christopher?"

I should have realized how transparent my

inquiries would seem, especially to another journalist. I decided to take a chance and trust him. "Yes, I do have another reason for these questions." I told him about my suspicions regarding the death of my uncle, and that I hoped I could count on his discretion until I'd finished my investigation of the matter. I know, I added, that it must seem impertinent of me, the newest board member, to pursue such inquiries of my fellow board members, but I assured him that it was not being done frivolously. I was fully aware that my pursuit of this matter, if it became public, could adversely affect the reputations of innocent people. That's one reason why I needed his understanding and cooperation. I then filled him in on what Sam had told me, about the threatening note she had received, and about everything else I knew. I added that, hopefully, if I were successful, it would exonerate once and for all, all of the innocent suspects.

He studied me for a full minute, though it seemed much longer. Finally, he said, "Why don't you just leave this in the hands of the police up in Salem?"

"The Salem Police, fortunately for them I suppose, have far less experience with homicide cases than the police here in Boston. They're not bumpkins —Salem is bigger than that, and a rich town, so they have a decent force, but they just don't see much serious crime. I do intend to talk to Chief Gormley, but I don't expect him to change his opinion of the case. A reversal would not enhance his reputation as a law enforcement officer."

"Perhaps you're not being fair. After all, you admit you haven't met the man yet."

"Perhaps," I conceded, "but I doubt it.

He leaned forward, placing his elbows on the battered surface of his wooden desk. He made a steeple with his fingers. "You do realize, Mr. Christopher, that talking with you could lose me my job here? If the board members learn that I'm talking with you about this, there's no telling what they'll do?"

"Yes, of course. And if you don't want to tell me

any more about this, I'll understand. If you do help me, though, be assured that it will be between you and me."

"Unless it leads to an indictment," said Zumbach.

"Yes, I suppose that's true. Hell, if this doesn't lead to an indictment, and my fellow board members learn about what I'm doing, they'll not take kindly to me, knowing that I suspect them of murder."

"That, Mr. Christopher, is an understatement. Look, I'd like to help you, but I'm not sure how much help I can be. The explanation given for Martin Van Zandt's murder never made sense to me. God knows, enough people hated him, but, as I said, he was good to me. I owe the old man something."

"What about some of the other board members? How did he get along with them?"

"I know for a fact that he didn't think much of Sebastian LaRue."

"Oh?"

"He thought him the worst type of lawyer, and he thought very little of lawyers in general."

"Didn't he approve of LaRue when he was first appointed to the board?"

"Yes, he came highly recommended by Mr. Van Zandt's bankers. I don't know how well you know Mr. LaRue, but he can be quite charming, if he's of a mind to be."

"So what happened to change my uncle's mind about him?"

"They quarreled about something. Things were never the same after that. Shortly after their row, Mr. Van Zandt appointed Mr. Friedman to the position of corporate attorney. Took the job away from LaRue."

"I don't imagine LaRue was happy with that."

"You imagine right. I wouldn't be surprise if your uncle had done it to force LaRue off the board, but it never came to that. LaRue fumed awhile, but stayed on."

"What was their quarrel about?"

"I don't know for sure. I've been told that LaRue felt that Mr. Van Zandt took too many chances editorially, that he put the magazine, and therefore the stock, at risk. I think he was afraid people would sue us because we said nasty things about them. Your uncle... and here's an example of what made him a great journalist... your uncle said that was nonsense. If our facts checked out, we shouldn't hesitate to print important pieces." Zumbach looked at me as if we were kindred souls. "Don't you love it? Your uncle was the kind of man I could hate and love at the same time."

"Did any of the other board members worry about the magazine taking too many risks?"

"Not that I'm aware of. They might have, but I never heard that any of them did. From what I could tell, even if they didn't care for your uncle, they acknowledged his skill as a journalist. If they disagreed with him, it was usually over money or a money-related matter."

"Who else disagreed with him—besides LaRue and Trampler?"

"I suppose when it comes right down to it, most of them did at one time or another. Those two, he fought with the most, but from what I hear, he had disagreements with Mrs. Neustadt and Mrs. Calore from time to time also. The only one he never fought with openly was his old friend Arthur Billingsley." He looked at the ceiling, as if a thought had just occurred to him. "I can't even say that, to be honest with you. I've heard them have words, too, but there was a qualitative difference, if you know what I mean."

"I'm not sure I do."

"Well," he grinned. "They would argue, but they would argue as equals. He didn't intimidate Billingsley the way he did most of the others."

I nodded my understanding. "I see. You said he argued with the two women members, too. Do you recall what Mrs. Neustadt and my uncle disagreed over?"

"No, I was never privy to what it was, but I do know they argued—and more than once."

I hesitated for a second before asking my next question, "You weren't personally privy to all of the arguments you've related to me, were you?"

"Some, but not all of them."

"So how do you know about the ones for which you weren't actually present?"

He smiled self-consciously. "I overheard some of them. Sometimes one can't help overhearing. You understand." I waited patiently for him to continue. "They weren't always discreet," he explained. "Some of what I've told you I heard from other sources. Reliable ones, I assure you."

"Of course. What about Mrs. Calore? Can you tell me anything about disagreements she might have had with my uncle?"

"No, I can't. I do remember that when she first came on the board—it must have been in '79 or '80—they seemed to get along fine." He paused as something came to him. "You know, don't you, that she inherited her directorship from her husband when he died a few years ago?" I nodded, and he continued, "Well, after a few months, their relationship changed. She seemed—I suppose you'd say—more deferential when he was around. But there was something else, too—almost a resentment on her part. Hard to describe it, really."

"You don't know why this change occurred?"

"No, I don't. Maybe you should ask her."

"Maybe I will."

Chapter 12 *Thursday the 11th*

The ringing of the front-door chime jolted me from the dreamless depths of a sound sleep. I blinked twice and looked at the time. Eight o'clock. I never sleep that late. The toll of recent events must have been getting to me.

I was still half-asleep. Normally I'd remain in that semiconscious state until I'd consumed my first cup of coffee. I couldn't for the life of me think of who could be calling at this hour. Eight might be late for getting up, but it was early for most callers.

Then it came to me. Charles Trimble was to start work today, and eight was when he was supposed to show up. I'd been so preoccupied with the murder of Uncle Martin, and the attack and threat on Sam that I'd completely forgotten about Trimble. And now the man was on my front doorstep. I was totally unprepared. What would I have him do first? Damn, I wasn't even dressed.

I hastily threw on my robe and slippers, ran a hand through my hair, and dragged myself down the hall to the front door. The house was still cold. I hadn't yet stoked the coal furnace, but I was waking up fast.

I unlocked the front door, pulled it open, and found myself staring into the alert eyes of my new manservant. Christ, the man was dressed better than I was at my businesslike best.

"Good morning, sir," said Trimble professionally. "I hope this isn't too early. You did say eight, didn't you?"

There was something about the way he said that. If he handled my visitors as skillfully as he'd just handled me, I'd stumbled onto a real find in Charles Trimble. The man was a pro. I had a feeling he was going to work out just fine.

I invited him in, and he soon had things well in

hand. I didn't have to come up with a list of things for him to do. Before two minutes had passed, I found him interviewing me without being the least bit impertinent. Within twenty minutes, he knew what I planned to do during the day, what he could do to make things easier for me, and where he'd be living (a small apartment on the third floor).

Seeing how competent he was, I gave him an unusual assignment. I asked him to find out whom we needed to contact and what would be involved in having a telephone installed in the house. Hearing this, he beamed whether from the challenge or from the knowledge that we'd have one of Mr. Bell's new contraptions under our own roof, I couldn't tell.

Through some kind of culinary magic, Charles managed to prepare a surprisingly edible breakfast from the meager stores I had on hand. I conjured up tantalizing images of what he might do for future meals, once he had the benefit of proper provisions in the pantry.

It was a few minutes before nine when the door chime rang for the second time that morning. Number 31 Beacon Street was becoming a popular place. I rose from my chair at the dining room table. Until today, I'd had my breakfast either in the kitchen or at a neighborhood café I frequented, more for its convenience than for the quality of its food. Before I'd gone two paces from the table, I was startled by Trimble's booming voice.

"I'll get it, sir."

I started to protest. After all, I'm not helpless. Charles held up a hand and patiently waved me back into my chair. He had me sized up already: A young man with too much money, who wasn't yet comfortable in the role of being a gentleman of substance. At least I hope that's what he thought. He may have simply considered me nouveau riche. Why was I concerned about what Charles thought of me anyway? It was he who should be looking for my acceptance. Dear God, life can be complicated.

He returned a moment later with a telegram. It suddenly occurred to me that, if the messenger had received a tip, it had come from Charles. I'd have to make some provision for reimbursing him. Or if he hadn't tipped the messenger, then the messenger was the loser. I shook my head at the permutations. Life was indeed complicated. I'd deal with this later.

The telegram was from Samantha, and the tone was urgent:

NEED TO SEE YOU SOON STOP WILL VISIT YOU AT BEACON STREET THIS AFTERNOON AT FIVE STOP IF NOT CONVENIENT PLEASE SEND TELEGRAM OR MESSENGER WITH TIME AND DAY CONVENIENT FOR YOU STOP PLEASE MAKE IT SOON STOP DO NOT COME HERE STOP
SAMANTHA

Something was seriously wrong. My first impulse was to set aside my other plans and go directly to Mt. Vernon Street to find out what the problem was, but the last sentence of her message sounded ominous. Obviously there was a problem, and apparently it involved Edward. Why was I not surprised?

I planned my day around a five o'clock visit from Samantha. The thought occurred to me that she would probably have preferred to come sooner, but realized that a midday visit would be more likely to interfere with any business I might have planned for the day.

I'd already made plans to go up to Salem today. My five o'clock meeting with Sam shouldn't alter those plans. I'd sent a telegram earlier in the week up to the Flicks informing them that I wanted to meet with them. They were expecting me. I suppose I could have worked on the *Gazette* series instead, but I knew I couldn't concentrate on writing until I'd gotten to the bottom of things closer to home. The series would just have to wait.

I walked east on Beacon until a horsecar came by. I boarded the car and took it into the North End, where I got off and proceeded to the ferry terminal on foot. I took the ferry over to East Boston to the Eastern Railway Station, where I took the train north to Salem. I was lucky. It took me only 45 minutes to get to East Boston from my home. I arrived at the station with five minutes to spare. It gave me time to buy copies of the *Post* and *The Globe* to read on the train. The timetable said I'd arrive in Salem at 11:09, which would leave me with plenty of time to do what I wanted to do and return to Boston in time for my meeting with Sam.

The train arrived in Lynn at 10:38, where we took on water for the engine while passengers got on and got off. Lynn was one of the bigger towns on the North Shore, but it wasn't that impressive from the train. We were only there five minutes or so. As you go north from Lynn, you pass through Swampscott, South Salem and finally the main Salem Depot.

The train pulled slowly into Salem Depot a minute ahead of schedule, its engine puffing and wheezing, sending out big clouds of steam from around the big wheels and from the gray stack in the front. A small boy waiting on the platform jumped as one particularly loud belch of steam burst across the platform less than five feet from where he and his mother were standing. A few feet farther down the short platform I made out the bulkily clad, slightly hunched figure of Everett Flick, his arms folded across his chest in order to ward off the bitter-cold gusts icy wind on this colder-than-average December morning.

As I stepped down from the car, he recognized me and hurried over.

"Mornin' Mr. Christopher. Good trip?"

"Fine, Everett, fine. Where's the buggy?"

"Right there, sir," He said, pointing to one of a half dozen buggies standing at rest not far from the platform. I stood there for minute, surveying the town.

I'd been to Salem numerous times over the years, especially when I was a boy, and, of course, I'd worked here for the Gazette, but I'd really never paid much attention to the town. As a boy brought up in Boston I'd been eager to get out to the house, where my aunt and uncle would treat me like royalty. Of course I'd heard about Salem's rich history—the great maritime tradition and the notorious Witch Trial era—but history has little appeal for young boys.

Now that I was a homeowner up here, I looked at things differently. I began to notice other houses—historic houses. Began to look into the history that not so many years ago had bored me. Now I was fascinated by what I was learning about my North Shore home. Fascinated to learn that America's military started here in 1637, that in the last century Salem's Elias Hasket Derby had become America's first millionaire by opening up America's trade with China and the rest of the Orient. Funny, the more you get into that sort of thing, the more fascinating it becomes.

Most of the towns and villages in Essex County had been named after places in England. A few were Indian names. Salem was different, it was apparently an anglicized version of the Hebrew word *shalom,* meaning peace. The early settlers called the place *Naumkeag,* an Indian name, meaning the fishing place. Within a few years the colonial leaders changed it to Salem. Today, a number of towns in the United States are called Salem, but all of them were named after this one.

I climbed up and into the buggy, and dropped into the seat next to where Flick was sitting. "The house, sir?" He asked.

"Yes. If I have enough time later, on the way back to the depot, I may ask you to take me to see Chief Gormley."

Flick nodded submissively. "Police station's only a few blocks out of the way, sir."

I grinned at Flick, "I know, Everett, I know.

Don't forget, I worked here for the last couple of years.

He looked embarrassed, turned his attention to the team, flicked his whip at the hindquarters of the two horses, and we started off for Chestnut Street.

Twenty minutes later, we were settled in the comfortable front room of the stately house on Chestnut Street. I marveled at how good the place looked, and was effusive in praising the Flicks for the wonderful job they'd done in keeping it in such fine fettle—both inside and out. Mrs. Flick had prepared a lunch for me and was about to serve me in the dining room. I told her I hadn't come all the way up to Salem to eat alone. I asked her to set two more places so that she and her husband could join me at the table while we discussed the house and plans for the future. She seemed startled that I would make such a request. I could see that she was both pleased and uncomfortable with the arrangement.

As we ate, I reassured the couple once again that I wanted them to remain on at the house, explaining that I probably wouldn't be up to Salem very often during the winter—except, of course, for the holiday dinner next Sunday. I did, however, expect to come up more often in the spring and certainly in the summer. Of course visits in the spring were subject to the weather. If it was a fairly dry spring, I'd come up. Rainy springs and springs following snowy winters meant muddy, frequently impassable roads.

Having hopefully set their minds at ease as to their continued employment, I turned the conversation toward a discussion of routine household affairs and questions of procedure that had come up since my last visit. There were repairs that needed doing, and they wanted my permission to obtain cost estimates for the big jobs and approval to proceed with the smaller ones.

The house was heated by fireplaces in each of the major rooms and Franklin stoves in the other rooms. As far as I knew the place had been heated that way for all of its eighty-three years. According to the papers I got when the property was transferred to me, the house had been built in 1801 by Samuel McIntire—Salem's famous architect and builder of that earlier period.

I told the Flicks that I was seriously considering putting a coal furnace in the cellar in order to heat the entire house. I could see their faces beam at the prospect of central heating.

I directed my attention to Mr. Flick. "Everett, you might go to a local merchant and get us an estimate for such a furnace. For that matter," I added, "You probably should get two estimates."

He nodded. "Yes sir. Be my pleasure."

"You might also look into what's involved in installing a telephone in the house. I suppose we should think about getting up-to-date. After all, it is 1884. And isn't this the town where Bell made his first long-distance call?"

At this, Mrs. Flick's hands flew to her mouth, and her eyes lit up. "My Lord, a telephone. Yes, Mr. Christopher, it was Salem. Just seven years ago. Me and Everett were outside the Lyceum the night Mr. Bell placed that first telephone call. All the way to Boston it was. Least that's what they said. Couldn't get inside, of course," she sniffed. "They only sent out invitations to the important people," she added in tone that said what else would you expect.

Everett, clearly the practical one in the family, just said, "Yes, Mr. Christopher." I don't think he thought much of the idea, but he knew where his bread was buttered. "I'll look into it," he added. "Not exactly sure where to begin, but I'll ask around town. Someone'll know."

"That sounds fine. There's really no hurry. We've gotten by just fine without one. I still don't have one in Boston, though I am getting one soon."

"Do you really think we need one Mr. Christopher?" It was Everett asking. I could tell that he viewed me as the city sophisticate who would know about such things.

I laughed. "Probably not. Who would we call? Hardly anybody has one. It's just that I rather fancy things that are new and innovative. Find them interesting. Besides, someday they *will* be more common. Might actually be useful, instead of just fun."

Miriam smiled approvingly. Everett just shook his head doubtfully.

I leaned forward, placing my elbows on the table. It was time to talk about the event I'd planned for next Sunday. "Here's what I'd like you to do for dinner on Sunday," I went on to explain how I wanted the evening to go. "I know it's a lot of work and that you'll be busy for most of the day and evening. Get someone from the area to help you if you need to." We went over everything twice, and then, after thanking them both once again, I told Everett that it was time to take me back to the station. First, though, I wanted to see Chief Gormley for a few minutes.

The sergeant at the desk looked to be a good ten years older than me. He seemed occupied with something when I entered the police station. After a full minute, he looked up, his face saying he resented the interruption.

"Yeah?" he said by way of welcome. "What can I do for you?"

"Is Chief Gormley in?"

"He expectin' ya?"

"No, but I'd like to see him."

"What's it about? Maybe I can help ya."

"It's about the Van Zandt murder. I'm his nephew and I'd really prefer to talk to Chief Gormley. What's your name, officer?"

"Haskins. Sergeant Haskins." I could see he wasn't happy with my request to go over his head, but after mulling it over a few seconds he grudgingly acceded. "Just a second. I'll see if he'll see ya. What'd you say your name was?"

"I didn't. It's Christopher, James Christopher. I inherited the Van Zandt place over on Chestnut—

where my uncle lived."

He forced a smile, but his eyes looked suspicious. Caution had taken over. "Ah yes, heard about that. Didn't expect you to be so young."

"I have a young face."

He raised his eyebrows as he went through a door into another room. There was agitated conversation in the other room for a minute or so, and then an older man appeared, followed by Haskins.

"G'day,sir. I'm Chief Gormley. Understand you're Mr. Van Zandt's nephew."

"You understand right, chief. Name's James Christopher."

He squinted. I could see he was thinking about something. "Say, there's a fella named Christopher works on the local paper. Writes these long investigative articles. You wouldn't be—?"

"Yes, though I'm no longer working at the *Gazette*—not since my uncle died."

He studied me for a minute, shaking his head as he processed all this. When he spoke his tone was friendly, but professional.

"Haskins says you want to talk to me. Why don't we go into my office." I followed him in, feeling Haskins' eyes boring into my back.

"Have a seat," said Gormley. "Only have a couple of minutes, so why don't you tell me what's on your mind."

"Well, I was—"

"No offense, Mr. Christopher," he interrupted, "but I was surprised to hear that the girl didn't get the place. Since you did, I can see why you stopped writin' stories for the paper. Got a lot more money now, and don't need to work for it, do you?" Clearly he felt no need to hide his disapproval. I had very little stature when I entered his office and was losing more with every passing moment.

"You mean my cousin Samantha. I was surprised, too, frankly." Then I added, trying to control my temper. After all, I needed him more than he needed me. "My uncle didn't leave her the house, but he did leave her a considerable fortune. You knew that, didn't you?"

I could tell that he didn't. He seemed almost disappointed that the rumors he'd heard were not accurate. "No, can't say's I did. Word around here is she got nothing—and you got it all."

"Well, that's not true." I was trying not to let the meeting become confrontational, though it seemed to be heading that way, despite my best intentions. I was not going to get anywhere with him if he was convinced I'd somehow benefited at Samantha's expense. I had to set the record straight. It was my only chance at gaining at least a modicum of cooperation. "It's really not my place to go into the details of her inheritance, chief, but I can assure you that Samantha Ridley made out quite well. It's true that her father didn't leave her the house, but he did leave her a large inheritance. And for what it's worth, she and I remain close friends." Before he could respond, I added, "By the way, I still write for the *Gazette*. Just not on staff anymore. I admit, I no longer need the work, but I write because I consider myself a journalist at heart."

His brow knitted and he squinted at me suspiciously. I could see that he wasn't sure what to believe. "I see," he said skeptically, obviously trying to remain patient. "So just what is it I can do for you?"

"I was wondering if you'd be willing to tell me what you remember about the night my uncle was murdered?"

He frowned suspiciously. "It's all in my report. Filed it with the county last March. Besides, it's police business. Why would you be askin'?"

"You were speaking a minute ago about my cousin Samantha. She's the one who's asking. She asked me to talk to you. I told her I would." I was deliberately placing this on Sam's shoulders, as I felt Gormley would be more inclined to offer up information for her than he would for me. So far, he'd seemed more concerned about her welfare than mine. I was hoping I'd read him right. I pushed on. "At the time of her father's death, no one took the trouble to explain any of the details of the murder to Mrs. Ridley. Her father's lawyer felt he was protecting her from the sordid details. She says that she never even spoke with you."

Gormley nodded, and I resumed my litany, "Mr. and Mrs. Flick over at the house couldn't give her much information, either. Or wouldn't. And her husband told her she should get on with her life. The sooner she put those terrible things behind her, the better. Everyone wanted to protect her, so no one told her anything except that a prowler or burglar broke into the house and killed him."

Gormley nodded again—a bit more emphatically. This time as if to say that he agreed with the way things had been handled. I looked him squarely in the eyes and waited. He finally said, "I hear what you're saying, Mr. Christopher. Don't see what the problem is, though. She is a lady. No need for her to know more than what she's already been told— 'specially seein' as it was her father this happened to. Best she knows as little as possible about the gory details. Just between you an' me, they were gory."

"How do you mean? I thought someone hit him on the head. I know that's not very pleasant, but as murders go, it doesn't sound particularly gory."

There was no one else in the office, but Gormley leaned forward, dropping his voice, as if there were. "There was sticky blood all over the side of the old man's head and on the carpet. Must of poured out of his head like Niagara. Whoever hit him, didn't hold back. Wasn't satisfied with just knockin' 'im out. Whoever it was, he wanted to do the old man in for good. Looked to me at the time like he was hit several times." A look of satisfaction came over his full face. "The county coroner—after he looked at the body—he said that's exactly what happened. Said old man Van

Zandt was killed by multiple blows to the head with a blunt object."

"You find the object?"

"Wasn't hard to find. Lying right there by the body. This green statue. Jade. Real valuable I'm told, and real heavy, too. Ten pounds if it was an ounce. Brought over from China by Elias Hasket Derby's *Grand Turk*, they say. Hell, you hit somebody with that and they stay dead." He smiled at his weak attempt at humor.

"You didn't think Mrs. Ridley should know this?"

"As I said, she's a lady. And she's his daughter. Best she don't know everything. Besides, her husband said not to tell her."

"Is that so?" Edward rears his unpleasant head once again. "I didn't know that."

"Yep, he came up here from Boston the morning after the murder. Said he'd handle all the details. Said he wanted to spare his wife all that. It was hard enough on her knowing her father'd been killed. I couldn't argue with that, could I?"

"No, I suppose not," I said with a disdainful expression that was lost on Gormley. "I'll try to spare her anything that's too ugly, but just to satisfy my own curiosity—after all, he was my uncle—do you think the killer had help?"

"I shouldn't be talking to you about this. The only reason I'm makin' an exception is because you're family, and you're the new man of the house out there." I could see that he wanted to show how knowledgeable he was, and that he felt better about it now that he'd given me his little preamble. He was visibly more relaxed now as he shifted his weight and continued, "I'd say he was alone. Wouldn't of needed no help to do what he did."

"I understand that there were several people at the house that night."

"That's right."

"Did you consider them suspects?"

"Nope."

I could see this wasn't going to be easy. "Seems strange," I offered.

"What seems strange?"

"That you wouldn't consider them suspects."

Gormley pursed his lips. I watched as he struggled to remain patient with me, the pampered young man from Boston who should have known better but didn't. "Why would I? They were gone when Mr. Van Zandt was killed. They couldn't've done it."

"I see." I really didn't, but I wasn't going to get anywhere arguing. "Bear with me just a bit longer, chief, if you don't mind. I'm sure you can guess my next question."

"If you mean do I have any suspects," he rubbed his chin thoughtfully before continuing, "you're not gonna like the answer, my friend. The answer is I don't." He drew in a deep breath, whether out of exasperation or from physiological need, I couldn't tell. "One thing I can tell you, though, whoever did it came in later—after those fancy dinner guests were long gone. Looked to me and my boys like it was a burglar. Old man Van Zandt must've caught him in the act, and the fellow panicked. Grabbed the first thing he saw and hit the old man on the head. Must've been panicky as hell 'cause he kept on hittin' him. Coroner says he crushed his skull. Awful mess. Never seen nothin' like it. Just awful."

"What'd he take?"

"Not a thing, far's we could tell. As I said, Mr. Van Zandt must've interrupted 'im before he could take anything."

"Any idea how he got in?"

He looked at me as if I were not too bright. "No doubt through one o' the doors. They don't lock up over there till everyone goes to bed. And sometimes not then."

"Isn't that a little strange—not keeping the doors locked?"

"Not really. This isn't Boston, you know." He

grinned mischievously. "Guess I don't have to tell you that, do I?"

I smiled appreciatively. "No, I won't argue with that. Still, anyone could wander in. There's a lot of valuable things out there."

"Well, sir, until last March, I would've said they were safe, no matter how valuable they were. People around here don't give much mind to locks 'n keys. Never been no need for 'em."

"Even the big houses owned by people with substantial means?" I persisted.

"Even those houses, and with good reason."

"Yes? Why is that?" I asked.

"They all have servants around the clock. Houses are never empty."

I nodded my understanding. "But now...?"

"But now, after what happened out there, people are a lot more careful."

"You're convinced that the killer was someone other than one of the dinner guests?"

"Like I said, the guests was long gone when this happened."

"Couldn't one of them have come back by himself?"

"Not much chance o' that. Others would'a noticed. Everett Flick says he dropped 'em all off at the depot. They was all together. If one of 'em took off on his own, the others would'a noticed, don't you think?"

I nodded. "Yes, I see what you mean." But I wasn't ready to abandon this thread yet. "By any chance, did you or one of your men happen to ask any of the guests if they remember anyone leaving the group when they got to the depot?"

"Nope."

Here was the opening I was looking for. "So it is possible that one of them could have gone off on his own?"

"Not really. And we didn't need to ask. Everett Flick says he stayed at the depot till the train came.

Says he watched 'em all get on board."

This was not what I'd been hoping to hear. I decided to pursue another angle. "Did the killer leave any clues?"

He shook his head. "Not that we could find. Lot of partial footprints around the place, but there were too many people there to tell who they belonged to."

"Did you look for footprints under the windows—in case the killer was waiting out there for the dinner guests to leave?"

He shrugged his shoulders. "Damned if I remember. Probably not to be honest with you." At that moment we were interrupted by Sergeant Haskins peeking around the door.

"Yes, what is it, Haskins?" said the chief.

"Joe Gagné is here to see you. Says it's important."

Chief Gormley turned to me. "That about it, Mr. Christopher?"

"Yes. Thank you. Appreciate your sharing that with me."

I wasn't at all happy with what I'd learned, but I didn't need Gormley as an enemy.

Chapter 13 *Thursday the 11th*

I'd managed to get back from Salem in time to receive Samantha at five o'clock for what I just knew was going to be an emotional meeting. I had just forty-five minutes to clean up and compose myself before she arrived. I shouldn't have been surprised when Charles opened the front door for me upon my return—but I was. His being there was going to take some getting used to. As I stood there on the front stoop reaching into my pocket for the key, Charles stood beaming out at me as if he'd accomplished a lot more than merely opening the door. He had, too.

"Mr. Christopher, I trust you've had a productive day so far?"

"I hope so, Charles. How did your first day go?"

"I'm really glad you asked, sir. Quite well, I think. Here, let me take your coat, and I'll tell you what I've done. I hope you'll be pleased." I raised my eyebrows at this. Just what had he done?

"So tell me?"

"Well sir, I hope you don't mind my moving on this so quickly, but seeing as you asked me to look into it, I've gone ahead and ordered you a telephone for the house. They'll be over tomorrow to install it."

I raised my eyebrows. "You do move fast, Charles. I don't even know the cost yet. I'll get myself a cup of coffee, and you can fill me in."

"No need, sir. I have coffee ready for you—and Mrs. Ridley, too, when she arrives."

I kept forgetting. I really wasn't used to being waited on. "Very good, Charles. I'll take it in the library. You can stay and tell me about the telephone."

As I took my coffee, Charles explained about

the cost of the telephone—it wasn't as much as I'd expected. He pointed out that the telephone company was keeping the fees down in order to attract as many subscribers as possible (No doubt they'd raise the prices once they had you hooked.). He explained that we could have the wires and the device removed at any time if we were not satisfied. Since there was minimal risk, Charles had gone ahead and ordered the telephone. I thoroughly approved his decision.

"Charles," I said, "I think we're going to work well together."

Chapter 14 *Thursday the 11th*

We talked a bit longer, Charles telling me something about himself and I filling him in on how I'd recently moved back to the city from Salem. I explained that I hadn't yet established a new routine-that I'd be dashing around the city at all hours for awhile and not to be surprised if my comings and goings seemed a bit strange. Soon I'd be into a more regular kind of schedule. At exactly five, the chimes rang, and Charles rushed off to answer the door.

A moment later, he ushered Samantha into the library. I'd resisted the temptation of meeting her myself, not so much because I wanted to impress her that I now had a manservant, but because I didn't want to confuse Charles. After all, how was he to know when I wanted him to answer the door and when I didn't, if I preempted him unexpectedly and arbitrarily? Besides, friends had told me to resist trying to appear too democratic with domestics in situations like this. It is generally misunderstood, and seldom does any good come of it.

As soon as I saw her I could tell that something was wrong. She was still beautiful. But her eyes were sad. She wasn't the Samantha I remembered from the day she first dropped in on me. Her expression was somber, and there was evidence of fatigue in her eyes and in little creases on either side of them and at the corners of her mouth. But none of this in any way detracted from her unmistakable beauty, her inner femininity. There was only one gas lamp burning in the library, and it was turned way down. The level of light in the room was accordingly quite subdued—especially to someone who'd just come in from the out-of-doors. Sam's eyes adjusted to the dim light quickly, though, and when she saw me, she ran across the room, into my outstretched arms.

It's impossible to accurately describe the feeling I had at that moment. In one sense, there was nothing intimate about it, but in a very real sense there was everything intimate about it. For the longest moment, I was aware of nothing but the scent of her and the feel of her warmth close to me. It was as if everything I'd concerned myself about for the past week no longer mattered. Only Sam, myself, and the moment were real. I was becoming very much aware not merely of her presence but of her body—and very definitely of my own.

Then she looked up at me, and that simple equation became more complex. Her eyes told me there was more to think about than just that precious, fleeting moment.

"Thank God you're here, James."

"I wanted to see you sooner, but from the tone of your telegram I thought it ill advised to see you at your house."

"It's best you didn't. No telling what he'd do if he discovered you'd come to the house. Damn it, James, what's to become of me?"

"Sit down and tell me about it. Would you like some tea—or coffee?"

Her face brightened for a moment. "I see you have a man now. What's his name?"

"Charles. I think he's going to be terrific." I then leaned to my right, found the bell cord, and gave it a tug. I'd never used it before, so I wasn't sure it would even ring, much less bring Charles. But in less than a minute he came. When he'd taken our requests and was gone, I leaned forward across the small coffee table and spoke in a serious voice. "Now tell me what's wrong?"

"He hit me again, James. Here." She pointed to a bruise on her cheek that was beginning to turn black and blue.

"Good Christ! The man's an animal. "When was this?"

"Six o'clock yesterday evening. He'd come home early for a change. I got all hopeful. Maybe we could have a nice evening together. I know, it was naïve of me, but that's what happens when you try to hold onto your memories of a person as he used to be. He was drunk as usual, but I didn't realize it right off. I was so delighted that he'd come home early that I began telling him things I'd kept stored up for weeks." At this, her voice dropped. Her next words were drained of emotion. "Unfortunately, I told him more than I should have."

"Like what that is, if you want to tell me?"

"Of course I want to tell you. I told him that I was seriously leaning toward voting against selling *Knickerbocker.*"

"Why should that bother him?"

"He was counting on a windfall of money from the sale. Apparently he's not doing as well at the bank as I thought he was."

"I'm not surprised, what with the way he treats people. But this is interesting. Is he counting on your money?"

"Edward lives for money, James. He makes good money at the bank, but he's not satisfied with that. As you well know, I just came into my inheritance, but I know he's already counting on it. He has big plans for the *Knickerbocker* stock. Apparently his plans, whatever they are, are too big for what he makes at the bank."

"But your stock in *Knickerbocker* is in your name isn't it?" I was hoping she hadn't changed the ownership to include Edward.

"Yes, but he's been urging me to convert it to a jointly held account. Says he understands money better than I do. He wants to sell the stock and invest the proceeds in this big business scheme of his. Says that if the board sells *Knickerbocker*, he'll have more to invest, and we'll be that much better off."

I sighed and shook my head. “Do you love him, Sam?”

She wasn’t as startled by my question as I thought she’d be. I could see that this wasn’t the first time she’d considered the question. She looked at me with reddened eyes. Her voice was scarcely a whisper when she finally replied. “God forgive me, James, I don’t think so. Not any more. He’s not the same person I married ten years ago.” As she said that, she obviously reflected on how it must have sounded, for she then added, “I know, none of us is the same after ten years. But Edward is not different in the ways most people become different—personal habits, interests, routines, idiosyncrasies and the like. We all change in those ways. The changes in Edward have turned him into a different person—and not a very likeable one at that. He’s become materialistic, hardhearted, ruthless, utterly cruel.”

“Do you think he still loves you?”

“Sometimes I wonder if he ever did.”

“Why did he strike you?”

She took a deep breath and let it out slowly. “It was something else I told him. It was this second thing that really angered him. Made him positively violent.”

“What in God’s name could you have told him that would make him angry enough to strike you?”

A trace of a smile flickered across her face. “I told him that I write articles for *Knickerbocker* and that I didn’t want to sell the magazine that had given me my first opportunity to have my work published.”

I looked at her in amazement. “You write for *Knickerbocker*? I’ve read the magazine for years, and I don’t recall ever seeing your name.”

She grinned. “Of course not, James. Do you know of any women who write for *Knickerbocker*—or for that matter, any serious magazine?”

Of course she was right. The only magazines women wrote for were women’s magazines, which by definition, at least according to modern convention—avoided serious issues. But now I discover that my cousin was writing for one of the most prestigious publications in the entire country. I kept learning of new ways that Sam had changed in the past ten years. I'd always admired her mind, though when we were younger I sometimes thought she wasted it. She'd obviously matured tremendously in the years she'd been with Edward. Perhaps I owed him that—though if he deserved any credit, I suspect it was because he forced Sam to become more self-reliant. I looked at her with even greater admiration. "Can't think of one offhand. Then you must be writing under—."

"A pseudonym, yes. Do you recognize the name Harcourt Evans?"

My hand flew to my forehead. "You're Evans?"

She laughed. "I take it you've read me?"

"Every month. Love your stuff." Harcourt Evans —or Samantha Ridley wrote about social issues, particularly issues that affected the average and less-fortunate souls who lived in Boston and New York. I knew that the poor lived in tenements, but I learned from one of her essays that many thousands of Bostonians and New Yorkers—mostly recent immigrants—lived in windowless apartments with nothing more than a central air shaft to circulate the foul odors of chamber pots, cooking, and garbage. Another of her articles told of children as young as eight years of age engaged in long hours of thankless labor in grim factories—never once having the opportunity to go out for air. Worse yet, these unfortunate urchins didn't go to school, so they never had the opportunity to better their sorry lot. As I recalled some of the articles I'd read by Harcourt Evans, I remembered that some had been about women and their second-class position in society. It brought back a conversation Sam and I had had at the Union Oyster House just a week ago—about her being involved in the women's movement. The more I learned about my cousin, the more interesting she became. We still had to have our conversation about her women's movement participation, but this was clearly not the time. I studied Sam's comely features.

She was beaming. I could tell that she was proud, and I didn't blame her. I was proud of her, too. Then I remembered what she'd said a moment ago.

"This is what made him violent, Sam?"

"Yes."

"But why. What could he possibly take exception to?"

"You have to understand what's important to Edward. To Edward's boss at the bank, Harcourt Evans is the vilest sort of bleeding heart, tantamount to being a socialist and someone who works at stirring up trouble in the press and strives to make businessmen look bad whatever chance he gets. If word ever got out that Edward's wife was Harcourt Evans, Edward believes his career would be ruined." She manages a smile before adding, "The fact that Harcourt Evans turns out to be a woman, and not just any woman, but Edward's wife, of all people, would embarrass him no end."

"I see what you mean. To be frank, most men would find it embarrassing."

"I know, you're right. Most men would find it hard to deal with. I suppose I should feel bad that I've put him in this position. But, James, my God, would most men get that violent?"

"Absolutely not, though, admittedly, many businessmen would be taken aback, embarrassed, even annoyed to find that their wives had been writing about such stuff. Especially if it was their business being written about. God knows, much of it's true, Sam. Business is far from perfect. It does have its hard side. And some businessmen do thrive at the expense of the people who work for them. Many factories don't pay their workers enough to live on. These are things that need to be written about, and I'm proud that you're doing it." As I spoke I could see that she was heartened to have some support, if only from me. I wasn't quite sure how she'd take what I was going to say next.

"I happen to believe, Sam, that all businesses are not the same. I know this sounds hopelessly naive and optimistic, but I also believe that American business, despite its warts, will eventually help to make this country become a great nation. Hopefully, someday, through the efforts of people like you and businessmen of good will—there are some, believe me —business will become a more positive force in American society." I reached out across the small table and held her hands. "A lot of men would be proud of their wives for writing about the abuses in our society. I know I would. And damn it, don't you dare say that you should feel bad about this. What you should feel bad about is the way your husband treats you. You can't continue this way, not after this latest incident."

"Do I really have any choice?"

"Do you want to have a choice?"

Samantha got up and walked across the room. She pulled a thin leather-bound volume from the shelves and fingered through its pages absently. After a few seconds, she replaced the book and slowly approached me. "Women don't have many choices. They can get married, raise a family, and grow old with their grandchildren." She looked back towards the shelves where she'd just replaced the book. "Or they can become old maids."

"Or they can become writers who argue persuasively about important issues. You've already made that choice, Sam."

"Only by hiding under the veil of an assumed name and an assumed gender. When people learn the true identity of Harcourt Evans, there'll be hell to pay. My choice has cost me dearly already."

"Are you willing to give it up?"

She made a graceful steeple of her fingers and slowly brought it to her chin as she considered my question. After a moment she grinned. "Probably not."

"Then perhaps you're ready to make other choices."

"I told you before, I can't leave Edward if that's

what you're referring to."

"That, indeed, is what I'm referring to. Why can't you leave him? Look at the way he treats you. And you've already admitted that you don't love him."

"We're back where we were the last time we spoke of this, James. Where would I go?"

"You could come live with me."

She laughed. "And what a scandal that would be. You're thinking like a loving cousin, James. That's nice, but not very practical."

"If only I *were* thinking like a cousin." No sooner had the words left my lips than I realized what I'd said. Sam's face registered something...I wasn't sure quite what. What had gotten into me? Why was I talking like this?

She recovered quickly and tilted her head to one side, looking at me as if I were out of my mind. "You're not saying what I think you're saying? My God, that's insanity."

"Is it? Is it really? We're not blood relatives."

"Yes, but everyone thinks we are. Besides, cousin," she drew the word out in a teasing fashion. "What makes you think I would even consider such a thing?"

I could feel my face flushing. What, of course? Who was I to presume that she shared my feelings? Seeing Sam after all those years, and seeing the woman she'd become had stirred something in me. Perhaps it was feelings that had lain dormant for nearly a decade. But, no, I didn't remember feeling that way ten years ago. Of course, Sam wasn't the same ten years ago. Neither was I, I suppose. My God! What the hell had I unleashed? What had come over me? Why hadn't I seen it creeping up on me? All I could manage was, "I'm sorry. I was completely out of line. I, I..."

Her eyes softened as she saw my discomfort. "You do care for me, don't you?"

"Yes."

"You were always my hero, James. When we

were growing up, all the girls were in love with Will, but I was in love with you." She was referring to my big brother. Will had been *my* hero. I was amazed to find now that he hadn't been hers. Looking back, I didn't see myself in the hero category. When we were young, everyone looked up to Will. Then he went off to war. He was killed a few months later in the Battle of Chickamauga—September 19, 1863. A date I'll never forget. Will had volunteered for the Union army the day he turned 17. We'd lived in Massachusetts then. Father had worked for a paper in Salem. Mother had been against Will's joining up; father was for it. Needless to say, the days that followed Will's enlistment were terrible days at home. Tempers on edge. We were all tense. What didn't get said was worse than what did. The strain got to all of us. As the months passed, though, Mother had just about accepted it. We'd gotten a few letters, and we all looked forward to the day when Will would come home. It seemed as if that would happen. Then those two smartly dressed Union soldiers came to the front door that awful day and told us what we knew they were going to tell us—that Will had been killed in battle.

I was sure mother would blame my father, but she surprised both of us. She never once—at least to my knowledge—even hinted that father, by his consent, had contributed to Will's death. It was her finest hour. Mother and I had always been close, but when I saw how nobly she carried herself after Will's death, I elevated her to sainthood.

The day I turned 15, I told my parents that I wanted to join the army. This was too much for mother. She just looked at father, without saying a word. He took me aside and told me that the Christopher family was not going to lose two sons to the war. Besides, he said, the war would be ending soon. All signs were pointing to a Union victory. I didn't put up much of an argument on the matter of my joining up, but father was wrong about the war. It lasted another full year.

I shook myself out of my reverie and looked up into the expectant eyes of Samantha. She was waiting for my response. "You must have been the only one," I said. "Will was everybody's hero—even mine. I was just an awkward adolescent. I can't imagine what you saw in me."

She grinned, "Neither can I."

I laughed, nervously. Then I turned serious. "You can't continue to live with him."

"If I tell him that I've told you about his striking me, he'll keep his distance."

"How can you be so sure? Beating up on women is not rational. Good Christ, you've already gone to the police about him. What good did that do you? Besides, even if he does keep his distance, what kind of a life is that?"

She sighed. "I know. I know."

"Then you'll think about my offer?"

"You mean live with you?"

"You could bring Elizabeth. And, as you see, I now have a man here to help me. If you feel it would be more proper, you could have your own apartment on the third floor." I grinned. "It would all be on the up-and-up. Simply sharing quarters with a relative."

"I'd pay rent."

I smiled. "If that would make you feel better. The important thing is to get you away from Edward. What do you think he'll do if you tell him you're moving out?"

"I have no doubt he'll fly into a rage."

"Then I'll be there with you when you tell him."

"No, that wouldn't be fair to him. His pride couldn't bear that."

"Then I'll wait outside. Just so long as he knows I'm there."

She nodded, then grew more serious. I could see that something else was troubling her.

"What is it, Sam?"

"This is all very well, but it leaves unsaid the

nature of our understanding."

"I don't follow you." I did actually, or at least I thought I did, but because of a certain perversity of character of mine, I wanted to hear her voice it.

She gave me a funny look. "Why do you think I'd even consider moving into this house?"

"For safety, and to get on with your life, and—"

"And what?"

"And maybe we might find that we actually enjoyed each other's company. That we *should* be together. I don't know Sam. That's not important now. What's important now is that you get out of that house."

Her expression softened. "I understand what you're trying to say."

I took this as a good sign, but then she surprised me.

"I have to go home now. I need to think."

"Why in blazes did you come here in the first place?" I blurted out harshly.

"You think there's an easy answer, don't you?"

"No, of course not. But you must have felt that I could help you."

"You have, James. You have. You have no idea how much. But I've got to go. I want to be home before Edward gets there."

"What are you going to tell him?"

"I don't know yet, but it'll be something about change."

"Don't be alone when you tell him. Please."

"I won't."

"Will you tell me what you decide?"

"Soon," she said tenderly as she rose to leave. "Thank you, James."

"For what?"

"For giving me strength."

Chapter 15 *Thursday the 11th*

I found myself brooding the rest of the evening. It wasn't a good time to brood—not that there ever is a good time. Charles had prepared his first dinner for our small household, and I'm afraid I didn't seem very appreciative.

I was not at all happy with the way things had ended with Samantha. She was going back to that house and a husband who, at the least provocation, could do her serious injury. Who knows, in a fit of rage he might even kill her.

Nor was I happy with the unresolved situation between us. Did she love me? Would she leave Edward and move into my house? If she didn't, what would happen to her? What would happen to us? All of this weighed heavily upon me when I went to bed. I didn't sleep well at all.

Friday morning I was greeted by a bountiful breakfast of truly gargantuan proportions. Obviously Charles had not been put off by my saturnine behavior at dinner the night before. This time, though, I at least made an effort to show my appreciation for his elaborate efforts, though I doubt it was in proportion to the size or quality of the morning's excellent fare.

I was about to take a sip from my second cup of coffee, when the front door chime rang, and I heard Charles' brisk step as he hurried to answer it. A moment later he handed me a thin, white envelope marked confidential. It was from Peter Zumbach at *Knickerbocker* and had been sent by messenger at eight o'clock the night before. I tore open the envelope eagerly, hoping for anything that might take me a little closer to finding my uncle's killer. The message was written on one of the magazine's new type-writing machines:

Mr. Christopher:

When you were here today, I neglected to mention something that I believe will be of interest to you. Frankly, I'd forgotten about it until just now. It may be nothing, of course, but I'll leave that to you to decide. Shortly before your uncle died, he showed me a sealed envelope containing what he described as an extremely important article he'd written. He said at the time that, if certain conditions were not met, he would give me the envelope on March 15 for publication in the April issue. When your uncle was killed earlier in March, things were so chaotic that I completely forgot the envelope. As you read on, you'll see that it was an important oversight on my part, and I hope that I haven't exacerbated the problem by my forgetfulness. I would be happy to discuss this with you at your convenience. I didn't read the article, but your uncle told me the essence of what it said:

In it, your uncle claimed that a reliable informant had told him that one of Knickerbocker's board members had collaborated with Charles Guiteau in the assassination of President Garfield. The article went on to say that the board member preyed upon Guiteau's known mental instability and encouraged him to assassinate the President. The article supposedly named the board member, though your uncle withheld the name from me, saying it was best I didn't know until the last possible moment. The article further claims that the board member convinced Guiteau that killing the President was the patriotic thing to do.

Mr. Van Zandt also told me that he said in the article that he planned to tell the entire board the identity of the guilty person, but preferred to have the person confess voluntarily. He went on to say that he'd threatened to run the article in the magazine if the board member didn't resign by the 15th of March, so if someone was reading the article, it meant that the guilty board member had not confessed. This was back in early March, just a few days before the dinner party at his Salem home at which he was murdered by an unknown killer.

As I said, Mr. Christopher, I would be pleased to meet with you about this at your convenience.

Respectfully yours,
P. Zumbach

I put the letter down and took a deep breath. I was shaking. This was craziness. If it were true, it was devastating news for *Knickerbocker* and its reputation as one of the most upstanding publications in the country. The official report at the time had said that Guiteau was insane and that he had acted on his own. That one of my fellow board members could have collaborated with Charles Guiteau was almost beyond comprehension.

I leaned back and rubbed my eyes. I'd only been up a short time, but I was suddenly feeling very tired.

As a journalist, and as a citizen, I had followed the Guiteau case closely. The strange facts of the assassination came flooding back to me as vividly as if the tragedy had happened yesterday—not three years ago. President Garfield had been shot just four months after taking office—only 16 years after Lincoln was shot by Booth. Good God, what kind of country was this?

Unlike Lincoln, Garfield never had a chance to show what he could do—and there are those, myself included, who feel he might have been a good president. As a journalist I'd followed his career with interest and appreciation.

In his 49 years, Garfield had been successful in almost everything he'd attempted. Like Abraham Lincoln, he'd been born in a log cabin. He'd worked as a canal-boat tow boy when he was 17 and 18. He seldom viewed his difficult early years as a handicap.

At 23, he left Ohio to attend Williams College in Williamstown, Massachusetts.

At 28 he won his first election, becoming a member of the Ohio State Senate. When war broke out in 1861, Garfield volunteered for the Union Army and received a commission as colonel in the 42nd Ohio Volunteer Infantry. He was given command of a Kentucky brigade and defeated General George Humphrey

Marshall, one of the few victories for the Union forces up to this time. In 1862, at the age of 31, he was promoted to the rank of brigadier general.

Later in 1862, Garfield was persuaded by President Lincoln to resign his commission and to run for Congress. By this time, Garfield had gained a reputation for his oratorical skills and his leadership qualities. He was the bright star on the Republican horizon, and Lincoln was looking for bright men of integrity to run for Congress. Garfield was also a man Lincoln liked personally. He enjoyed a good joke, and he wasn't so political that he followed convention just to please a constituency. He was elected to Congress and repeatedly won re-election for 18 years, becoming the leading Republican in the House.

In the four months of his presidency leading up to the shooting, Garfield launched a serious attack on political corruption. He invited all of the nations of the Americas to a conference to be held in Washington in 1882 in order to relieve tensions between countries of the Western Hemisphere. Unfortunately, because of the assassination, the conference was never held.

I fingered the letter from Zumbach. Good Lord, what terrible things had been set in motion. A man of integrity like Garfield shot down in his prime by a man like Guiteau. I remembered the assassin's background vividly.

Charles Guiteau had grown up in Illinois, the fourth of six children. He'd attended the University of Michigan for awhile, but was unhappy there. Hoping to find purpose in his life, he joined the Oneida Community in Upstate New York.

He soon became disenchanted with the Oneida Community and headed for Chicago, where he took a job in a law office. Guiteau quickly grew tired of that position and moved back east to New York City. He bounced between jobs as a journalist before managing to pass the bar. He then married Annie Bunn, and it was about this time that his behavior, always erratic and unpredictable, became even more bizarre and downright frightening. He abused his wife on a number of occasions, at one point threatening her with an axe.

Since childhood, Guiteau had been fascinated with politics. He considered himself a Republican, and at first, he leaned toward the Stalwarts, the wing of the party urging the nomination of Ulysses S. Grant for a third term. When Grant failed to gain the nomination, losing to Garfield, Guiteau quickly changed his allegiance, moved to Washington, and tried to get himself a government appointment in the Garfield administration. After repeated rebuffs, he again changed sides and once more supported the Stalwarts.

It was in mid-May of 1881 that he dreamed up the idea of "removing" the President. Less than two months later, on July 2nd, he shot Garfield twice,once in the arm and once in the back. Garfield didn't die, though, until September 19th.

To say that Guiteau was a strange man would be an understatement of monumental proportions. According to documents he wrote before the assassination, he checked out the jail accommodations before going ahead with his wretched mission because he wanted to be sure they were satisfactory. Creature comforts were important to Guiteau, it seems. Other documents, as well as statements he made upon his arrest, indicate that he did not consider the deed murder, but simply "a political necessity." He told one attorney that he'd acted in accordance with God's will and in that manner it was an "act of God."

Chapter 16 *Friday the 12th*

Less than two hours after receiving his letter I was sitting in Peter Zumbach's office. I'd decided that I should learn as much as possible about this new development before pursuing anything else. Zumbach seemed pleased, but hesitant when he saw me.

"Again I have to apologize for not mentioning this when you were here Wednesday."

"Please, I understand completely," I said. "It must have been hectic around here when the news of my uncle's murder became known. I'm just glad you remembered now. Tell me, is there anything else you remember. Anything at all?"

"I remember screwing up my courage and asking Mr. Van Zandt why he would run the article in our own magazine when he could have simply exposed the culprit to the authorities. Naturally, the fact that the guilty party was on our board was bad, but not as bad, in my opinion, as publicizing the shameful news to our own readers. Why advertise the awful deed in our own magazine?"

"Why indeed? Did he give you an explanation?"

"Yes. He said we'd gain more than we'd lose, if we disclosed the guilty party ourselves." Zumbach smiled. "Your uncle always had a flair for the dramatic. It was typical of the way he thought. Who knows, he may have been right.

Before arriving at the magazine, I'd been convinced it would have been a terrible mistake for *Knickerbocker* to publish the story. The more I thought about it, though, the more sense it made. Perhaps this was this kind of thinking that had made my irascible uncle the journalistic genius he was.

"I don't suppose you have the envelope now?" I said.

He smiled wanly and shook his head. "No. After he showed it to me, he took it with him. That was just a few days before he was killed. I don't know where the envelope is now. Perhaps in his office. Or in his home up in Salem—or here in Boston."

"Does anyone else know about the envelope?"

"No one that I'm aware of. No one, that is, except the board members. Presumably he told them the night he was killed." Suddenly his eyes narrowed and he got a curious expression on his face. "Say, you don't suppose—?"

I nodded. "That he was done in by one of the board? Yes, I do believe it's possible. As you know, I was wondering about them before I learned of this Guiteau thing, though I had no real evidence that any of them were involved in my uncle's death. This Guiteau thing, though, and the timing of my uncle's apparent announcement of his intentions to tell all, only adds to my suspicions." I sighed, "God, I wish I knew. This whole thing has happened so fast, I don't know what to believe. But I must look into it."

"Well you'll be looking into one of the most bizarre incidents in American history."

"Guiteau was a strange character, if that's what you mean."

"He was indeed, but he's only part of what makes the Garfield assassination bizarre. You remember, of course, that the President didn't die immediately upon being shot by Guiteau?"

"Yes, he was shot on July 2nd, but didn't die until mid-September."

"September 19th to be precise."

"He must have suffered terribly."

"He did," said Zumbach, "but it's possible he would have lived, but for a number of blunders made by the very people who were supposed to be caring for him. But I'm getting ahead of myself. Guiteau passed up one opportunity to kill the President because the First Lady was present.

"Then, on July 2nd, the President was at the Washington railroad depot waiting to leave for his reunion at Williams College in Massachusetts. Guiteau was waiting at the depot and fired two shots at the President. Now here's where our man shows just how strange he was. He had a hansom cab waiting for him to take him to jail. He thought this wiser than being attacked by an angry mob that might form when they realized what he'd done. He didn't get a chance to ride in his hansom, though, because the Washington police dragged him off to the jail.

"Garfield never lost consciousness. For the next two-and-a-half months, 16 doctors were consulted about his condition. The generally accepted courses of action physicians have in cases of gunshot wounds is 1)If a bullet penetrates an organ, it means certain death unless you operate to remove it, or 2) If a bullet doesn't hit an organ, the victim's chances of recovery are much better if you delay surgery until the patient's condition has stabilized. The only way to find the precise location of a bullet is to probe with instruments. The first doctor, Willard Bliss, stuck his finger into the wound in the President's body to try to find the bullet. He had no luck, so he then probed with an instrument. He never did find the bullet, but the channel he created in search of it misled other doctors into thinking it was the actual path of the bullet. As a consequence of this, they believed the bullet had entered the liver. They therefore concluded that surgery wouldn't help." Zumbach paused and looked at me to judge my reaction to the tale he was telling. I nodded that he should go on, and he eagerly proceeded. It was a story that clearly fascinated him, and I confess it held me in its spell, too.

"Then the Army Surgeon General stuck his finger into the wound in another effort to find the bullet. This was to no avail, either. Next the Navy Surgeon General gave it a try. He accomplished what the bullet had failed to do. He punctured the liver. He concluded that the President would die in 24 hours. He was wrong, of course. The President had a fever, and it grew worse. But he didn't die. Other doctors got their fingers into the act." Zumbach smiled wryly at his play on words, and when he got no reaction from me, continued, "This further widened the wound, which was now festering."

"The doctors knew that continued probing exacerbated the risk of infection." Zumbach pursed his lips dramatically. "Their concern was a little late. The damage had already been done. Newspapers across the country began running editorials about the indecision of the President's doctors and how he was dying while they did nothing to save him. People from all over America began sending packages containing home remedies, herbs, teas, and poultices. Others, with medical degrees, sent letters giving their opinions on what should be done." Zumbach paused. "Am I boring you?"

"On the contrary, this is fascinating. Please go on."

"It only gets better. A man from Baltimore named Simon Newcomb had been experimenting with running electricity through coils and what happened when metal was placed next to the coils. He'd found that if the metal was close enough to the coils a faint hum could be heard. He was interviewed by a reporter for a Washington paper, and in the subsequent article, he said that he might be able to perfect the device so that it could be used to help the President. The only thing was, he said, it would probably take too long to perfect. Alexander Graham Bell read this article and thought that the telephone might be used to amplify the sound made by the coils."

"I remember the incident, though not the details," I said. "Go on, you obviously know a lot more about this than I ever did."

He grinned. "I have well-placed friends in Washington. I get a lot of good stuff. Anyway, the more

I learned, the more fascinating this whole situation became. Bell, as you no doubt know, contacted Newcomb and proposed that they work together to help save the President. Newcomb agreed and together they created a contraption that they proceeded to test in various ways. They would hide a bullet in their armpit or mouth and pass the wand of their device over the area, and the bell would go off. Every time they tried it they succeeded. They found that the closer the wand was to the object, the louder the buzz. The maximum distance that the hum could be heard was five inches. Then they took it to the old soldiers home in Washington where they tested it on veterans from the war, many of whom still had bullets somewhere in their bodies. The device worked every time.

"Finally, they were ready for the President. Bell, his assistant Tainter, and Newcomb went to the White House. There were five White House doctors present and several presidential aides. The effort turned out to be a complete failure. No matter where they scanned with the wand, they heard a faint hum. But the strength of the hum never varied. Bell and Newcomb left and became the subjects of scorn and ridicule in the press, as you no doubt recall. Bell, in particular, was accused of trying to gain publicity at the President's expense. The fact that *his* device—they conveniently forgot about Newcomb—failed, only added fuel to the whole affair.

"Bell, was not discouraged. He and Newcomb went back to their lab in Baltimore and ran more tests. They all worked fine. They went back to the White House to try again and got the same dismal results. No matter where they passed the wand, they got the same hum. This second try was the last day in July. Bell gave up after that."

"Yes," I said, "I recall it vividly, though I never did find out why the device didn't work on the President."

Zumbach laughed. It's unbelievably stupid

when you look back on it. The President had been lying on one of these new coil-spring mattresses. They were so new that no one even thought to move him onto a normal mattress. The metal detecting contraption was detecting the springs. Didn't matter where they passed the damned wand, the reading was always the same. If someone had thought to ask about the mattress, it's very possible Garfield would be alive today. Is that the damnedest thing you ever heard?"

I was stunned. "No one ever knew this."

"They weren't supposed to."

"What happened after Bell's fiasco?"

"Things only got worse, sad to say. Bell and Newcomb had the right idea. They just never thought of the mattress. The doctors then decided to cut Garfield open and look for the bullet. Eventually what had started out as a relatively small wound became a deep, festering infected channel, oozing with pus and close to 20 inches in length. President Garfield finally died of a massive heart attack a month later and 80 days after that crazy bastard Guiteau shot him. The autopsy concluded that the President would have survived the initial bullet wounds, if the doctors had just left him alone." Zumbach looked up, a sad expression on his handsome face.

I was dumbfounded. "I had no idea."

"It's not the kind of thing the medical profession would want the press to get a hold of. But the craziness doesn't end there. Believe it or not, Guiteau's attorney had the audacity to argue that his client had not killed the President, his doctor's had. Admittedly, the autopsy reports lends some credence to this, but thank God the tragedy wasn't made worse by the court's accepting that reasoning. Though I suppose one can't blame the attorney for trying."

"After what you've told me, I'm amazed they did convict Guiteau."

"You want more?"

"There's more?"

"I'm telling you, James, this story just gets

better and better. There's one final bizarre note in this whole crazy affair."

I shook my head in amazement. "After what I've heard so far, nothing would surprise me."

"Don't be too sure. After Guiteau was hanged in June of '82, the government refused to return his body to his family. They stripped his corpse of flesh—right down to the bones—and planned to display his skeleton to the public. Fortunately sanity prevailed in the end, and they never did it."

I sat there stunned. "This was never in the papers. I never saw any reports of this when I was working in Salem as a journalist."

"Very few people know this. I told you I had good contacts. I assure you, everything I've told you is true, though I'm not sure how useful it will be to you."

"I'm not sure, either. I need to give it some thought. In the meantime, I don't suppose you'd know if any of the board members had any connection with our Mr. Guiteau?"

"No, I don't. Sorry. That would be too easy, wouldn't it?"

I smiled. "I suppose it would."

"Well, can I help in some other way?"

"Maybe you can." An idea had taken root in my head, and I decided to trust Zumbach. I quickly explained what I had in mind.

He raised his eyebrows and looked at me as if he'd suddenly seen a new dimension to my personality. "Are you sure you know what you're doing? Isn't that rather dangerous?"

Chapter 17 *Friday the 12th*

Margarita Scharf Calore was a Latin beauty. I could see why men might have been willing to pay her for sexual favors. I had called on her at her Back Bay apartment after sending a messenger first to alert her that I'd be dropping in.

If the elegantly marbled lobby of her building was any indication, I could expect her fourth-floor apartment to be quite comfortable. The doorman sent a boy upstairs to alert her that I was downstairs. He came back in a moment and told me I could go up.

She was waiting at her door when I reached the top of the landing. Her face broke into a smile.

"Mr. Christopher, what a pleasant surprise. Do come in." She turned and spoke to a young woman standing silently a few feet behind her in the apartment. "Ingrid, take Mr. Christopher's coat, please. And bring him a drink." She turned to me then and asked, "What will you have?"

"Coffee will be fine, thanks." It was, after all, early afternoon.

The room was magnificent. Whoever decorated it had to have been to Florence. The Italianate influence was unmistakable. The room was elegant and enormous with a magnificent high ceiling. I assumed the apartment was part of her inheritance from Mr. Calore, and as I took in the exquisite furniture, objets d'art, carpets, and Renaissance paintings, I concluded that Mr. Calore must have done quite well for himself. That is, before the TB got him.

"So," she said, "How do you like being part of *Knickerbocker*?"

"I like it very much. Though, I must admit that I'm a bit troubled."

She looked puzzled. "How so, Mr. Christopher?"

"I'm concerned that my uncle's killer was never found, and that that doesn't seem to concern most of the people on the board." I knew that plunging right in like this was rude, and that she would very likely take offense, but I'd convinced myself that a little shock value might not hurt. It might even shake people enough to loosen up their tongues.

"You don't mince words, do you?"

"I'm sorry, I'm not always this direct. I can't believe that everyone on the board was unaffected by my uncle's murder. But frankly, I haven't seen much evidence of their concern. If anyone cared, they haven't expressed it to me."

"It may be because he wasn't. . ." She pursed her lips thoughtfully before continuing—obviously trying to choose her words carefully. ". . .because he wasn't, shall we say, well-liked."

"You don't mince words, do you?" I said wryly, not hiding a brief smile.

"Touché." She grinned. "Shall we try again?"

"I'd like that. I guess I came in here like a Hessian cavalryman. I know my uncle wasn't Father Christmas, but he was my uncle. I just want to get to the bottom of things. Sometimes my frustration gets the better of me especially when I realize that a killer is still running around free."

"I know it's not very original, but you might try honey instead of vinegar."

I laughed. "I'm sure you're right. Perhaps I'll start now. Do you mind if I ask you a few questions?"

"Not at all, though I'm not sure I'll be of much help. What do you want to know?"

"Do you know of anyone on the board or connected with *Knickerbocker* who would have wanted my uncle dead?"

She laughed, a look of irony on her face. "You can start with me. I was not too fond of Martin. Everyone else at *Knickerbocker* knows that, so you might as well, too. You'll find out soon enough, anyway. You might as well know why, too. I have a past that I'm not proud of. Something that happened when I was much younger."

"I've heard." It was almost imperceptible, but I'm sure I saw her flinch. I was uncomfortable acknowledging her past so openly, but it was important that she knew how much I was aware of. We'd be able to move our conversation along a lot faster, if we didn't resort to verbal fencing.

"I see. Have you heard what it was?"

"Yes, I was told that when you were younger, you were a courtesan, and that my uncle knew about it and was blackmailing you to gain your support in the battle for votes against the proposed sale of the magazine."

She nodded grimly. "I see. And how does that sit with you?"

"It's no concern of mine what you did in the past. I like to think I take people for what they are now." She studied me as I said this. I'm not sure if she believed me. I continued anyway, "So it was true that he was blackmailing you?"

"Yes. He threatened to tell the board and a few other people important to me." She had grown serious. I could barely hear her words.

"As far as you know do any other board members know about your past?"

She shifted in her seat and spoke more audibly now, "Not to my knowledge. No one's ever said anything or treated me in such a way that indicated they knew. If they did know, Martin's threats would have had no power over me."

"I realize that. I was just wondering. Sometimes such ironies occur."

"Of course. I don't think so in this case. I'm sure I'd be able to tell by their behavior." She leaned back in a self-assured manner, stretching a graceful arm over the antimacassared arm of her Italian sofa. I'd never seen a women sit in that manner before. It was both titillating and disquieting. I somehow had the feeling that I was being manipulated by this woman.

She stared me straight in the eyes and said, “Do you think that I killed your uncle to silence him?”

“I’d like to think you wouldn’t, but the truth is I don’t know you.”

“You're very direct, Mr. Christopher.”

I laughed nervously. "We've already established that. Anyway, I apologize if I’ve offended you, but someone killed him, and until I find out who, a lot of people are possibilities.”

“Even a woman?” she said, coyly.

“Let’s not play games, Mrs. Calore. We both know that the stakes were high, and you are not some innocent girl who just came in from the country.”

“Ouch. So I can’t hide behind my petticoats. So be it. It so happens I didn’t kill your uncle. God knows I wanted to. I may have had a motive, but I’m not the only one on the board who did. Why single out me?”

“I’m not. As I said, until I find out who, I can’t rule out anyone with a motive.”

“Then you don’t accept the conclusions of the police—that he was killed by an itinerant burglar?”

I laughed. “Not on your life. The facts don’t support it. Tell me, what other board members had a motive?”

“It might be easier to list the people who didn't. But if you want motives, you can start with Hugh Trampler. He needed money from the sale of the magazine in order to keep his business afloat.”

I nodded. “So I’ve heard. Could you see him killing anyone? What I mean is—.”

“I know what you mean. Is he the type of person who could kill? I don’t know. He’s got a violent temper. Who knows what someone will do when they lose control? Still, I rather like Hugh. I can understand how desperate he was.... and is, for that matter. But I honestly don’t know.”

“Anyone else with a motive?”

She smiled. “Of course. I told you there were

plenty. “Take, for instance, Sebastian LaRue. He couldn’t stand Martin. Martin treated him like dirt. LaRue’s a lawyer.... you probably know that. Well, Martin ignored him and chose someone else as the corporate attorney. That had to be humiliating. He never forgave Martin. Can’t say that I blame him. Still, you may have concluded by now that Sebastian is not the nicest person himself.” She smirked, as if sharing an inside joke. “You may also have concluded that the board has more than its share of prima donnas.”

"It’s beginning to look that way. Could you see LaRue killing anyone?"

"I really don't know. He, too, has a temper, though I have a feeling he can turn it on and off at will. Not like Hugh, who just loses control when something bothers him."

"Who else would have been upset enough with my uncle to want him dead? How about Mrs. Neustadt?"

"Winnifred and I are good friends. You're not going to get me to talk against her?"

"Even the affair she had with my uncle?"

"Damnation! You do get around, don't you? Who told you that?"

"It doesn't matter. Was she bitter about it?"

She shrugged her shoulders. "I really don't know."

I could see that she was growing tired of my inquiries. Can’t say that I blamed her. “Look,” I said, "I don't like asking these questions any more than you like hearing them. I'll just be a bit longer, if you'll bear with me."

She shrugged again. This time it was clear that she was becoming impatient with me. "Might as well. If we don't deal with them now, you'll just come back with more later. What else do you want to know?" Her voice was flat. No attempt at charm.

"What about the others?"

"There's just Billingsley. He and Martin were very tight—at least as far as I could tell. They went way back together. No motive there, Mr. Christopher." Then she forced an insincere smile. "And of course there's you and Mrs. Ridley. . . . but you and she know more about your own motives than I do."

"We weren't on the board when my uncle was killed."

"No, but you clearly stood to gain by his death."

I didn't bother to protest that I didn't know the contents of my uncle's will until after his death. She wouldn't have believed me anyway. As for Samantha, I found it hard to believe that she would kill her own father. Maybe I was blinded by my own interest in her, but I just didn't see that in Sam. I decided to take a different tack before leaving Margarita Calore's apartment.

"I understand that when you and the other board members left my uncle's house the night he was killed, you all left together?"

"That's right. We left in a buggy driven by Martin's estate man. I forget his name."

"Everett Flick."

"Yes, that's it. His wife prepared the dinner. Quite good, too."

"You all took the train back to Boston?"

"Yes, of course. How else would we have gotten back?"

"Bear with me a minute, if you don't mind."

Her impatience was near the surface now, but she nodded tolerantly.

I said, "Did you all sit in the same car on the train?"

She frowned as she thought about my question. She seemed to be concentrating on bringing back the scene as she remembered it. Finally she said, "That's interesting. As I recall, we did at first—all five of us. Then, I think, one or two of the others left and went into the next car. I remember thinking it a bit odd at the time, but not that strange. Some people just like their privacy. Or prefer to read."

"They could read in the same car," I pointed

out.

"Yes, but they might consider it rude to read while sitting with people they know."

"And they wouldn't consider it rude to get up and leave these people?"

"Like I said, it did seem a bit odd."

"Do you remember who it was who left?"

"No, I really don't. It wasn't such a big thing, you know, that you'd make it a point to remember. I'm surprised I recall it at all."

"Would you happen to remember anyone who remained in your car?"

"Yes! Yes, I do." She grinned victoriously. "I'm not a complete doddering old lady, am I? I do remember at least one person because we sat together chatting the whole trip."

Chapter 18 *Friday the 12th*

It was just after six o'clock Friday evening when I got back to Beacon Street. Charles greeted me at the front door, took my coat and hat efficiently, and handed me a whisky. Just the way I like it, too. I was beginning to like having him around. I was about to go upstairs to freshen up before dinner—which I could smell the moment I came in—when he drew me aside and said, "Ah, sir, you have a visitor." He tilted his head ever so slightly and nodded towards the front parlor where a smartly attired Sebastian LaRue stood studying a portrait of one of Uncle Martin's ancestors. One of mine, too, come to think of it. The little brass plate on the massive frame identified the stern-faced gentleman as one Henryk Van Zandt. His dress indicated that he did his frowning sometime in the middle of the last century. I'd have to ferret out his place in the family lineage sometime in the future, a time when I had a bit more leisure time on my hands. Not that I wasn't curious. I was, but it wasn't high enough on my list of priorities for me to set aside what I already had on my plate.

Right then I needed to satisfy my curiosity as to why this elegant and sometimes abrasive gentleman had decided to call on me. I entered the parlor and extended my hand.

"Mr. LaRue, this is indeed a surprise. Can I have Charles bring you a drink?"

He'd heard me come in. I know he had, but he didn't turn around till I spoke. "Thank you, Christopher, but he's already taken care of me." He pointed to what appeared to be a double whisky on a table next to one of the sofas.

God, I thought, what I wouldn't give for a voice as resonant and deep as that. "Please sit down," I said, pointing to the sofa nearest to both him and his drink. "So," I drew the syllable out as I chose my words carefully. "What can I do for you on a Friday evening?"

"I don't plan to stay long, Christopher. No need to concern yourself." He drew himself up and took a long breath before continuing. "Mind if I smoke?" He waved a cigar in front of him that looked to be half the size of my arm.

I nodded and motioned for him to go ahead, but he'd already begun to light up.

"I've been hearing some things that concern me, Christopher. Thought I'd better find out if they're true."

I managed to keep my expression deadpan. I wanted to hear what he was going to say next. "I don't quite understand, LaRue." He winced at my use of his surname. Apparently only others were fair game for the use of the surname. Without the "mister," that is. "Just what is it that concerns you, and why should it concern me?"

"You're a cheeky one, aren't you. I came here to give you a chance to explain. Looks like you prefer to play word games with me."

I was beginning to think my initial impression of this man had been accurate. I hadn't liked him the first time I met him, and he wasn't doing anything now to change that impression. I was finding it hard to control myself. "Do you generally make it a practice, sir, of going into a person's home and insulting him? I suggest you come to the point and take your leave."

I could see that he was debating with himself as to how to react. He was obviously used to getting his way. It was also obvious that his natural inclination was to be contentious. Still, it was quite apparent that he'd come to my house with the intention of learning something. As contentious as he was, he wasn't stupid. He could see that a continuation of hostilities would get him nothing. It must have killed him, but he calmed down and made a valiant effort to be civil. "All right, I suppose I did come on a bit strong, but—"

"A bit strong—"

He reached for his drink and drained half the glass. "All right, I was presumptuous and maybe even a little rude. I'm sorry."

That was about as much as I was going to get from him.

"Accepted. What is it that you've been hearing that concerns you so much?"

"I hear you've been running around town accusing members of the board of killing your uncle."

"Well, I'm afraid you've heard wrong."

He raised an eyebrow and said deliberately, "Then you're not making inquiries about the board?"

"I didn't say that." I knew I was jousting with him, but the man was impossible. I couldn't help myself. "I've been making a few discreet inquiries, but I certainly haven't accused anybody of anything."

LaRue scowled. "What gives you the right to inquire into the lives of your fellow board members? You're a newcomer to the board. Young, too. You think it's proper to question the lives of people you don't even know?"

"I think it's proper to find out who killed my uncle. Do you think the killer should be allowed to run around Scot free?"

"Of course not," he snorted. "Unfortunately, he's long gone by now. He's certainly not one of us."

"How do you know that?"

"The police themselves said it. Said it was a burglar or some such thing. My God, man, you're running around accusing proper ladies and gentlemen of murder. You can't do that. Don't you see that?"

"I'm not accusing anyone of anything. I'm simply asking questions. And I can't believe you accept that police report. The investigation was a joke. Nothing was taken from the house. What kind of burglar kills, but takes nothing?"

He shrugged. "No one ever said burglars were smart. The man obviously panicked and bolted."

"I don't buy that. He didn't have to kill my uncle, even if he did panic. Besides, there were too many other inconsistencies." I took a long pull on my drink and lowered my voice. I wanted LaRue to know that what I said next was well considered, "In the course of my inquiries I've learned that several board members had reason to see my uncle dead."

"Damnation! You *are* accusing us." I don't think you realize who you're dealing with here. Some of your fellow board members have important places in the community. I, myself, am well connected here in Boston and in Washington, too, for that matter. You're not talking about a bunch of common criminals." The blotches on his fleshy face were redder than usual. "You have no right to do this."

"I repeat, I have not accused anyone of anything. As for my rights, I believe I have every right to know who my uncle's killer is. I find it interesting that you don't share my interest in seeing justice done. As a board member I would think you'd want to know who killed your chairman. And if the killer happens to be on the board, I'd think you'd want to see him rooted out."

"Don't put words in my mouth, Christopher. Just because I don't sanction you as an officer of the law doesn't mean I don't want to see the killer get his due. It so happens, I'm inclined to accept the word of the proper authorities; not some amateur who's decided to take the law into his own hands." He sneered; then took another healthy draught of his drink, nearly draining it.

It took every bit of willpower I could muster to keep from throwing him out of the house bodily. Assuming I could do it. He was a lot older than me, and extremely overweight, but one never knew. In any event, I restrained myself. Since he was already in my house, I might as well make the most of a bad situation and get something out of it. In that regard, it seemed, we were of a mind. Clearly, that was the only interest we shared. I could see that we were well past any pretension of civility or tact, so I didn't even try.

"From what I've heard, you, yourself, hated my uncle. I understand that he bypassed you and selected an outsider as the corporate attorney."

His eyes grew larger, and, for a moment, I thought the man was going to explode. "Who told you that?" His emotional voice was little more than a whisper.

I ignored the question. "Do you deny it?"

"I don't deny that I resented it. That doesn't mean I'd kill the man."

"No, but you admit you may have felt like it."

"I admit no such thing. See, this is just what I was talking about. You're probing into business you have no right, or, for that matter, authority to get yourself into."

"All I'm trying to do is show you how it's possible that someone close to my uncle—yes, even someone on the board—could have had a motive to want him dead. I'm not accusing you of anything."

"You're harassing me. I've a good mind to report you to the police."

"You came here, uninvited, sir. I doubt that—in light of your impertinent and provocative visit—the police will view my responding to your rude questions as harassment." Before he could react, I got in another question. "Since you deny having even the desire to kill my uncle, do you know of anyone else on the board who might have had a stronger motive than yours?"

"Hell, most of them did. Your uncle was an insufferable, arrogant egotist, if you must know. He treated people as if they were objects to be manipulated at his personal whim. One minute he'd turn on the charm; the next, he'd walk all over you."

“I would say you had a lot in common.”

“Nobody speaks to me like that, sir. You don’t

even know me."

"I believe I know you as well as I want to."

To say he was livid would be a huge understatement. I suppose I should have feared for my life, but by now his power to intimidate me was past. I just watched, wondering what he would do or say next. I didn't have long to wait.

"Don't trifle with me, Christopher. Bigger men than you have lived to regret it."

"I understand you know Edward Ridley?"

He hadn't expected this. It seemed to put him off balance. For a moment he was at a loss for words.

"We've met. His wife's on the board. What would you expect?'

"Did you know him before she came on the board?"

"Yes, I suppose I did," he said offhandedly, waving his cigar as he spoke. By now the monster had grown an ash over an inch long, and I was wondering how long he'd let it get before disposing of it or before it dropped on my expensive Persian rug. I was growing tired of his cigar smoke and tired of his presence. LaRue seemed oblivious to my concerns. Not really a surprise. I bit my tongue as he made a sweeping motion with his cigar hand and continued, "I did some work for his bank. Didn't know him well. Still don't, for that matter. What's he got to do with all this?"

"Probably nothing." I shifted direction again. My only hope was to keep him off balance and hope he might let something slip. "So you believe everybody on the board had reason to kill my uncle?

"There you go putting words in my mouth again. I said they all hated the bastard. They had different reasons, maybe, but they hated him. Well, maybe not Billingsley. But the others, yes." He took a long draw on his cigar and slowly exhaled. The house would reek for days. "I didn't come here to be interrogated by you, Christopher. You can play detective all you want, but I'm telling you, you're barking up the wrong tree. The killer is some street thief, and he's long gone." He looked towards the door. "That's what I'm going to be, too. Before I go, though, I'm leaving you with a warning." He stuck his cigar in my direction and jabbed a couple of times, the ash, for some uncanny reason, still adhering to the burning baton.

"You've already offended your fellow board members," he continued menacingly. "The only thing you could do to make it worse would be to vote against the sale of *Knickerbocker*. If you do something stupid like that, I wouldn't be surprised if one of the board members killed *you*."

I pride myself on my self-control, but this was too much. "I suggest you leave my house now, sir, before I really lose my temper and do something we'll both regret." I then raised my voice a level and said, "Charles, get Mr. LaRue's hat and coat. He's leaving."

Chapter 19 *Saturday the 13th*

I'd managed to make at least one enemy and probably more since I'd returned to Boston a little over two weeks ago. They were enemies not to be trifled with, either. One of them was very likely a killer. It was entirely possible that he—or she—would try to kill me in the next few days, either before the dinner I was holding on the 21st up in Salem or before the 22nd, when the board was to vote on the sale of the magazine.

Needless to say, my return from Salem was not getting off to a good start. Not the sort of triumphal return I'd envisaged when I first learned that I'd inherited a fortune from my disputatious Uncle Martin.

It had all started when Samantha Ridley called on me that fateful day earlier in the month and asked me to play detective. In retrospect, I suppose I could have refused. No one could have blamed me for saying that police-type investigations were not my responsibility. Granted, the police had not done the job, but that was still no reason to drop the investigation into the hands of a private citizen. Of course that private citizen happened to be Sam's cousin, and I was always a sucker for Sam. And she knew it.

And, of course, Martin Van Zandt was Sam's father. . . and my uncle. And his killer was still running around free. And I am a damned good investigator. That's what they liked about me at the *Salem Gazette*. At the risk of being immodest, I was the best investigative reporter up there. I enjoy the investigative process, the thrill you get when a lead you're following suddenly turns up something and then leads to something else, eventually taking you where you want to go. It's hard to say just what it is that's so gratifying about this, but there's something to it that I can't get enough of. Maybe it's the sense that the information you turn up wouldn't have seen the light of day, if you hadn't set things in motion in the first place. I'd like to think that there's something creative about it, too, or that it's at least akin to the creative process. Whatever it is, I'm hooked like a big trout. But the attraction ends when my life is at stake. It's not as much fun now as when I first got involved. But there was no going back. The horse was out of the barn, and I'd have to see it through.

My dilemma was made even more difficult by knowing that my killer very likely had two motives for dispatching me. He wouldn't want me to vote against the sale of *Knickerbocker*, and he wouldn't want me to reveal that he had been involved in the Garfield assassination. Both good motives for killing someone, if you were so inclined. There was a third motive too, now that I think of it. By now, the killer no doubt knew I was investigating my uncle's murder. He certainly wouldn't want that to proceed, either. Good Christ, what a vile person he had to be.

I couldn't help thinking back to Garfield. The thought that the man I was after—it didn't have to be a man, I suppose—could have conspired to kill a President was almost too much for me to deal with. I, along with most Americans, had believed that Guiteau had acted alone, as the deranged person he was. Was it possible that he'd been acting in consort with someone on the board—someone I knew? My God!

I'd followed Garfield's career ever since I learned that Will had served under him at Chickamauga. The letters we got from Will praised the man as being fair and courageous—a true leader. Ironically, Garfield had emerged from Chickamauga as a strong national figure. Ironic because Rosecrans, the general in charge of the Union forces there and Garfield's immediate superior, had been considered a strong presidential contender until that fateful battle. Unfortunately for Rosecrans and the Union forces, he received some bad information, and, based on that, gave an order that subsequently opened a gap in his defenses. Longstreet, the Rebel general, poured through the lines and insured the defeat of the Union forces. This disastrous defeat at the hands of the Rebels destroyed Rosecrans' chances for the presidency, but enhanced Garfield's.

Eighteen years later, during the Hayes administration, the Republicans were torn apart by party struggles over reform of the civil service system. A group called the Stalwarts, led by Roscoe Conkling, the powerful senator from New York, was against reform. Ulysses S. Grant had given Conkling the power to make all Federal appointments, and he and his cronies weren't about to give it up. The Stalwarts supported Grant for a third term in the 1880 election.

The other wing of the party, the Halfbreeds, supported moderate reform and a more lenient treatment of the South. They were led by James G. Blaine. After 35 votes at the convention, the Blaine group and Grant group remained hopelessly deadlocked. The party finally turned to someone entirely different—Ohio's favorite son, James Abram Garfield. Congressman Garfield had just been elected to the U.S. Senate, but never got to serve there because the party drafted him as its candidate for President.

Garfield went on to defeat the Democratic candidate, Winfield Scott Hancock, for the Presidency and immediately became embroiled in battle with his fellow Republicans over Federal appointments. He launched an investigation into the corruption-riddled U.S. Post Office, and found his party divided over that, too. He began to defy Conkling by making appointments that the New York senator opposed, and stood his ground in the investigation of the Post Office, despite constant harassment by the Stalwarts.

Conkling soon resigned. His power had gradually given way under the pressure exerted by Garfield's administration. Unfortunately, Garfield's victory over the Stalwarts cost him his life.

It had been a good start for a presidency. I often wonder how good a president Garfield might have become if he'd had more than a mere four months in office.

I couldn't help feeling badly for Bell and Newcomb, too. Since Garfield's death, Bell has been the subject of an enormous storm of criticism. Some say he used his device to promote himself. Hah! Some promotion. Where's it gotten him? Others even go so far as to blame him for the President's death. Admittedly, it was a terrible error of judgment not suspecting the mattress as being the source of the metal his device detected, but I often wonder whether I would have thought of it. After all, those coil-spring mattresses are still relatively unknown. And why single out Bell. Not one other doctor present thought of the mattress either.

Newcomb, too, was considered a laughingstock. Good God, the man is not some eccentric tinkerer. Since talking with Zumbach, I've learned that he's one of the nation's foremost scientists. Mathematician, astronomer, physicist, economist—the man is brilliant. Probably no one in the history of this country has made a greater contribution to astronomy. His analysis of stellar and planetary positions and his computations of the motions of the moon, the planets, and the sun have advanced the entire science. The poor man makes one miscalculation, and he becomes the subject of ridicule. The sad thing is, the device he and Bell devised did work. It's a marvelous invention. One unfortunate oversight, and nobody cares.

Chapter 20 *Tuesday the 16th*

Monday morning the workmen from the telephone company arrived to install our telephone. It took us 20 minutes to decide which room to put it in. We finally decided on the rear parlor. My first inclination was to put it in the library, but the telephone men pointed out that that would preclude Charles using it if I were in there working. I then said, put it in his apartment or the kitchen, but the problem there quickly became apparent. I'd have to go to his apartment or to the kitchen to use the gadget. The rear parlor seemed a good compromise. Two hours later they were finished. I decided to test it while the men were still there—in case I couldn't make it work. I asked them to demonstrate by placing a call to Mrs. Samantha Ridley. Sam had given me her telephone number when I told her we were getting one of the contraptions.

The older of the two men picked up the part of the thing that goes to your ear. I've since learned it's called the receiver—and spoke into the part that captures your voice. He spoke to someone called an operator, giving him the number. The operator eventually connected us with the telephone at Sam's house. The telephone man spoke to someone there and said that I would be talking to them in a minute—to please hold on. The whole process took less than five minutes. Amazing. The man then handed the receiver to me, and the two men left the room so that I could speak with Sam.

"Mr. Christopher?" It was Elizabeth.

"Yes, Elizabeth. Can you hear me?"

"I can hear you, sir. Quite loudly, actually." I realized that I must have been yelling.

"Is Mrs. Ridley there?

"She's out, sir. Visiting a real estate agent, I believe. Shall I tell her you called?"

"Yes, please do." I gave her my number and asked her to have her mistress call when she felt she could talk freely. The thought occurred to me that someone should compile a list of telephone numbers and sell it to people with the instrument. In the meantime, I supposed, I'd have to make a list of my own.

So Sam was seeing real estate brokers. What ever for? Could she be looking for a house or an apartment for herself? There couldn't be any other explanation. Good Christ, how would Edward react when he found out? Here I was concerned about my own safety, while all the while Sam was just as vulnerable. My God, she lived with a violent unpredictable man. And she was very likely vulnerable to attack by her father's killer, too. She'd already declared her intentions to vote against the sale of the magazine. If the killer was as desperate as I thought he was, he might want to make a preemptive strike against Sam and myself before the vote took place. For the first time since I'd agreed to look into all this, I was beginning to have doubts. Maybe I'd bitten off more than I could chew. Worse, maybe I'd exposed my cousin to great risk—something I'd live to regret. That is, if I lived.

My thoughts were in turmoil. I couldn't get Sam out of my mind. It was obviously more than the affection one feels for a cousin. It was evocative of the passion I'd felt eight years ago when I'd fallen in love with the nubile Mary McCafferty. Ah, the divine Mary McCafferty. I couldn't believe my luck when it happened. How she'd twisted me into a helpless semblance of my former self. My senses had taken control of my very being. But that was eight years ago. Nothing came of it. I suppose, in retrospect, it was better that way. It hadn't been my idea to end it, though. I was right originally not to believe my good luck. But while it lasted—pure euphoria. Everything I did in the course of a day brought pleasure to me. The smallest things. Nothing bothered me. Things that would normally irritate me were as nothing.

It was that same feeling now. I wanted to be with Sam every waking moment. It wasn't good to think about it because I only realized how much I wanted her—in every sense of the word.

The thought of Edward laying a hand on her was more than I could bear. I wasn't sure that I could do anything about it, either. The unfortunate truth of the matter was they were married. In marriage in Victorian America, if a husband deems it necessary to keep his wife in line, a certain amount of violence is overlooked. Married men in our society have most of the rights in a household. It's a woman's duty to obey her husband, and if she veers far from his wishes, not many will interfere if he punishes her to teach her a lesson.

It wouldn't be easy for Sam to gain her independence, assuming that's what she wanted, and I dearly hoped it was. Not everyone condones it when men resort to striking their wives, not by a long shot, but it's widely enough accepted to make it difficult for women to seek their independence. Virtually all judges are men, and they tend to share the prevailing thinking of the day. Extreme cruelty, of course, is not condoned, but it's not easy to prove a husband guilty of it.

If Samantha were looking for a new place to live, I prayed to God it wouldn't provoke Edward to do something we'd all regret. I feared that the matter would come to a head in the next few days. And I had no idea what I could do to prevent a possible tragedy—a tragedy I may very well have had a role in creating.

Chapter 21 *Thursday the 18th*

I wanted to speak to the two remaining board members before my dinner party up in Salem this Sunday and the board meeting the next day. I'd met with Margarita Scharf Calore and Sebastian LaRue last Friday, and Trampler before that. That left Billingsley and Neustadt. Billingsley seemed to have had no motive—at least none that I was aware of. I decided to visit Winnifred Neustadt next—in case I didn't get to Billingsley before the weekend. Since I had no idea whether she had a telephone—more than likely she didn't—I'd already sent a messenger to let her know that I'd be calling on her in person at two.

Lunch had been magnificent. A small steak accompanied by sautéed potatoes and a green salad. Every meal now seemed to eclipse its predecessor. Having Charles about was like having a culinary magician on the premises. Greens were almost impossible to come by in the winter. When I asked where he got them, he just beamed. He enjoyed amazing me.

Winnifred Neustadt lived west of Boston, out in Brookline. I left the house and walked out into Beacon Street to wait for the next horsecar. I didn't expect to wait long, as there were over 8,000 horses engaged in pulling horsecars in the city. I savored the mid-day sun as it warmed my face. Another exceptional December day.

The trip out to Brookline on the horsecar would give me some pleasant time to savor the crisp December weather, not to mention the less-than-savory redolence of my fellow Bostonians. I opted for a horsecar. I was in no hurry. As I looked up and down Beacon, I heard my name above the din of the street.

For a minute I was at a loss as to where it was coming from.

"Mr. Christopher." This time it was louder, and I saw the man who'd said it. He was young, perhaps a few years younger than me, and wearing a gray suit at least as good as mine. He was standing next to a well-appointed carriage, which had pulled up to the curb. He saw that he'd caught my eye, but that I didn't recognize him. I hesitated, certain that he must have mistaken me for someone else. "Mr. Christopher, it's me," he said familiarly as if I must have known him, though his face still didn't ring any bells. But he did know my name.

Not wanting to offend someone I'd apparently met sometime in the past, I approached him.

"Yes, do I know you?"

He laughed nervously. "No, you don't know me, sir, but you know the man inside." He extended his arm, suggesting that I take a look in the carriage and see for myself. I stepped up and peered in. Before my eyes could adjust to the darker interior, I was pushed from behind and thrust headlong into the carriage. It all happened so quickly and so forcefully that I found myself sprawled awkwardly across the interior of the carriage, one arm on the back seat; the other on the floor. Anger welled up in me as I looked up at the two men above me on the rear seat. They were not gentlemen. They looked more like street toughs. Boston had more than its share of them. I turned to the front seat to find a third man staring down at me. He didn't look friendly. He was wearing a dark suit that looked a size too small for him. Why would I notice something like that at a time like this?

“What the hell's going on? Who are you?” I blurted out with more bravado than I felt.

“Keep your mouth shut and listen,” Said the man in the dark suit, barking out the orders in a stentorian voice. He was facing the rear of the carriage and looked down at me contemptuously. He wore an evil-looking black handlebar mustache with side-whiskers down the side of his pockmarked face. "Get up and sit between these two gentlemen," he snapped. "NOW!" he bellowed for emphasis. He motioned impatiently toward the middle of the seat between the other two. They didn't look like gentlemen to me. Then he wrapped on the ceiling and yelled up to the driver. "Okay, Johnny, move it." The carriage began to leave the curb, gradually picking up speed as it entered the traffic.

I pulled myself up slowly, trying to stall for time long enough to figure out what my options were. It was pretty clear that I didn't have many. With odds of three against one, patience appeared to be the better part of valor—at least until I had a better idea what my new friends wanted. "If you don't mind, I'll sit next to you. It's a little crowded back there."

"I do mind," roared the one with the loud voice—actually the only one who'd spoken so far. He was obviously in charge. "Sit the fuck between the boys—like I told you. And make it fast."

His loudness was beginning to annoy me. I might have abandoned my newly acquired wait-and-see attitude, if I hadn't noticed that he was holding a revolver and was aiming it precisely at the point where the lapels of my new suit coat overlapped each other. Back to patience.

"All right, Mr. Christopher. I suggest you listen to what I have to say. You won't get another opportunity."

"And I was so looking forward to doing this again."

"You gotta mouth on ya, ain't ya? Wiseacre comments ain't gonna help you, my friend." He paused—for dramatic effect, I suppose—then pointed a long finger at me. "You been sniffing around business that's gonna get you killed. That plain enough?"

"I'm afraid I must be dense. What business is that?"

"The Guiteau business. Leave it alone. Guy was a lunatic. Nobody else was involved. Nobody. You're giving my friends a bad name."

"And who might they be?"

He leaned forward and down—slowly at first—as if to pick something off the carriage floor. Then, without warning, he reared up and backhanded me across the face with his gun. It was all done with the deliberateness of a golfer's swing.

"I don't think you're taking me seriously, Mr.Christopher."

I felt something warm running down my cheek and reached up—tentatively at first—fearing the worst. The side of my face was wet. I knew it was blood—my blood. I pulled my handkerchief from my lapel pocket and held it to my face, hoping to stanch the flow.

"You bastard!"

My tormenter reached over and stuck the gun in my face. "Just a little reminder that we're not playin' games here, bucko." The gun was so close I could have grabbed it with my teeth. I'd never had a gun pointed at me before, and it was not a good feeling. Come to think of it, I'd never been this close to a gun before—certainly not the business end.

It wasn't good for the nerves, I admit, but I didn't think he wanted to shoot me. I was more concerned about his pulling the trigger accidentally. As we traveled down Beacon Street, we were jostled unmercifully. The horsecars ran on rails, of course, which made the trip smoother than the old horse-drawn omnibuses of thirty years ago. The omnibus ran directly on the cobblestone surfaces, and a ride was enough to shake your teeth out of your mouth. But horsecar travel was still at the mercy of the horses. These miserable, overworked beasts often moved in fits and starts for any number of reasons. They might be startled. Sometimes they were simply exhausted. And then, when they were going uphill, they would often pause to collect their breath or gather their strength.

We slowed down as we approached the next

intersection. I inched tentatively towards the door. My two silent buddies may not have been the brightest, but they weren't stupid, either. They grabbed me by the arms and pulled me back onto the seat.

"Don't be foolish, my friend," barked His Loudness with a sneer at what he no doubt perceived to be my own stupidity. "You think I'd hesitate to pull this trigger if you try to get away?" The sneer became a leer as he added, "Or if I thought you weren't takin' me seriously?"

"No, I'm sure you wouldn't hesitate," I said, mostly, but not entirely, to placate him. "Where are you taking me?"

"Depends on your attitude in the next coupla' minutes. Say the right things, I let you go a few blocks from here. On the other hand, I don't like what I hear, we take a little trip over towards the river. Am I makin' myself clear?"

"Very clear." I brought my handkerchief away from my cheek and looked at it. It was damp with blood—a grim reminder of the deep gash my pockmarked friend had made in my face. I'd never make the cover of *Knickerbocker* now. I returned the handkerchief to my cheek.

The carriage was moving now—not as fast as before, but moving. It was normal for traffic to become more congested as you got closer to Massachusetts Avenue. Our present slow pace was about as fast as you could expect to go in this part of the city.

"Okay, then. Let's be sure we understand each other." He kept waving that damned gun in my face as he spoke. "You go about your business and make sure nobody prints no articles about Mr. Guiteau. You with me so far?"

My nod was almost imperceptible.

"Answer me, you fancy son-of-a-bitch. Don't fuck with me, you hear?"

"I hear you."

"All right. Next, you get any information—like a letter or somethin'— sayin' somebody helped Guiteau, you burn it. Ya hear? You don't show it to nobody. Nobody, you understand?"

"I understand."

"Cause, if you got somethin' like that, it's not true. Right?" He reached across and pushed the gun into my face again, this time flicking it against my nose for good measure. Something snapped. I felt rage. It was all I could do to keep from lashing out. He started to say something else when we hit a pothole and the carriage lurched sideways. The gun swung away from my face, and I grabbed it from him, launching myself from the seat as I did so. I placed my back to the door and directed the gun at my captors, pointing it first at one; then the next. I felt my hand shaking. I don't know if they noticed. Better, I suppose, if they did.

"All right, gentlemen, there's been a slight change of plans. Here's what we're going to do now."

"Billy, do somethin'" It was one of my former seatmates. His voice was shaky.

"Shut the fuck up, and stop usin' names you dumb shit. Mr. Christopher ain't gonna pull the trigger, are ya?" He stared me in the face, daring me to call his bluff. I honestly don't know what I would have done, but I never got the chance to find out because at just that moment one of our wheels hit another pothole or something. The carriage lurched so badly we careened off to our left and into the path of an oncoming horsecar. We'd have tipped over, had we been going any faster. One of the horses of our team apparently stepped on the leg of one of the tram horses causing a loud commotion.

The horses in both teams reared and whinnied —their drivers bellowing orders as they tugged on the reins, trying to regain control of their charges. By now, the carriage was stopped dead in the street, though it continued rocking and shaking as the horses reared and lunged, trying in their panic to free themselves from their frightening entanglement.

In the midst of all this, the four of us in the

carriage were thrown together like a mixed salad. I tried to get to my feet and realized that I'd somehow lost the gun. My three chums were scrambling about the floor of the carriage trying to find it. Ever mindful of the maxim *carpe diem*, I decided to get the hell out of there while I still could. I fumbled desperately with the door latch. Finally it opened, and I leaped down to the street, already running as I hit the pavement.

"Remember what I said, Christopher," roared His Loudness from the carriage. "We know where you live."

I reached the other side of the intersection before I turned around. It was a busy intersection, and people were milling around, attracted by the collision in the middle of the street. Billy, apparently thought better of chasing after me with so many possible witnesses. I watched him as he stood there by the carriage glowering at me as I waved to him.

Why did I taunt these people? Clearly they were capable of anything. As I reflected on this, I felt something trickling down my cheek and realized that I'd forgotten just how ruthless they could be. My face must be a mess. I also realized that I'd lost my handkerchief. My face was bleeding, and I had no way of stopping it. And I was due at Winnifred Neustadt's out in Brookline in less than an hour.

Chapter 22 *Thursday the 18th*

She seemed like a real lady, but she couldn't keep her eyes off my face. I couldn't blame her, really. I'd seen myself in a mirror in my bathroom back at my house. I'd retreated to the house after the attack in order to clean up and to see how bad the damage was. It was worse than I'd expected. Fortunately, Charles was out shopping for dinner, so I didn't have to endure his fussing. There was a deep slash about three inches long down my left cheek. When it healed, I'd look like a pirate. I should have pulled the trigger when I had the chance.

I was more than an hour late getting to Winnifred Neustadt's place. When I'd seen my face in the mirror, I'd decided to find a doctor to get it sewn up. I had no doctor I called my own. I was possessed of that arrogant confidence young people like to flaunt —a sense of immortality. But time was of the essence, so I had to resort to the resourcefulness that had served me well as a journalist. A policeman on the corner a block from my house gave me the name of nearby sawbones the coppers use when they need to fix up a victim of street crime. At first he'd been suspicious, but when I mentioned John Holland and that he was a friend of mine, the copper had been willing to at least listen. It took some explaining before he came through, though. I didn't want to tell him what really happened, so I made up a story about how I'd fallen. I don't think he bought it, but what else could he do.

The doctor had been more than willing to see me. I think he could tell that he was likely to get more out of me than the usual street victim brought there by the cops.

Winnifred Neustadt was trying not to be too obvious, but the prominent bandage on my left cheek was hard to avoid. I smiled as I pointed to the bandage.

"This is the reason I'm late." Better to satisfy her curiosity. Besides, it would add credibility to my mission.

"My goodness, what happened to you?" She was a large woman. Not fat, but tall, nearly as tall as I was, and I'm close to six feet. She probably weighed as much as I did, too. I'm not that heavy, but I'm not slight. She was what I suppose you'd call handsome, in a womanly way. I know I'm not explaining this well, but suffice it to say that I found her attractive for a woman I guessed to be in her early fifties. She had a great smile, too.

"I was abducted by three men in a carriage." She looked at me like I was from another planet. I could see that she was not sure whether I was jesting or being serious.

"Goodness, what on earth happened? I mean why?"

I smiled. My cheek hurt when I did it. "It's a rather long story, but I think you'll find it interesting. May I sit down?"

Her hands flew to her face. "Dear God, what kind of hostess am I. Here, please sit down. It's just that." She indicated my cheek with a self-conscious gesture of her hand.

"Of course, I understand. Please, don't apologize." I took a moment to survey my surroundings. Her house was not as magnificent as that of Margarita Scharf Calore, but it felt more like a real home. There were more of those personal touches —things from her past, family daguerreotypes, other reminders of people dear to her. More like a true home and less like a place meant to impress. It appeared that she lived in the entire brownstone; not just one floor. A great deal of space for one person. I couldn't help but wonder about how she occupied her time.

A deferential young lady in a prim black dress and crisp white apron brought us coffee and almond-flavored cake. We'd been making idle small talk more or less pleasantly, but now, as the shy girl exited silently from the room, Mrs. Neustadt grew more serious.

"You were going to tell me what happened to you."

I gave her a brief version of my harrowing experience and was about to explain how it related to my visit when she interrupted me.

"This Guiteau business—his being encouraged or helped by one of our board. You think there's something to it, don't you?"

"Mm— I don't know yet," I said noncommittally.

"You do. No need to deny it. I received your letter this morning. It said that you have in your possession an article that Martin wrote last spring. You went on to say that this manuscript claims that Guiteau was a member of a radical offshoot group of the Stalwarts that plotted the assassination of President Garfield. You say that the manuscript reveals the name of someone on our board who was active in this radical group—someone instrumental in encouraging Guiteau to shoot the President, no doubt because this person knew the man was unstable and could easily be blamed for the assassination.

She stopped for a moment, probably for the dramatic effect. When she continued, she spoke deliberately, studying my reaction to her words. "You may not realize it Mr. Christopher, but this is not the first I've heard of this."

"Oh?"

"No, your uncle raised the ugly matter last March at a dinner he held up at his Salem mansion the same night he was killed. Did you know that?"

"Yes, I've been told that he brought it up. I can see how it would make for rather unpleasant dinner conversation."

"An understatement, I assure you. I remember his words fairly clearly. He was addressing all of us in the room, but he was directing his words at the person he believed to be guilty. He said something like:
'If you tender your resignation by the end of this month, I'll allow you to voluntarily throw yourself on the mercies of the authorities. God knows how merciful they'll be, but that's as much as you'll get from me. It's more than you deserve, but my objective in this is to minimize the negative impact on *Knickerbocker;* not to protect you. Should you fail to submit your resignation by March 15th, the April issue of the magazine will run a story about your vile part in the assassination, and I'll personally tell the authorities everything that I know.'

"I remember the scene so vividly. I knew then that he was deadly serious." She sighed and looked away for a moment before continuing, "I've wondered ever since which of the people I've been associating with is a killer—a two-time killer at that. Believe me, it is not a good feeling to wonder which of your colleagues is a killer. How do you concentrate on the magazine, when you keep envisioning the worst possible things about the people sitting in the room with you? To be quite honest, I'm frightened every time someone calls on me. After all, one never knows, does one?"

This was new information—and a new insight into how my uncle operated. My curiosity was aroused. "I can understand how you would feel that way," I said. Then I got back to the matter at hand. "Why didn't my uncle simply take what he had to the authorities instead of putting you all through hell?"

"I guess you didn't know your uncle as well as you thought you did. That was the way he was. He never did the conventional thing. What I thought you were going to ask was why didn't he come right out and name the person."

I grinned. "That was going to be my next question."

"He explained it that awful night. Said he was 95 percent certain that the person he named in his article was guilty of aiding and abetting Guiteau. But then Martin said that he was waiting for a specific bit of confirming information to be delivered in the next few days." She paused to see how I was reacting.

"Ah, that explains it." I wondered as I said that just what confirming information he'd been waiting for, and if, in fact, it had ever arrived. What I wouldn't give to have it in my possession.

"So tell me, Mr. Christopher, which one of us plotted to kill the President?" She leaned back in her seat and eyed me expectantly, a wry smile transfiguring her fine features.

This was not going the way I'd planned it. Last Friday, when I'd been with Peter, I'd told him that I was going to inform each of the board members by letter that I'd found the article Martin Van Zandt had planned to run in *Knickerbocker* last spring. I told him that my letter would conclude by saying that I was considering reading from the manuscript at my dinner party on the 21st, or perhaps even offering it to another magazine or newspaper for publication. Any publication would love the opportunity to get their hands on such a scoop. My hope was that the guilty party would be provoked into revealing himself, or herself. After all, there were two women on the board. Peter was instantly smitten with the scheme. I think he enjoyed being part of this little counter-conspiracy. He thought it might even work, but he also thought it was risky.

I'd mailed my letters yesterday afternoon, thinking they'd arrive tomorrow, Friday, at the earliest, but preferably Saturday. I didn't want the letters to arrive too soon, as I was sure that most of the recipients would be after me as soon as they'd read the contents. At best, they'd want to know whom the article named; at worst they'd try to shut me up—maybe permanently. I didn't want to have to deal with that before the dinner party. The less exposure—verbally or physically, the better.

I was hoping the guilty party would give himself away during dinner. I know it sounds crazy, but barring that, I was hoping he'd attempt to kill me either before the affair or possibly afterward. The possibility that the killer might do something after dinner was not lost on me. My guess was that he considered himself part of some sort of noble historic mission. There'd be something symbolic about doing in two members of the same family in their own house—and after they'd hosted a dinner for virtually the same people.

"I can understand why you'd hesitate to answer," said Neustadt, interrupting my thoughts and reminding me that her question remained unanswered. "It's a serious allegation."

"I'd rather not reveal my hand just yet. When I first came across the article, it was in a sealed envelope with a brief description of the contents written on the front. At first I couldn't contain myself, and was about to tear open the envelope to find out who the guilty person was. But then an idea took hold of me. I would reveal the contents of the letter to the entire board, or maybe even the entire world through the pages of some competing publication. Anyone who'd conspire to assassinate a President and kill my uncle didn't deserve anything less ignominious." I took a deep breath, and seeing the look of fascination transfix her pleasant face, was reminded that she and my uncle had engaged in a tempestuous *affaire de coeur.* How foolish my uncle had been to have cast aside such an elegant woman.

"But why didn't you look to see who it was?"

I grinned. "I finally did look. I now know who it is, but I suppose I have this propensity for the dramatic. I prefer to do it my way. You, of course, know about yourself. But for the present it's only a short wait now. I prefer to keep the identity of the guilty party my secret."

Since only Peter Zumbach and I knew that I hadn't really found the manuscript, it wasn't going to be hard to keep the identity of the killer a secret. I had absolutely no idea who it was, though I had my favorites. I was counting on my letter to frighten the guilty party into some sort of reckless action. It was risky, but I could see no other way of ferreting out the killer.

"You're a strange man, Mr. Christopher. I'd think that you'd want to take this information to the police, and the sooner the better. If you're right about this, and if the guilty board member knows that you alone possess this incriminating information about him, your life is in danger. Why are you taking such a terrible chance?"

"I have my reasons. Someday, if you're still interested, perhaps I'll tell you." I couldn't risk sharing with her the knowledge that I really didn't have the article, else I'd lose whatever leverage I had with the board members. If my plan was going to work, they all had to believe I had the manuscript. "By the way," I said, "On that night that you and the others were at my uncle's for dinner last March?"

"Yes, what about it?"

"I understand that you all left together on the same train."

She nodded.

"Did you sit with the others?"

She thought for a moment before answering. "Most of us were in the same coach. I seem to recall that one or two of them got up and went into another car. That was shortly after we left the depot"

"Do you remember who they were?"

"Yes, two of the men. Mr. LaRue was one of them. I remember that for sure. And I think Mr. Billingsley left, too. Yes, Arthur Billingsley."

"Anyone else?"

She brought her long, well-manicured fingers to

her forehead, trying to recall. “Did Hugh—? I can’t be sure, maybe Hugh Trampler, also.”

"Were there many cars on the train, do you recall?"

She thought for a moment. "I don’t think so, no. There couldn't have been more than three or four cars in the entire train. I'm sure of that."

"But there were more than two?"

"Yes, yes. Definitely three, probably four." She gave me a quizzical look. "Why in the world would you want to know how long the train was?"

I ignored her question and said, "You know, I can think of more than one reason someone would have wanted my uncle dead."

"You have a wonderful imagination, Mr. Christopher. The Guiteau cabal seems more than adequate."

"And it may well be. Nevertheless, until I know which of the several possibilities was the actual reason, I can’t help being curious about all of them. I understand you and my uncle were very close at one time."

"You seem well informed."

"And I heard that, when the affair ended, it was not your decision—and that you were quite angry with him."

She gave me a cold look. "I suppose I was, but I got over it.” Slowly her expression softened. “A long time ago. I'm not one to live in the past. I don’t dwell on spilt milk. You may find this hard to believe, but despite Martin's cavalierly throwing our relationship away, we maintained a deep respect for each other's abilities. Your uncle was a very talented man. He made me very angry when it happened, but my resentment didn't last. Believe me."

“I’d like to.”

Chapter 23 *Thursday the 18th*

When I got back to Beacon Street, Charles met me with a pot of tea and an assortment of cookies he'd baked while I was away getting my face slashed. He took one look at my face and realized that tea and cookies were not what I needed at that moment. He turned on his heel and was gone before I could say anything, returning in less than a minute with a tall whiskey, which I accepted gratefully. After a great deal of fussing about my bandaged cheek and the events leading up to it, he told me that I'd had four telephone calls in my absence. The instrument had only been in the house two days and already I'd received four calls. I had a good idea who they were from, too, as I'd only given the number out to four people. Charles, of course, had written down the names of the callers and the times of their calls.

I looked at the first slip of paper. John Holland. He'd called from the Police Department. My heart started to beat faster in anticipation of what I hoped he might have for me. I picked up the receiving end of the device and placed the first telephone call of my life, that is, the first without the help of someone else. After a wait of just a few minutes—I still can't get over this magical invention—the operator put me through to the Police Station, and I asked for Inspector Holland.

"Jimmy, you rascal. You got yourself a telephone. Gotta spend that money, right?"

I laughed. "I suppose you're right. Already I love the blasted thing. Have you got something for me, John?"

"Well, m'boy, maybe I do. Maybe I don't. Would you believe you got a guy on your board who used to attend political meetings with that nut Guiteau? Some sort of secret society or something. A fanatical group that broke off from the Stalwarts. They were both members. I don't know if that's any help, but it sure is interesting. Oh and James?"

"Yes, John?"

"This guy matches the physical description of the guy who sent the note by Western Union messenger. This any help, m'boy?"

"It most certainly is, and you know it. You going to tell me who it is?"

"Yeah, I'll tell you."

* * *

The next message was from Justin Case at the *Globe*. When I reached the City Room, the person who answered told me that he would fetch Justin. I found out later from Justin that the executive offices at the *Globe* had the first telephone at the paper—naturally, but that, finally, only two months later, the city room had its own separate telephone instrument. Clearly the *Globe* was doing well. Justin sounded breathless when he came to the telephone. Apparently it's located some distance from where he sits. Anyway, he seemed pleased that I'd gotten back to him as soon as I had.

"James, I'm glad you called. I think I've got something for you. I did a search of those names you gave me. As I expected, I didn't find much of anything on these people other than some business-related stuff. This Trampler fellow's been skating on thin ice for years. Nothing really illegal, but to extend the metaphor, he's definitely been skating on the edge. And one of your lady board members, this Neustadt woman, she's loaded, you know. Ever since her husband died. Piece we did on her husband after he died says he left her a fortune—over four million."

I whistled. I knew she was well off, but had no idea how well off. "Justin, I knew about Trampler. What you told me about Mrs. Neustadt is news, though I don't see how that gives her a motive for murder. If anything, it tends to exonerate her."

"Assuming money was the motive."

"Yes, point taken. You come up with anything else?"

I could almost see his grin. "As a matter of fact, my friend, I've saved the best for last. This man LaRue is really fascinating. And there's one other person I want to tell you about, too. . ." There was silence for a few seconds, and then I heard him again. "Sorry, James, someone else needs to use the telephone. I shooed him away, but he'll be back. You have to be persistent, or you don't get to use this thing. Let me give you a quick report of what I have before he returns."

* * *

The third message was from Peter Zumbach at *Knickerbocker.*

When I finally got through to the magazine, a young woman answered. She sounded like the woman who'd interrupted the board meeting ten days ago to tell Arthur Billingsley that Samantha had been attacked. I told her it was important that I speak with Mr. Zumbach. She said to me he was in a meeting, but that she'd interrupt to let him know I was calling. I took a long pull on my whiskey and beat an impatient tattoo on the table as I waited.

"Mr. Christopher?" It was Zumbach.

"Yes, Peter, you called while I was out."

"I can't talk long—people keep coming in and out of this room—but I was just curious as to how things were going with your investigation. By the way, Mr. LaRue was in the office earlier today, fuming as usual, saying he'd received a distressing letter from you. Asked me if I knew anything about it. As you and I agreed, I told him no."

So another copy of the letter had been delivered ahead of schedule. Why wasn't the Post Office this efficient when I wanted them to be? So be it, the cat was out of the bag. As for Zumbach, I'd told him that there was no reason for him to tell anyone that he'd given me help with this matter. It would only put him in a bad position at the magazine and compromise him in the eyes of the other board members. After all the help Zumbach had given me, the last thing I wanted to do was make him lose his job.

"So what did LaRue say?"

"He asked me if any other board members had received a letter from you, and I said I had no idea. I asked him why in the world he thought I would know anything about the mail that board members received? He told me I was insolent and stormed out of the building."

"Sounds like the LaRue we've grown to love. Apparently the Post Office has suddenly become super efficient. Mrs. Neustadt told me she received her letter, too."

"How'd she take it?"

"I think she took pity on me because of how I looked." I could tell from the dead air in the receiver that he hadn't the faintest idea what I meant by that. I told him about being shanghaied earlier in the day by the shady characters in the carriage and how I'd barely escaped.

"What reason did they give for abducting you?"

"They said they wanted to convince me that I should forget about the Guiteau business. That it was a wild-goose chase—a waste of my time because there was absolutely nothing to it."

"Which, of course, means—"

"That there definitely is something to it."

"They don't sound too smart."

"No, but they mean business, I can assure you." I reached up and touched my bandaged cheek gingerly. "They obviously belong to a group of fanatics that will stop at nothing to achieve their ends. They've already killed a President, and probably my uncle, too." I realized I was getting wound up, so I paused for a second. When I continued, I tried to sound more in control. "Anyway, I think Mrs. Neustadt was more fascinated by the letter than threatened by it. We'll see how good a judge of character I am."

"I hope you're right about her. I sort of like her."

"Anything else for me, Peter?"

"No, wish I did have. I take it that you're now convinced that your uncle was killed to prevent him from revealing the name of the Guiteau accomplice, and not to prevent him from selling the magazine?"

"No, I'm not entirely convinced. They're both good reasons, of course, but I suppose I am leaning more towards the Guiteau motive."

"Might be a case of eliminating two problems with one stone, so to speak."

"You could very well be right, Peter."

My final message—the one I'd saved for last—was from Sam. I'm not quite sure why I saved it for last, but I suppose it's because I wanted more time to talk to her —and to be as up-to-date as possible when I did. It was barely five-twenty, so I was fairly certain that Edward wouldn't be there when I returned her call. She must have been waiting near the telephone, for she herself answered—and on the first ring.

"Sam, this is James."

"Oh, James, I'm so glad you called. Wait, let me close the door so I can talk." I could picture her in my mind's eye moving effortlessly across the room to close the door. "I'm back," she said. "Do you have a few minutes? I want to tell you what's happened."

"Yes, yes. Of course. Are you all right?"

"I'm all right, but I'm not happy. I know Elizabeth told you that I'd gone to see a real estate agent about finding a place of my own to stay."

"She didn't say why you'd gone, only that you had. But why on God's earth didn't you just come here?"

"You know why, James. What would people say? Besides, it was only going to be temporary—until I could figure out what to do. At least I'd be away from him."

"You're talking as if you couldn't find a place. What happened?"

"Oh there are places to be had. That's not the problem."

"What is it, then?"

"No one will sell or rent to me without getting Edward involved."

"That's ridiculous, you have your own money—and a lot more than he does." To be honest, my outrage was more a show of support for Sam, than heartfelt. I was well aware of how things worked.

"That may be true, but no one is going to deal with a woman and leave her husband out of it. If I were a dowager, maybe they'd take me seriously, but as long as I'm married, they want Edward's signature on the documents. Damn, James, I'm so mad I could kill."

"Come live here. Get yourself out of that house. Bring Elizabeth with you."

"I'd like to, James. Believe me. It would be wonderful."

"But you won't."

"I can't."

"Even knowing that you risk being physically abused by him?"

"He's aware now that you know about his behavior. I think he'll restrain himself. It won't be pleasant around here, but I think he'll stop at violence."

"You told me the police were aware of how he'd beaten you, and that didn't seem to make a difference."

"Yes, but Edward was never concerned about the police. The old-boy network, you know. He sees *you* as more of a threat. I think he fears you."

He had to be the first person who did. Not that I was timid or small, but I was not by nature an aggressive sort. I didn't get satisfaction from intimidating others.

"I must see you," I said.

"And I you, but it's not easy for me to get away, now. Edward has become extremely suspicious."

"Of what?"

"He thinks I'm fond of you."

"We are, after all, cousins." I was hopeful that she wouldn't let this pass.

"But we're not really, are we?"

"And are you still fond of me?"

"Yes." Her voice was scarcely a whisper. "But I'm married, for God's sake. What in the name of heaven is wrong with me?"

"The same thing that's wrong with me."

"But you're not married. There's a difference."

"You're married to a man who doesn't deserve you."

"No, I must have done something to deserve this. He's not perfect, but he is my husband."

"You've done nothing to deserve this man. We need to meet soon. Maybe up in Salem on Sunday. In the meantime, don't leave your house without an escort of some sort. You could be in danger, at least until the vote has been taken at Monday's board meeting. Someone, as we both know, want's to prevent our voting against the sale. By the way, you will be coming to the dinner up in Salem, won't you?"

"You think it's important?"

"I know it's a trek up there, but I think you'll find it interesting. I'll have Everett Flick meet you at the Salem Depot." As I spoke, a thought crossed my mind. "You'd better ask Edward to take you up. He's not great company, but it's better than traveling alone, under the circumstances."

Chapter 24 *Sunday the 21st*

The cocktail hour passed without incident—fortunately.

I was not deluding myself. I expected tempers to flare before the evening was over, but I wanted to orchestrate things according to my own plan.

In the parlor, my guests gravitated to one of two small groups—based on gender, of course. The conversation was light. Everyone appeared to be at least superficially relaxed. Margarita Scharf Calore and Winnifred Neustadt seemed sincere in welcoming Samantha into their little conversation circle. Sebastian LaRue told a risqué joke that had Trampler, Billingsley and Edward roaring.

Yes, Edward came. I'd thought he would. I was glad he did. I hadn't invited any other spouses, just as my uncle hadn't back in March. Edward, of course, could, by social convention, be the exception, since it wouldn't be appropriate to let his wife go off to Salem by herself. The reason I'd given for not inviting the other spouses was that I intended this to be a working dinner, and I was sure that the men's wives would find it dreadfully dull listening to us discuss business. Since Winnifred Neustadt and Margarita Calore had no spouses anyway, Edward was the only exception. I'd given Samantha the obligatory social kiss when she and Edward arrived. I don't know if anyone else noticed but she responded with what I perceived to be something more than what was obligatory. I also thought I detected a brief flush on her usually porcelain-like complexion. Glancing at Edward, I couldn't help but feel a combination of guilt and satisfaction.

My real reason for not inviting spouses was that I wanted to come as close as possible to approximating the conditions of my uncle's infamous dinner last March—in case one of my guests was inclined to attempt something untoward after the dinner was concluded. If someone was going to act, I didn't want him to feel inhibited by the presence of a spouse.

Mr. and Mrs. Flick had done a superb job of preparing for the occasion. They seemed to relish the thought of having some activity in the house after so many months of quiet sadness. I'd asked them to do everything as they'd done it in March. Even the menu.

Everett was about as dashing as the poor man could be in his ill-fitting black tailcoat. He busied himself serving drinks to the guests with an aplomb I confess I wouldn't have expected from him. Not surprisingly, Miriam was unflappable.

Surprising myself at what a solicitous host I'd become, I found myself popping into the kitchen more than once to check on progress there. Miriam had brought in a girl from the village, and the two made an efficient team.

We finished the main course without serious incident. I could tell that my guests were becoming restless, despite—or maybe because of—the alcohol they'd consumed. So far, we'd avoided any talk of company business, or any reference to the Guiteau connection. If anything was going to happen, now was the time.

"I hope you all enjoyed dinner," I said, smiling. "I understand we have some excellent vanilla ice cream for our dessert. I imagine this will be the first of several holiday meals you'll be having. I hope that this is a memorable one."

"You had us fooled for awhile, Christopher." It was the booming voice of Sebastian LaRue from the far end of the table.

My eyes met his, and I furrowed my brows quizzically. "I'm afraid I don't follow you."

"Pretending this is a holiday gathering, when, in

reality it's a way of getting us here so you can continue your interrogations and harass us with your wild accusations. Only this time you want to do it in front of everyone else. I have to say, Christopher, this is becoming a bit tedious." He caught the eye of Everett Flick who was passing by with a bottle of vintage Chateau Petrus. "I'll take a little of that."

LaRue was goading me, hoping to provoke something, so I obliged him, "I don't appreciate your use of the terms interrogations and accusations, Mr. LaRue. My inquiries have been conducted with the best interests of all of us in mind. I don't think any of us feels comfortable knowing that there's a murderer in our midst."

"If that were true, I'd agree with you," snapped LaRue.

"I take it, then, that you're quite comfortable with the conclusions of the Salem Police Department?"

"I dare say we all are. Only you have this crazy idea that one us did your uncle in. I hate to tell you this in your own house, Christopher, but I think you're suspicions are ridiculous."

"Thank you for not hiding your feelings, sir." I looked around the table, meeting each pair of eyes before moving on to the next. "Do all of you share Mr. LaRue's views?"

No one responded. The silence was uncomfortable, and I began to doubt the wisdom of having this dinner. For a second it looked as if Margarita Calore were going to speak, but then she leaned back in her chair.

Obviously nobody was going to volunteer anything. I turned my attention to Hugh Trampler. "Mr. Trampler, do you believe that my uncle's killer was a passing burglar who panicked when he was caught in the act of robbing the house?"

On the few occasions I'd seen Trampler before, he'd exuded extreme confidence plus more than his share of bluster. Right now he shifted about uncomfortably in his chair. At length, he cleared his throat and said, "I don't believe I'm qualified to make that sort of judgment, Christopher. What's more, I don't think you are, either. I think you should leave matters alone."

I wasn't at all surprised by his little speech, but I looked at him as if he were from Mars. "Am I to understand that, even if there is a murderer among us, you don't want to know about it? You can live with that?"

"I didn't say that. What I said was I don't think you're qualified to play detective. You don't have the authority to run around poking your nose into other people's business."

"Forget me for a moment, sir. How do you feel knowing that one of the people at this table might be a killer? Surely you must have an opinion on that."

Trampler frowned, looked around the table and saw that all eyes were focused on him, waiting for his answer. He was angry, but knew he had to say something.

"Who in blazes *would* like it if he knew he was eating with a killer?" he blurted out. But it's preposterous, and you know it. Or if you don't, you should," added Trampler with finality. He pushed back from the table and folded his arms. He'd said all he was going to say.

"Preposterous, you say." I stared at Trampler for a minute; then I leaned back in my chair and studied my other guests. I was hoping that at least one of them would feel uncomfortable with Trampler's cavalier dismissal of the notion that one of them might be a killer. Barring that, I hoped that at least one of them would be concerned with the head-in-the-sand attitude of the other fellow board members. After what seemed an endless period of time, I wasn't disappointed. Winnifred Neustadt squirmed in her chair and began to speak.

"It's probably true that the police should be doing what you're doing, Mr. Christopher." Hearing this, a smug expression formed on LaRue's pudgy face. Mrs. Neustadt continued. “I can understand why you feel you need some answers, and since the police don't seem to be interested in further investigation, I don't blame you for asking a few questions."

I glanced at LaRue again. His smugness had evaporated, only to be replaced by a look of apoplexy. I feared for a moment he'd have a stroke. I caught a glimpse of Trampler, and noted that his face, too, was a bit flushed. Turning back to Winnifred Neustadt, I said, "Thank you. I appreciate your understanding."

"This is ridiculous," muttered LaRue, barely audibly.

I ignored the remark and turned to Arthur Billingsley, who so far had not uttered a word. "How about you, sir. Do you share the opinions of Messieurs Trampler and LaRue? Or that of Mrs. Neustadt?"

Billingsley cleared his throat two or three times and said, somewhat diplomatically, in comparison to the directness of the two men before him, "I do understand your wanting to know more about the dreadful incident last March. Believe me, I do. But I can't say I endorse your efforts to badger—" I was about to interrupt when he corrected himself. "Forgive me. Poor choice of words. I have to agree with the others that it's not your place to pursue this." I started to open my mouth again, and he quickly added, "I know, I know. If you don't do it, who will? Well perhaps you should direct your efforts towards persuading the proper authorities that they should reopen the case. Or perhaps you should reexamine your view of what happened. Maybe it did happen just the way the police up here in Salem say it did."

I'd hoped for something better from Billingsley, who'd in the short time I'd known him, seemed the most level-headed of the three male board members—excluding myself, of course. I nodded and turned to Margarita Calore, the only board member I hadn't heard from. "How about you, Mrs. Calore. Do you agree with Mr. Billingsley?"

"I agree that it's a bit irregular for a private

citizen to be pursuing this sort of investigation, but on the other hand, I don't blame you a bit. No one else is going to do it."

LaRue motioned to Everett Flick to add more wine to his glass. He raised the refilled glass and took a deep draught of the crimson fluid, wiping his mouth with the back of his hand. "Christopher," he said in a softer tone than he normally used. "I don't know what kind of game you're playing, but since you've come into your uncle's money and since you've gotten your seat on the board of *Knickerbocker*, you've created havoc. Good God, man, don't you see what you've done to the rest of us? You've sown seeds of distrust among people who used to get along fine. You've accused us of killing your uncle—"

"Hold it just a minute," I thundered.

"No, sir, let me finish. I've had just about enough of your interference."

"I think you've said enough, Sebastian." It was Billingsley. "I don't happen to think Mr. Christopher's on the right path, but I respect his right to look into what he sees as unfinished business."

"But you just accused him of poking his nose into other people's business. Now you're changing your tune."

"When you bully him the way you've been doing, you force me to defend him, Sebastian. I suppose, he doesn't have the right to play detective, but I think he believes there was something fishy about Martin's death, and there's something wrong with not getting to the bottom of things. I know it's disruptive, and I know it's inconvenient. I happen to think he's wrong, but I understand how he feels." "That's absurd, Arthur, and you know it."

"Then why should you mind if Christopher looks into it? If you have nothing to hide, it shouldn't concern you."

LaRue's face was livid. He started to rise from his chair. "How dare you accuse me of—"

Billingsley interrupted quickly, "Calm down,

man. Christ, get a hold of yourself. No one's accusing anybody. As I said, I don't think Christopher's right. I'm just saying you should welcome getting this business cleared up. Then we can all stop looking over our shoulders at each other and get on with our own affairs."

LaRue frowned and slowly sat down. It was clearly an effort for him to refrain from saying something else. I glanced at the others around the table. Samantha, who'd been the silent observer all evening, looked like the cat that had swallowed the canary. I think she was secretly enjoying this. Edward appeared sullen and quite drunk.

LaRue, now barely in control of himself, said, "You may be right, Arthur. Still, our host does tax the patience and the good grace of us all." I smiled. The man's precarious control was ebbing fast. He was already getting wound up again. He gestured in my direction with his cigar as he continued in his booming voice. The ash on the cigar was now of such proportions as to make me wonder whose plate or wineglass would have the unexpected pleasure of its imminent presence.

"As if holding up the specter of a murderer in our midst wasn't enough," said LaRue, "our host now wishes to taunt us with the further accusation that one of us collaborated with that wretched Guiteau in the assassination of President Garfield. Where does the man get such ideas? Are we to sit back and take these insults? I don't know about the rest of you, but I will not tolerate it."

Margarita Calore cleared her throat softly in order to get our attention, and everyone turned to look at her. "Mr. LaRue does have a point, Mr. Christopher. Your letter to us says that you have information claiming that one of us collaborated with that crazy man. That's a terrible thing to say about one of your own colleagues. Either you should tell us who this collaborator is or retract what you said in your letter. It doesn't seem fair to allow this shadow of guilt to be cast over all of us."

"I must agree, James," chimed in Billingsley avuncularly. "Either produce the name, or admit you were wrong. Perhaps you've been misled. People make honest mistakes. I'm sure all of us would understand. Better to admit you've made a mistake than to allow this to hang over the heads of all of your associates. It's tearing the board apart. You must see that."

I could see that even my allies were beginning to resent the pressure brought about by my allegations. I couldn't blame them, either. Now my uncle's oldest and most trusted associate was talking to me as if I were an irresponsible child. All the while, in the back of my head was my knowledge that I really didn't have my uncle's article, which meant that I really didn't have the name. Nevertheless, in for a penny, in for a pound. There was no turning back now. I had to hope that the guilty party would make his move soon and vindicate me. In the meantime I would continue bluffing. What else could I do?

"I appreciate your feelings," I said, meeting the eyes of Billingsley, first, and then the others successively as I scanned the table. "Believe me, I haven't raised these issues without first giving the matter a great deal of thought. I do understand the implications here. And please keep in mind, it was my uncle who first learned of this person and wrote about him, not me. My uncle had his faults, but this is not the sort of thing he was likely to be wrong about." I paused to let that sink in, taking a deep breath before continuing. I pulled an envelope from my inner coat pocket, and held it up so that all could see it. "The article my uncle wrote is in this envelope. In the article, he identifies the person who collaborated with Guiteau. Until I leave for Boston Monday morning, the envelope will remain in my library here in Salem." All eyes were on the envelope.

"I plan to reveal the name at the board meeting tomorrow. I had thought that I might be able to reveal it tonight, but I'm waiting for confirmation of one more bit of information. I expect to have that confirmation by tomorrow morning, in time for the meeting. Then, once you know all the facts, I'll be counting on you to provide me with guidance as to the proper action to be taken. I realize how you must feel about this matter being further protracted, but I'm sure you'll agree that it's best that I be certain before I reveal the person's name. As several of you have already pointed out, this is not a matter to be taken lightly."

I paused again before adding, "While most of you may be disappointed that this business has not been cleared up tonight, I'm sure you can imagine how the guilty party must feel. No doubt it's a mixture of relief that his culpability remains undisclosed for the present, and anxiety that his secret will not be secure much longer. The rest of you should have no anxiety, for you know you are innocent." All heads nodded their grudging acceptance of this logic. I had a pretty good idea which head had nodded insincerely.

Chapter 25 *Monday the 22nd*

It was quiet now. My guests had been gone since just after ten. Through my open window I could hear the comforting chirps of tree frogs and other sounds of the rural night. But that was all.

As I lay quietly on my back in the big four-poster I'd inherited from my uncle, my thoughts prevented me from sleeping. It was just past one, and my guests had been gone for the better part of three hours. They'd stayed longer than I'd expected them to, no doubt because they'd continued to hold out hope that they'd learn more than they had, which was essentially nothing. My planned event had been, to put it bluntly, a fiasco. As a holiday get-together it was a joke. None of my guests had expected, nor, to be honest, experienced, anything remotely like the spirit of Christmas. As an inducement to provoking the killer to action, the evening had also been a failure.

No one had broken into the house, set fire to it, or attacked my person. I'd remained dressed till just after midnight before finally going to bed. Could Sam have been wrong from the start? Was my uncle wrong about Guiteau? Was I wrong about believing both of them?

No, I couldn't have been that wrong. You couldn't ignore the telegram that came to Samantha's house when I was there. And you couldn't ignore my abduction and beating in the carriage. Nor could I ignore what I'd learned from Peter Zumbach, Justin Case, or John Holland. No, it wasn't my imagination, or anyone else's imagination. Something was rotten in Denmark, and that something or, more likely, someone, was very close.

But was I going to discover the identity of that someone by today, when I'd be expected to reveal the name at the board meeting? If I didn't know the killer's identity by then, I'd not only look foolish; my reputation and credibility would be so tarnished that no one would take me seriously from that point on. I'd be the laughingstock of my colleagues and of my friends. I might even be sued for defaming the character and reputations of the other board members. And, of course, the killer of my uncle and the co-conspirator in the assassination of the President of the United States would get away with murder.

What was that? Nothing. I'd lived in cities so long that I wasn't used to the absence of sounds in the country. When I did hear the occasional rustling of wind in the trees or some animal in the distance, it startled me. So odd, when you think about it. In the city, there are hundreds, perhaps thousands of noises, and you don't hear any of them.

There it was again. Probably just a tree branch scraping against the side of the house. I'd have to remember to have Everett prune the branches that were growing too close to the building. Now my mind was really active. I wasn't going to get much sleep tonight. There. Definitely something. Not a branch, either. More like a footstep. Another one. Someone tiptoeing. Slowly. Was it on the stairs? No. Downstairs. I tore the bedclothes off of me and slowly rose from the bed. The bed creaked. Damn! I stood there silently, holding my breath. It was quiet. Had he heard me? Were we both waiting? A long minute passed. Should I risk it? No. Wait a bit longer. Another minute passed, though it seemed like ten. I was about to take a step, when I heard another creak below. Then another. He was getting bolder.

I could hear my pulse beating in my ears. I took a deep breath. Stay calm. Nothing to fear. I was prepared for this, after all. Before going to bed, I'd placed a loaded pistol on my night table, and now I reached for it. Cautiously I left the bedroom and stealthily covered the few steps between the door and the landing, where I stood silently for a moment, holding onto the banister.

Another footstep. Definitely coming from below. Either the main hallway or the library. If it was who I thought it was, there was really nothing for me to do. The killer had gone for the bait. Still, I was curious, so I gingerly took a few steps down the staircase—a staircase I'd admired even as a child on those cherished occasions I'd come to visit Uncle Martin with my parents. It was perhaps six or seven feet wide at the top and flared to twice that when it reached the main floor.

It was to my advantage that my feet were bare. It was easier to move about silently on hardwood floors than if I'd been wearing leather-soled shoes. Still, my 185 pounds was enough to produce an occasional creaking of boards as I placed my weight on a step. I braced myself for the sudden appearance of my uninvited visitor.

I was a third of the way down the staircase now, and I had not sighted him yet. He was there, though. I could hear him moving about in the library. He'd leave after another minute or two. Wouldn't risk staying longer. No need to. He'd leave by the same way he'd come in. I was curious as to how he'd entered the house. I'd made sure that all the doors were locked. It had been reported after my uncle's murder that the doors to the house were seldom locked, so I didn't want to alert my visitor by continuing that careless policy. If he had to work at gaining entry, he'd be less suspicious. At least that's the way my thinking went.

Then I saw him emerge from the library. It was fairly dark, so I couldn't make out who it was, though it was clearly a man. Not really a surprise. He looked first to his left and then to his right. He glanced at the staircase, but I'd already scurried back up and stretched out in such a way that my body lay prone behind the part of the landing that overhung the staircase. I peeked around and under the landing so that I could barely make him out without being seen myself.

He seemed satisfied that he hadn't been spotted and started off in the direction of the back of the house. I descended the stairs and hid in the shadows as I tried to determine where he was now. It couldn't be the main back door, as that was locked. It couldn't be the outside kitchen door, as I would have heard him enter. The door between the hallway and the kitchen was kept closed most of the time and tended to squeak when opened. Then I heard a rustling sound. It was either the rear parlor or the large walk-in pantry adjacent to the kitchen. I proceeded cautiously down the hall, stopping every few feet to listen. There! The rustling again. He was in the rear parlor.

I peered around the doorjamb into the parlor just as he was making his escape through one of the large windows that let in so much of the bright eastern sun on clear mornings. It was a perfect opportunity to capture him now, as he was on his stomach, easing his way out over the windowsill. I noticed now that most of the pane was missing from the window. At this juncture he paused, felt his breast pocket, no doubt to be sure he had the envelope then pushed himself away from the sill and dropped to the ground. I walked over to the window and saw that my visitor must have used a diamond cutter to cut the pane free from the frame. I peered out and saw the glass lying intact on the ground. There were two gray objects attached to its surface. The light was poor, but they looked very much like two lumps of clay. No doubt he'd used these to hold onto the glass as he cut it free from the frame. My visitor had already vanished into the night. So far so good.

Chapter 26 *Monday the 22nd*

It was six in the morning and bitingly cold in my bedroom. It had flurried during the night and there was a light dusting of snow on the floor near the window. It was still dark outside. The sun wouldn't show itself for another hour, at least. I was surprised at how alert and rested I felt. Normally, after having gotten so little sleep, I'd be reluctant to get out of bed. After my late-night intruder had departed the house, and I'd sealed the opening in the window frame with a makeshift piece of canvas, I'd gotten, at most, three hours of restless sleep.

Downstairs, in the dining room, I told Mr. and Mrs. Flick about the break-in. At first, I wasn't going to tell them that I suspected that the intruder was the same person who'd killed my uncle—my first inclination being to leave them with the idea that it had been some random burglar. But then, I thought better of it. If the Flicks believed the house was going to be subjected to random break-ins, they might not want to continue in my service. Better to share my suspicions with them and pledge them to secrecy until the matter was resolved. This I did.

Miriam had prepared a hearty early breakfast for me, and Everett hitched up the team to take me to the Salem Depot so that I could make the 7:59 train to Boston. We were in the buggy now. I sat next to Everett up front. As we jostled and bounced along the rutted frozen street, I noticed a few snowflakes coming down around us. The sky was a slate gray, and you could see your breath. Halfway to the station it began to snow seriously.

"Looks like we might be in for a good one today," said Everett sagely, shaking his head as if to confirm his own wisdom. "Good thing we left when we did, Mr. Christopher. Another hour and we might'a had trouble gittin to the depot. We'll get you there now, though. Only a few more blocks. Don't you worry."

"I'm not worried, Everett—if you're not." I studied his lined face. He was concentrating on keeping the buggy's wheels in the ruts as it made for easier negotiating of the snow-covered street. It was easier on the horses and easier to steer. Flick was an uncomplicated man, but someone you could count on. "You might have trouble getting back to the house," I added with sincere concern.

"Shouldn't be no problem if I turn right around after I leave you off. That be all right?"

"Of course. By all means get back to your wife."

He made a funny expression and snorted, but said nothing.

I arrived in East Boston at 8:30 and took the ferry over to Boston, where I was lucky to find a horsecar that took me to within a block of the *Knickerbocker* offices. Everett had been right about the snow. It had been coming down hard since the train passed through Revere. I couldn't wait to get to my destination and get in out of the blowing wind.

I arrived at the *Knickerbocker* offices at 9:20 and spent a few minutes conferring with Peter Zumbach in his office before going into the boardroom. Peter pointed his chin toward the boardroom and told me that the other directors were already in there. When I left Zumbach's office a few minutes later, I felt confident that I was up-to-date on what I needed to know.

There was a great deal of buzzing in the boardroom as I approached the entrance. When I entered, the buzz subsided. I had the distinct impression they'd been talking about me. I nodded to each of them and then proceeded to say good morning to the ladies and shake hands with each of the men. I took a seat between Hugh Trampler and Winnifred Neustadt. It was ten o'clock and time for the meeting to begin.

Everyone in the room seemed eager to get started. The innocent board members would undoubtedly want to know once and for all who the killer in there midst was. Their thoughts, no doubt, were racing from one possibility to another. Over and above curiosity, though, they were probably more than a little uncomfortable knowing that they'd done business with and socialized with a two-time killer. And not just any killer, a killer who had the blood of a president on his hands. I couldn't help but sympathize with these people. They'd feel both relief and sadness when they learned who the killer was.

The killer, of course, would be gloating. He'd be anxious to proceed because he would take enormous satisfaction from having outwitted me. He'd cleverly broken into my house and taken the only evidence that could have incriminated him. I could only imagine the smug sense of victory he must now be savoring. As these thoughts flashed through my mind, I directed my attention to him. I was unable to detect the slightest hint of smugness on his countenance. I had to admit he was a clever son-of-a-bitch.

Arthur Billingsley asked Sebastian LaRue to close the door so that the meeting could begin. Billingsley, as board chairman, was sitting at the head of the table. He cleared his throat, more to get peoples' attention than to rid himself of any congestion. The room became quiet almost immediately. Clearly, everyone was eager to get on with things. All eyes darted between me and Billingsley, who now raised his hand as if to calm the room—though it wasn't necessary. The room was so quiet you could almost hear the snow falling in the street.

"The December 1884 meeting of the *Knickerbocker* board of directors is now in session," said Billingsley. After the secretary's and treasurer's reports were read, the chairman then said soberly, "I suggest we waive the reading of the minutes. I'm sure most of you would prefer to read them later at your leisure. I also suggest that we reverse our normal procedure and go to new business before we go to old business. I know we all want to dispose of the vote on the sale of the magazine, but I think it would be more properly dealt with after we confront the new business that Mr. Christopher plans to introduce this morning. I don't think that should wait. If there's no objection, perhaps someone would like to make a motion to that effect? Margarita Calore moved that the board go directly to new business and then come back to old business as soon as the board deemed it appropriate. There was no objection, and the motion carried unanimously.

Billingsley was efficient, I'll say that for him. I could see why he was such a successful businessman in his own right. He knew the importance of things what should be considered a priority and what shouldn't. He knew that the only thing on the minds of everyone present was what I was going to say. The sooner the board got to that matter, the better. Billingsley held up his hand again to signal for quiet. I could definitely hear the snow falling now. Billingsley smiled for the first time as he looked at me and said, "Is there any new business?"

I felt my heart beating heavily in my chest as I rose to speak. "Yes, Mr. Chairman, there is. You have all received a letter I sent you last week in which I explain that I have in my possession a document written by my uncle. This document, actually an unpublished magazine article, claims to have information about a conspiracy or collaboration by one of the people in this room with Charles Guiteau, the man who shot and killed President Garfield three-and-a-half years ago." I stopped and gazed around the room, pausing briefly to make eye contact with each person in the room. There was electricity in the air, as each pair of eyes returned my gaze with a look of expectant anticipation. When I came to Sam, I smiled, hoping she'd smile back. She'd looked serious up until now, but she did return my smile. I took a breath as I realized that what I said in the next few moments would affect us all, especially Sam, myself, and the killer for the rest of our lives. My guess was that, for the killer, that life was going to be a short one.

I had never liked public speaking, and, considering what I was about to do, my knees should have been shaking. I was nervous—you don't accuse someone of two murders and feel nothing. But my voice didn't quaver, thank God, and I don't think I appeared particularly nervous to the others in the room. I hoped not. I wanted what I had to say to come across with some authority. It was time to get on with it.

"When I was first alerted to the inconsistencies that seemed to abound in the matter of my uncle's death," I said, "I began to look at each of you and any possible motives you might have for wanting him dead. Aside from the fact that he was at times an extremely irascible man, I wasn't aware of any. But then, I didn't know you very well when I first joined the board. I had to dismiss irascibility as a motive, else half the people on the planet would be dead." This brought a brief murmur of nervous laughter from two or three of the people sitting in front of me.

"Over the past three weeks I've met with each of you and with others who know you. I gradually began to discover that most of you had what the legal profession would consider a motive. Some of you had more than one motive." A few frowns and glares formed on the faces of my audience. I was not making any friends at this point. "I realize that you may view my investigations as impudent and invasive—especially from someone so new to the board. Believe me, I appreciate how you might feel that way, but I appeal to you to understand how both Mrs. Ridley and I must feel, believing as we do that our father and uncle respectively was killed by someone he'd worked closely with. Imagine how we must feel believing that that person has a voice in the running of the magazine that Martin Van Zandt founded. Imagine how we must feel knowing that we sit in the same room with a murderer—a murderer who remains free to this day." I lowered my voice now and continued. "If I'm wrong about this, you have every right to expel me from the board and treat me as a pariah. I wouldn't blame you if you did. But if I'm right, I would hope that you would want to know what I'm about to reveal. I would hope that you'd want to rid *Knickerbocker* of such a person. And I would hope that you'd want someone who'd collaborated in the assassination of your president to be brought to justice. I realize that it won't look good that such a person has been a member of this board, but it will look a lot better that we have rooted the killer out ourselves, forcing him to face the consequences of his vile actions." A few nods of agreement.

"All right, all right, Mr. Christopher," interrupted Billingsley impatiently. "We understand what you're doing. Let's get on with it—please."

"I'm getting there. Bear with me a minute or two longer. Last night, a few hours after you had all gone home after joining me for dinner up in Salem, the killer broke into my home." There was a collective gasp. "Yes, it was well past midnight when it happened."

"But we're all here," interjected Hugh Trampler from the seat to my left. I thought you said one of us was the killer? If that's true, then—?"

"Then why didn't I capture him last night?"

"Well, yes," said Trampler. "That, of course, but that's not what I meant. What I meant was how do you know it was one of us, if we're all here? Surely, if you'd confronted the intruder, he wouldn't be here today."

"Exactly. Either he'd be arrested, or if he'd gotten away, he'd avoid this meeting because he'd know that I could identify him."

"That's more or less what I was getting at," said

Trampler uncomfortably.

Sebastian LaRue leaned back in his seat, one arm thrown nonchalantly to his side. He had a cocky smirk on his face when he spoke, "Obviously, Christopher, you can't identify this man. You didn't capture him last night because he doesn't exist. Aren't you getting a little tired of making a fool of yourself?" He looked at Billingsley. "Mr. Chairman, I would like to move that Mr. Christopher be removed from the board forthwith on the grounds that he's an embarrassment to the board and a deterrent to the proper conduct of our business."

Billingsley quickly looked around the table, and said, "Is there a second?"

"Excuse me," I interrupted, directing my words to the chairman. "Mr. LaRue is out of line with his motion. I'm not finished with what I have to say. If, after I've finished, the board agrees with Mr. LaRue, it should consider his motion at that time." I wasn't familiar enough with *Robert's Rules* to know whether my objection was justified or not, but I was counting on my fellow board members being as ignorant as I was.

Apparently they were, since no one challenged me. Either that, or I'd guessed right about what was proper procedure. In any event, Billingsley nodded that I should continue. He didn't look too happy about it, though.

"The killer is with us this morning," I said ominously. "Unfortunately, he's one of us.

I turned and directed my attention down the length of the long table in the direction of the chairman. In the soberest of tones I could muster I said, "Mr. Billingsley, you were one of my uncle's closest associates for 20 years. You invested in the magazine when others wouldn't touch it. He respected you more than most people." Billingsley smiled, but I didn't return it. Instead, I said, "But you had your differences, didn't you?"

Billingsley frowned. "Well, yes. Of course we

did. You don't work closely with someone for 20 years and not disagree occasionally."

"But you sometimes disagreed violently, I'm told."

"I don't deny it. So did everyone else in this room. That doesn't make us killers." He shook his head derisively at the very implication.

I turned to my left. Hugh Trampler was leaning back in his seat with his arm crossed over his chest and a smug expression on his face. He was enjoying this. I turned my attention to him.

"Mr. Trampler, you and I both know that my uncle angered you by his reluctance to sell *Knickerbocker,* especially at a time when the sale could have saved you from serious financial difficulties." Trampler frowned, but I ignored him. "Such a situation could be considered a motive for murder. Some might even say you had the best motive of all." He was about to protest, but I preempted him. "Happily you did not see it that way." I smiled and turned away.

I then directed my gaze at LaRue. "Sir, you and I have not seen eye to eye on much since we first met a few months ago. It's no secret that you and my uncle were at odds throughout much of your tenure on this board. He was not an easy man. We all know that. When he selected Mr. Friedman as attorney for this board, it must have galled you. I know it would me. I understand that you eventually overcame your pique and put the issue behind you. At least on the surface. Still, many believe that you continued to harbor resentment toward my uncle for what you believed to be a public insult. Your behavior toward me, the nephew, bears testimony to this. I couldn't help but think of this as a motive for murder."

"Now wait a minute, Christopher," blurted LaRue. His full face was flushed and he looked like he might explode in the next few seconds. "I've heard about as much from you as I'm going to take."

"I'm afraid you're going to hear a bit more. Mr.

Chairman?" I looked at Billingsley, in an appeal to be allowed to continue. He nodded and said,

"Proceed, but try to be less direct if you can."

"I'm getting to the point, Mr. Chairman. Mr. LaRue, it's unfortunate that you and I could not have had gotten along better because I sense that in some ways we have much in common. I'm hoping that when this is over we can achieve some sort of rapprochement." I didn't like LaRue, but I thought that I understood him. He'd been treated badly by Martin Van Zandt, as had a lot of people. I couldn't entirely blame him for being bitter.

My eyes now met those of the lovely Margarita Scharf Calore. "Mrs. Calore, I know you, too, bore resentment for my uncle. I think I understand why." Her eyes bore into me now. I realized that she feared I might reveal her past as a courtesan. I had no intention to get into this, but, of course, she didn't know that. It was enough that she knew that I knew. Since she'd clearly turned her life around, it was probably unfortunate that she even knew that I was aware of her seamy past. "I know that you and Martin Van Zandt had your differences," I said, "but there is no evidence that these differences ever came to much. Besides, I know you were not the one who entered my house last night." As it became obvious that I was not going to reveal her past, she visibly relaxed. I then turned to Winnifred Neustadt.

"Mrs. Neustadt. You, too, had reason to resent my uncle." She was glaring at me as I spoke. I pretended not to notice and went on. "You would not be the first to kill for such a reason. But I believe that, despite your anger at Martin Van Zandt, and despite what you must have perceived as a terribly embarrassing situation, you rose above it. No doubt you didn't completely forgive and forget, but I see you as a woman incapable of letting such an incident, no matter how embarrassing, prevent you from getting on with your life. Besides, I know that it wasn't you who broke into my home last night." Seeing that I was finished, she breathed what could only be described as a sigh of relief.

I looked across the table now at Samantha. She returned my look with one that was difficult to fathom as if she were surprised that I would address her at all under such circumstances. “Mrs. Ridley,” I said, trying not to betray the feelings I had for her. “It’s no secret that relations between you and your father were often strained. Some might say that is putting it mildly. For a number of years you were estranged. Someone who didn’t know you well might suggest that you had reason to kill your father.” At this, her eyes widened, and I detected something between alarm and disbelief. I smiled, hoping she’d read the right meaning into it. “I think I do know you, and I know that even throughout the years of estrangement, you continued to love your father.” I smiled again. “And he wasn’t an easy man to love.” This time, she smiled. “There is no way you could have murdered your father. In fairness to everyone here, though, I had to say what I did."

I looked up and quickly surveyed the table. "So then, we see that virtually everyone at this table had some reason to do in Martin Van Zandt. And yet, you all know, just as I know, that all but one of you is innocent. Only one person killed Mrs. Ridley's father and my uncle. Only one person conspired with Charles Guiteau to assassinate President Garfield."

I realized that, by revealing so many motives of these colleagues of mine, I was very possibly burning my bridges. Certainly I wasn't endearing myself to these people. At this point I didn't care that much. Most of them had scoffed at my concerns when I'd discussed with them my suspicions that the killer might be one of them. I could understand how that wouldn't be a very popular idea, but they were grown adults. They had to see that I wasn't imagining things. They had to see that I might be on to something. So, no, I wasn't all that concerned about whether I'd be alienating myself from them. I'd take my chances.

I turned my attention once again to the head of the table.

"And that one person is you, Mr. Billingsley." At this, I heard a gasp from Winnifred Neustadt. I could see from the stunned expressions on the faces of the others that they couldn't accept what they'd heard. Sam stared wide-eyed in disbelief. Billingsley glared at me and seemed to be searching for words. Finally he regained a measure of his normal composure and managed to speak.

"This is outrageous. Ridley told me months ago that you were a bad risk that we shouldn't allow you on the board. I didn't believe him. Being a friend of Martin, I felt obligated to bring you on the board. I should have listened to Ridley."

"You were no friend of my uncle's. If you were, you wouldn't have killed him. I have to admit, you were the last person I would have suspected. But when I saw you sneaking around my house last night, I had no choice but to accept what my eyes told me."

Billingsley snorted angrily. "You, sir, are a raving lunatic. I left your house when everyone else left. Ask them if you don't believe me." He stabbed a well-manicured index finger at each of the people sitting around the table. “Ask them, he roared.”

“He’s right,” said Margarita Calore. He was with us when we got on the train.

“Yes, it’s true, Christopher,” said LaRue, almost reluctantly. At that very moment I had the feeling he was disappointed that Billingsley might be getting away with something. I think LaRue liked it when others suffered.

I held up my hand. “I’m sure he was with you when you got on the train. But did he ride all the way to New York with you?”

“Well of course he did,” blurted Trampler. “What kind of question is that?”

“Did you see him the entire trip?

“No,” said Winnifred Neustadt thoughtfully. “Now that you mention it, after we’d been on our way for a few minutes, he left to go into the car behind us. I remember thinking it a bit strange, but not so terribly strange. He may have wanted to sleep."

"Exactly," said Billingsley. "I was tired and didn't wish to sleep in the presence of the others."

"That, sir, is a lie," I said. "You were in that rear car only as far as Swampscott, whereupon you got off the train and hired a carriage to take you back to Salem. Once in Salem, you had the driver let you off a few blocks from my house. You then walked those few blocks to the house and broke in through a rear window."

Billingsley threw up his hands in wonderment. "That's preposterous. This is the most ridiculous nonsense I've ever heard. My God, James, if your uncle could hear this, he'd turn over in his grave."

"He'd be disappointed, I'll grant you that, but in you, sir; not me. There's no need to pretend anymore. I hired a man to follow you last night. He was on the train and got off the train in Swampscott when you did." By now everyone at the table was staring in disbelief. Could this man, the most respected person on the board, have done such a thing?

"Even if I did get off in Swampscott, which I completely deny, that wouldn't mean I did it to break into your house."

"No, it wouldn't," I conceded, but I'm afraid I have you dead to rights. I truly wish it were not the case." I then directed my next question to the table. "I assume you all know what albumen paper is? The chemically treated paper used in photography." Most of the people at the table nodded.

"Well, having some knowledge of both photography and chemistry, I prepared a crude form of albumen paper and attached it to the envelope containing my uncle's article— the article naming Mr. Billingsley as collaborator with Charles Guiteau in the assassination of President Garfield." There was no way I was going to lose everyone's attention now. They were hanging on my every word. "As you may or may not know, albumen paper becomes light sensitive when coated with albumen or the white of an egg plus a salt such as ammonium chloride followed by a second coating of silver nitrate. The albumen paper process is now more popular than the daguerreotype process because it's impossible to make additional copies of daguerreotypes. With the albumen process, you can." I paused to see if they were still with me. They were.

"One annoying property of albumen paper, though, is that it is very messy to work with. If you touch it, and your hands are the least bit damp, it leaves a black mark. The mark is almost impossible to remove. Eventually, over several days, it will wear off. But you can't wash it off." I paused briefly; then said quietly, but dramatically, "What does that have to do with us?" I could see a couple of heads nodding now. Obviously they were with me. "It means that whoever stole that envelope, would have black stains on his hand."

I turned to Billingsley. His eyes had the look of the hunted animal. "Would you mind if we took a look at your hands, sir?" He remained seated with his palms facing down upon the table. He made no move, and I could see that he wasn't sure now what to do. His usual composure was gone, and I sensed that panic was about to replace it.

"I think you should know," I added parenthetically, "that Detective Inspector John Holland of the Boston Police Department is waiting outside this room with a constable. If there is no mark on your hands, you should be eager to show us and be done with this business." Our eyes met and I didn't waver. He began to tremble. Still he didn't move his hands. Until now there'd been a part of my brain that harbored doubts. I must admit that I wasn't sure what I would do if his hands were free of black marks. I drew in a long breath and said, "Well, sir. Why don't you just show us, and get this over with."

He slowly turned his left hand over. Nothing. It

was the well-manicured hand of a gentleman. I nodded in the direction of his right hand. Slowly he turned it over. There were no black marks. My heart skipped a beat and I grabbed his wrist and studied the hand closely. Sweet Jesus, what was I going to do?

Then I saw it. The tips of his index finger, middle finger, and thumb looked raw, almost as if they had been abraded with sandpaper. I wrenched his wrist and displayed the hand so that others could see what I'd seen. I pointed to the three fingertips and said, "What happened here, Mr. Billingsley? It looks as if you've worn your fingertips away."

"I slipped last night getting out of a cab. I had to brace myself as I fell to the street." He looked slightly relieved, as if he felt his explanation made sense to the others who were listening.

"That seems a little implausible." I looked around the table, trying to read the minds of my fellow board members. It was impossible to tell what they were thinking. "Tell me," I said, "what time did you arrive home last night?"

The color had returned to his face, and so had his confidence, apparently, for he now smiled smugly and said, "I'm getting a little tired of your questions, James. But since I have nothing to hide, I'll tell you. It must have been a bit past midnight. Certainly no later than twelve-thirty. Now, may we get back to—"

"I'm afraid not. You've just told another lie. You broke into my house in Salem around one this morning. You couldn't have gotten home at midnight."

"I've already denied your ridiculous charge of breaking into your house. Besides, how the blazes do you know when I got home?"

"Because, sir, I had someone stationed outside your house to observe exactly when you did arrive home. He's outside now with Detective Inspector Holland. He'll testify that you didn't get home until 3:45 this morning." Upon hearing this, Billingsley closed his eyes, and his head slumped to his chest.

I looked up and faced the others at the table.

They sat stunned. I said, "This is the most unpleasant thing I've ever done. Yet it must be done. I think when you consider the evidence I've presented that you must agree that the man we've all come to respect has not deserved our respect. He has betrayed all of us. Worse, he’s betrayed his country.”

Chapter 27 *Tuesday the 23rd*

"So much for quiet dignity," roared Zumbach with an ear-splitting laugh. The rest of us joined in.

A day had passed since the arrest of Arthur Billingsley by John Holland. The chairman of *Knickerbocker* magazine had been arraigned and was now in jail.

Justin Case of the *Globe*, John Holland of Boston's finest, Peter Zumbach of *Knickerbocker*, and myself were now sitting around a table at the Union Oyster House, discussing the whole sordid affair.

Case, who'd been relatively silent since we'd arrived almost an hour ago, now leaned forward with a glass of ale in hand and offered his thoughts on the matter.

"Dignity, my friends is only skin deep. Scratch a gentleman, and he's just like the rest of us—human."

"That's a bit cynical don't you think, Justin?" said Holland, who should have been the most cynical of us all, considering what he saw day in and day out. "What do you think, James," he said with a wink, "since you're a gentleman yourself now?"

I took a long pull on my lager, and, when I spoke, I tried to sound serious. "I suppose I'm old fashioned, but I believe in dignity. True dignity is more than a thin veneer one decides to adopt as a face to put on for the rest of the world. Arthur Billingsley was the real thing. I would have sworn it." I shook my head in disbelief. "I still find it all very hard to believe."

"I'm confused, James," said Zumbach. "Why'd he kill your uncle? Of all the people on the board, he would appear to have the least reason of all. I thought he liked the old curmudgeon." Upon saying that, he looked at me. "Sorry, James."

"Don't apologize, my uncle was a curmudgeon—at his best. At his worst, he was mean and ruthless. You're right about Billingsley being the closest thing to a friend my uncle had despite the fights they sometimes had. It was Trampler, actually, who had the best motive. My uncle's unwillingness to sell *Knickerbocker* cost him a fortune. Nearly ruined him. Turned him into a bitter, resentful man, and I wouldn't have been at all surprised if he'd turned out to be the killer."

"Your Mr. LaRue was right behind him," chimed in Holland. "He's a nasty character, and I'm not the only one around this town who thinks so. He's spiteful and vindictive, and when your uncle gave the job of corporate attorney to that other fella—what's his name—Friedman, I imagine your Mr. LaRue was fit to kill. I'm amazed he didn't."

Zumbach was nodding vigorously.

I nodded, too. "I agree. I wouldn't have been shocked, either, if he'd been the one."

Zumbach was still waiting for an answer to his original question. "So why did Billingsley do it, James?"

"Because he'd collaborated with Guiteau, and Martin Van Zandt knew it and was threatening to tell the world."

"It, it, just doesn't make sense," stuttered Zumbach. "What in God's name was a man like Billingsley doing associating with an unbalanced fanatic like Guiteau? For one thing, Billingsley must have been 20 years his senior. And as far as I can see, they had nothing else in common, either."

"That's why he was able to exert so much influence over Guiteau. Billingsley was like a father to Guiteau. Guiteau's own father was everything Billingsley wasn't. He wasn't exactly a failure, but he was a real plodder. Had no imagination and cared little for anything save the mundane obligations of putting food on his family's table, at least so far as I can tell. Apparently he was a colorless, dull man. Guiteau, though, was a dreamer. Had been since he was a child. Billingsley represented the kind of inspirational man his own father never was. First and foremost, he was a man of ideas. He was vibrant, committed to politics, and capable of persuading others to follow him. A true leader. To Guiteau, he was a hero." I stopped and shook my head slowly from side to side as I thought of what a waste his talents were.

I took a deep breath and resumed where I'd left off. "Arthur Billingsley appeared to be the kind of man you'd trust with your life. Unfortunately, in his case, appearances were deceiving." I sighed and took another draught of my beer. I'd already had two pints and was beginning to feel it. I pushed the glass away and continued.

"He was a Stalwart, you know. Fought under Grant in two different campaigns. Opposed Garfield from the first. Well, of course, a lot of people opposed Garfield. He only won the election by 40,000 popular votes. But Billingsley wasn't one to accept the vote of the people. Garfield's victory meant possible ruin for him. His business, it turns out, wasn't built through any commercial genius on his part, but because of favors granted to him by the Grant, and, to a lesser extent, Hayes administrations. Since the first days of the Grant administration, Billingsley has profited beyond your wildest imagination from the Spoils System. Why do you think his import-export business is so successful? Roscoe Conkling loved him." I was referring, of course, to the senator from New York who'd become the unofficial dispenser of favors and contracts for the Stalwarts. Billingsley knew that all this could end under a Garfield administration. Garfield could be his undoing. When Garfield was elected, Billingsley felt he had no choice but to do something about it. The sooner the better.

"Billingsley devised a Machiavellian plan to get rid of the President." I paused, realizing I'd been going on for some time now. Was I boring them? Apparently not, for they appeared eager for my next words. Maybe it was the beer, but I thought I was making sense. "Billingsley methodically set out upon a deliberate course of action aimed at persuading some vulnerable, unbalanced younger man to carry out his plan for him. He had no one in mind yet, but he had no doubt that he'd find such a person. He diligently attended Stalwart meetings. You can imagine his distaste at associating with such political rabble. Billingsley enjoyed the fruits of their politics, but he had little taste for the local ward politicians and their noisy, sweaty meetings. In short, while he shared their beliefs he had little in common with most of these people other than their politics. But he was driven, and he was willing to make sacrifices in order to find the right kind of person to carry out his plan. Then he met Guiteau, and he knew he'd found his man."

"Guiteau may have been a loony," interrupted Holland, "but how the hell did Billingsley get him to kill the President?"

"Guiteau'd been thinking about it for some time, so the idea wasn't entirely new to him. He just needed a little encouragement. As crazy as Guiteau was, he thought of himself as a good person. Basically, I think, he needed someone to come along and give him moral justification for something he wanted to do anyway. Billingsley provided that moral justification. With his fatherly manner and his gentlemanly carriage, he elevated murder to political assassination and gave it a moral stamp of approval. It then became a holy mission that Guiteau felt privileged to carry out."

"All of what you say makes sense—in a sick sort of way," said Case, "but when Guiteau confessed, he denied having any collaborators."

"When I visited Billingsley in his cell last night, he told me that he'd convinced Guiteau that he alone should have the honor of eliminating the President. He told me that he'd explained to Guiteau that, since he,

Billingsley, represented thousands of Stalwarts who all wanted the same thing the elimination of Garfield. Guiteau would look like little more than their instrument, rather than the true crusader of righteousness that he was. Our Mr. Billingsley is a clever one. I'll give him that. By appealing to the fragile ego of that wretched, pitiful little man, Billingsley convinced him he was a warrior of heroic proportions, rather than the contemptible murderer he was."

"But didn't Billingsley take a huge risk?" asked Zumbach. "What if Guiteau had had a last-minute change of heart? Or what if he decided that Billingsley was such a fine fellow, he deserved to share the credit?"

"Good question. Billingsley had that one covered, too. From the very first Stalwart meeting he attended, he'd used an assumed name. If Guiteau for any reason had decided to implicate him, the authorities would never have made the connection to Billingsley.

Chapter 28 *Wednesday the 24th*

It was eight o'clock Christmas Eve, and it was snowing again. Until a few days ago, Boston had gotten off without any snow this winter season. Since that first snow, though, at least some of the white stuff had come down every day. This morning, under a warming sun, yesterday's new-fallen snow had turned to slush in the streets. Walking around town was a messy, difficult proposition. If you didn't slip and fall—as I'd seen a poor elderly woman do this morning while she was crossing Boylston Street—your clothing became spattered with sooty-gray slush, and your shoes or boots became sodden.

It was dark out now. It had been for several hours. The temperature had dropped, and the slush had frozen solid. The falling snow had turned the city into a white paradise. A fresh blanket of snow had a way of hiding the city's poverty and grime. Temporary, but nice while it lasted.

Looking down the length of my dining-room table at Samantha, whose lovely face was highlighted by the soft light given off by the silver candelabra, I was willing to believe that the fresh blanket of snow could work magic for both of us.

My thoughts drifted back two days to Monday's board meeting. After that eventful meeting, Sam had taken me aside. I'd seen from her expression that it was something serious. When we were far enough away from the others, she told me that Edward had left her. Apparently the bank had discovered serious indiscretions and had accused him of being responsible. Rather than face up to these improprieties, Edward told her he was sailing for Europe on the next ship. He'd be in touch eventually.

"You mean he's already gone?" I said incredulously.

"Yes, the ship sailed on Saturday," she said.

"Good riddance. You're better off without him." As soon as I'd uttered the words, I realized I'd said the wrong thing. Her eyes told me that. She was trying hard not to weep. Obviously I didn't understand women as well as I thought I did.

"I'm sorry," I said. "I just thought you'd be glad to be rid of him. I see that I was wrong. You obviously still feel something for him."

"No, I am glad that he's gone. It's just that my life is a shambles. What do I do now, James? He may never come back." She sighed. "I suppose it's just as well. There's too much between us. We had problems before this, as you well know, but now things are worse. He as much as admitted to me that he'd embezzled bank funds. I've tried to understand him, James. Until this. But out-and-out criminality on such a scale is asking too much. I've reached the limits of my patience. I suppose I am better off without him. But where does that leave me?" I can't live with him, but now I'm not only the spouse of a wife beater, but also the wife of a thief. No one will come near me."

She was distraught, and for good reason. But it didn't have to be. "Look," I said, "Right now things look grim. But believe me, they'll get better." I hesitated, but only for a second before I went ahead with an idea that had just popped into my head. "Wednesday is Christmas Eve. Why don't you come over to my place on Beacon Street so that we can have a family holiday together? It's been a long time since I've had one, and I suspect even longer for you. I know this won't solve all of your problems, but you'll feel better, and maybe when we put our heads together we'll be able to come up with some ideas for your future."

She'd looked at me with those eyes that had had such a powerful effect on me from the very first time I'd looked into then many years ago—a time when we were both too young to think about what I couldn't escape thinking about now. Her next words were not what I wanted to hear:

"James, that's so nice. . . and I'd love to, but you know that I can't. Good Lord, when people learn that Edward has taken bank funds, things will be bad enough. If they find out that I've visited another man's house, imagine what they'll say then?"

"Bring Elizabeth," I'd said, thinking quickly. "Charles will be here, too, of course. The entire situation will be a model of propriety. Besides, I am your cousin." I winked, and she forced a smile.

So she'd come. We'd been sitting at the table for some time. The meal Charles had prepared had been perfection. I was happy. I couldn't tell from Sam's face what she felt. Her next words gave me no clue to her feelings, either.

"Do you mean to tell me that Arthur Billingsley hired those ruffians who abducted you in the carriage? I can't believe it. Where would he find such people?"

"He'd met a number of toughs like them at the Stalwart meetings he attended. Don't get me wrong, the Stalwarts weren't a group of criminals. Most of them really believed in their political cause. But some of them were street toughs and thugs, and our Mr. Billingsley, ever alert to opportunity, had no problem hiring them when he needed them. They, of course, thought, in their own twisted way, that they were doing it for the cause. There was no risk to Billingsley in hiring them, because he didn't use his real name. They could, therefore, never reveal his identity to the police or anyone else if they happened to get caught or somehow botched the job, which, it turns out, they did." I grinned.

I was tired of the Van Zandt affair. I supposed I should have thought of it as the Guiteau affair, or even more accurately as the Billingsley affair. In any event, I'd lived this nightmare for over three weeks—

not counting the nine months since I'd first heard of my uncle's murder—and I was eager to turn to more pleasant things. Looking down the table now, I couldn't imagine anything more pleasant than Samantha. She'd come without Elizabeth, who'd told her she'd been invited to a gathering of expatriate Irish relatives living in South Boston. Sort of a family reunion, she explained. Sam had told her to go ahead, enjoy herself, and have a Merry Christmas. So it was just the two of us. Sam's big eyes sparkled with reflected candlelight as she spoke:

"I'm glad this whole thing is finally done with. I'm glad my father's killer has been caught, and I'm glad that the man behind the President's assassination has at last been brought to justice." Her eyes were watery now, "But I'm saddened that it turned out to be Arthur Billingsley. I've known that man since I was child. He was like an uncle to me, James. Why did it have to be him?"

"I wish I knew, Sam. I know it sounds terrible, but I wish it had been LaRue."

"I know what you mean," she grinned. "He's a lot easier to hate, isn't he?" She turned serious and looked down for a moment before saying, "I'm glad it's over, though. I'm ready to get on with my life."

"It's not entirely over," I said. "I still have to contend with the other board members. Who knows how they'll regard me in the wake of all this. I treated them all as suspects, you know."

"I think you may be pleasantly surprised. At least by some of them. After all, they know that you were the one who got to the root of all this. And you were the one who removed a two-time murderer from their midst."

"I hope you're right."

"I think I am, James."

I smiled, "I'll take your word for it. All right, that's settled. But there's one more thing we may have to contend with."

"And that is?" she said, suddenly tense for fear

of what I was going to say.

"I can't help but worry about how the public is going to react to *Knickerbocker* magazine when they learn that its chairman helped assassinate the President of the United States."

When she spoke it was clear that she shared my concern:

"Only time will tell, I suppose. We have to count on the public's understanding, don't we? Hopefully they'll see that Billingsley was rooted out and removed by the board itself. Led by you, I might add."

"The public is hard to figure, Sam. Let's pray that you're right about them."

As I said, the supper for our Christmas Eve had been marvelous. Charles had started us off with a succulent appetizer of tender spiced oysters and followed that with a halibut au gratin that exceeded anything I'd had at the finest restaurants. Earlier in the day I'd invited Charles to join us, for I knew he had no relatives in the city, but he'd declined graciously. I think he appreciated my invitation, but I believe he felt he'd be uncomfortable dining with us. He may even have felt that he'd get in the way of any amorous overtures I might make to Samantha. He didn't say any of this, of course, but Charles was very astute when it came to understanding human behavior.

It was now a few minutes past ten o'clock, and, so far, I hadn't made any such amorous overtures. But as the night wore on and the eight-year-old vintage claret began to warm my insides and reduce my inhibitions, I found myself feeling less interested in talking about my departed uncle and more interested in Sam. Unless I missed my guess, she felt the same way. She was staring at me now. Not a penetrating stare, but a stare that expressed the mood of the hour. Her elbows were on the table, and her chin was resting in her hands. She smiled wistfully as she spoke:

"When Elizabeth told me that she was hoping to

go over to South Boston, I wasn't sure how I should feel about coming here alone. At first I thought it would be terribly indecent. Perhaps I shouldn't come at all. Then, the more I thought about it, the better it sounded." Her smile widened into a wry grin. "I'm so glad I came, James. I suppose that makes me positively wicked."

"You've already made my Christmas," I said as Charles poured more wine for Sam and then topped off my glass. Ever discreet, there was a knowing look on his face as he wiped the neck of the bottle. He was the consummate professional, and it was time for dessert. He directed his words to Samantha:

"Would you care for something light, Mrs. Ridley? I have some fruit and cheese—grapes, apples, oranges, and figs. The cheeses are Edam and Brie."

We both went for grapes with the Brie, and rich, aromatic coffee. I then excused Charles for the night, telling him that we'd be just fine. I added with a wink, "Just leave the claret bottle. And thank you, Charles. Oh, by the way. Merry Christmas."

"Yes, Charles," interjected Sam. "Merry Christmas. The supper was wonderful."

"Merry Christmas to you both. It's nice to see people enjoy themselves."

We finished the fruit and cheese matter-of-factly. Our conversation was light and of little substance. We laughed a lot. I loved it when she laughed. As we tossed down the last of our coffee, neither of us said anything for a minute or two. We just sat there looking into each other's eyes.

That's when I suggested that we adjourn to the rear parlor for a nightcap of claret, or some port, if she preferred. I realized that I was getting myself and Sam into dangerous waters. She didn't object, however, and we were now about to settle ourselves into the warm embrace of the heated back parlor. Earlier in the evening Charles had gotten the coal stove going. He'd stoked it less than half an hour ago, from the look of it. Funny, I'd told the Flicks up in Salem that I was thinking of installing central heating in the Salem house, but I still didn't have it here in Boston, where I spent most of my days.

The stove in the parlor was throwing off a great deal of heat, or maybe it was the wine. Whatever it was, I was feeling quite warm. I leaned over to place the claret bottle I'd carried from the dining room onto a side table. I was quite relaxed now. I turned from the table, *sans* bottle, expecting to see Sam waiting a few feet behind me. As I turned, I was wondering how we'd resolve the delicate matter of how to seat ourselves. Would we sit in separate chairs, or would we sit together? Either way, I thought, it could be awkward. Our relationship was still more than a wee bit ambiguous. Were we cousins, or were we lovers?

It turned out not to be awkward. She'd come closer as I was setting the bottle down, and as I turned to face her, our bodies met. I immediately sensed the warmth of her body and felt the rise of her breasts and the sweetness of her breath on my face. I know for certain that she could feel me.

"Charles?"

"He won't bother us," I assured her.

That night we reached boundless heights of ecstasy. But something far more memorable than any physical pleasure remained beyond that rapture of the flesh. I experienced a tender passion I never imagined possible. A bonding of souls. A oneness heretofore undreamed of.

There was something inevitable about our union. I know that now. Neither of us felt uncomfortable with it. Neither felt guilty. She knew that our relationship was a kinship of spirit; not of blood. If she needed any kind of justification for spending the night with me, Edward's criminal behavior and now his flight from the authorities were more than enough. They were for me.

One week later I asked Samantha to marry me. In light of Edward's behavior and record, it was obvious that she'd have no trouble getting a divorce.

She didn't accept. She made it clear that she wasn't actually refusing. She loved me, she said, but she needed to stretch her wings again. I reminded her that the last time she'd done that she'd ended up with Edward. She laughed and said that was a long time ago. She was a different person now. Besides, she said, with the money she had now, she could afford to be more independent. I said being married to me wouldn't restrict her all that much. I was a modern man with modern views about women. She said she knew that, but one of the things she wanted to do was get more involved with the women's movement. Maybe even travel with Mrs. Stanton or at least write more about women and their place in American society.

"You remember," James, "that day Edward and I came knocking on your door and I told you that I was attending a speech by Elizabeth Cady Stanton. I've attended others, too. Last year I wrote about her and what she stands for in one of my articles for *Knickerbocker.*" She grinned. "You know. One of my Harcourt Evans pieces." I nodded resignedly, "It was one of the articles in *Knickerbocker* that Edward hated the most. You can imagine the scene when he learned that I was its author." She closed her eyes as it all came back to her. She shook her head slowly and deliberately at the thought. Then she perked up and went on. I can't tell you how much hearing her speak affected me. What a magnificent woman. She awakened me to the potential we women have had locked up for centuries. She awakened me to my own potential. She's years ahead of her time. She introduced me to ideas that made so much sense. I've always been a rebel," she grinned, "as you well know. But she showed me something I'd never have seen by myself. She showed me that women weren't meant to live in the shadow of men."

I must have frowned, for she then said, "Nothing personal, James. As you've pointed out, you're not like most men anyway. But you must know that something's wrong with the way women are treated in this country."

This was not going the way I'd expected. What in God's name had gotten into her? I think that she could see that I was thrown by what she'd been saying, for she then said, "Oh look at you. You look like a little boy who can't have his way. I thought that you were a modern man, with modern views about women."

"It's just that I'm surprised to hear you speak this way about men. I know that Edward's a cad, but that doesn't make all of us cads. Don't you think you're getting a bit carried away with the radical thoughts of this Stanton woman?"

"No, my darling, I don't. Her thoughts are only radical because they're new to you. Someday, women will have the right to vote. Someday women will be treated equally in every way."

"Dear Sam, that sounds very nice, but don't get your hopes up. It's not very realistic. Good God, you must see that. This Stanton woman is a dreamer."

"She's not the only one who sees a different future for women, James. Look at Susan B. Anthony, and Carrie Chapman Catt. They believe as she does. It's going to happen, James. It's just a matter of time."

I sighed. "Where does that leave us, Sam. Are we enemies because of these women and their crazy ideas?"

It was the wrong thing to say. I knew that as soon as the words left my mouth. It's not that I completely disagreed with her. Certainly many women were capable of doing more than most of them did. Sam certainly was. I knew that. But was it we men who kept women down, or was it simply social convention? Or perhaps even the way things were meant to be in the scheme of things. If it was so wrong, why would the roles of men and women have been what they were for so many centuries? Perhaps that's the way God wanted it. I wasn't about to share these thoughts with Sam, though. At least not right now, judging from the look in her eyes.

"If you believe they're crazy, James, then maybe we are enemies."

"I don't know what to believe, frankly. You're talking about things that are so new, that they seem totally foreign, Maybe it's me who's not making sense."

"Do you believe women are not smart enough to vote, James? Do you believe they're incapable of doing the kinds of work men do?"

I laughed nervously. "Of course not, as far as the vote is concerned. As for work, I suppose it depends on what kind of work. Though I tend to feel that a woman's place is in the home—unless she has no other source of income, that is. How'd I do?"

She was exasperated, but she made an effort to laugh patiently. "You got it half right. A woman may want to work even if she doesn't need to, don't you see that?"

I had to confess I didn't. "Why in the world would she want to do that?"

"For the mental stimulation, James. Do you have any idea how boring it is to stay home seven days a week, especially when you have help to run your house and there's really nothing to do?"

"I go back to what I asked before, Sam. Where does that leave us?"

"I love you, James. I hope you know that. We have a great deal in common. We both care about issues. We both care about a lot of things things that are important. Do you realize how rare that is these days? Most people in this modern era care only about money, fashion, and making the right impression on the right people. Especially here in Boston.

"We're not like that, though. Just look at how you did something that the police in Salem and Washington couldn't do. You were a better detective than any of them, and you brought a dangerous killer to justice at great risk to your life and your standing in the community. And you did it because I asked you. I had no right to ask that of you, I realize that now. I owe you so much, James, my darling. My God, we all do. The nation does. Yes, you care, and you take action. A rare combination. You're not afraid of responsibility. I wonder if you're afraid of anything."

"I assure you I am."

"Well, I doubt that very much. But let me get back to us for a minute. More than all the rest, we have fun together, and," she smiled coyly, "you're also a great lover. But too much separates us right now. You know that, and I know that. You're uncomfortable with my views on women's rights, I can tell." I started to protest, but she held up her hand.

"I may as well tell you what I'm planning to do next week. I'm going to work with Elizabeth Cady Stanton. I want to do what I can to help her achieve her goals. I guess I just want to make my life worth something, James."

"Can't you continue to write articles in support of her?"

"Yes, and I will. But I want to do more. I can afford to do more. I'll help her financially, of course, but I want to travel with her, and help her prepare for her rallies and speeches. I even hope that I'll be able to help her exert enough influence to convince President Arthur that he should get involved with helping women achieve true equality. If that could be accomplished, I'd feel that I was doing it in memory of President Garfield and of my father so that their deaths may not have been totally in vain. Look at you. I can tell this isn't sitting well. See, there is just too much between us."

"My God, Sam. My head is spinning. Maybe for the present you're right about us. I don't know. Maybe I just have to get used to this. You're right, I do admire you for caring about things things that matter. And I'm impressed that you don't just care, but that you take action. God knows, when you decide to act, you don't do it on a small scale either. But you have to understand that you're talking about changing things that I grew up with. That my father and his father grew up with."

She smiled understandingly. "And that I grew up with, and my mother, and her mother. Yes, change is always difficult especially since we come to accept the status quo as that which is proper. I do hope you come to accept what I do, for I *am* going to do it. Maybe someday, if that happens, there'll be a future for us."

END

About the Author

Richard Scott is a retired editor, writer, and publisher, having been president and publisher of the David McKay Company and president and publisher of Fodor's Travel Publications. He's also been managing editor of *American Bookseller* and *Bookselling this Week*. In the 70s Mr. Scott was co-host with Isaac Asimov, Brendan Gill, Nat Hentoff and others of the talk show *In Conversation.* The show ran on radio station WOR in New York and eleven other stations around the U.S. He's a former trustee of Historic Salem, Inc. and of the Salem Athenæum in Salem, Massachusetts. He lives in Salem.

You can contact him at richard.scott2000@comcast.net.

31070848R00168

Made in the USA
Middletown, DE
17 April 2016